MANY SORRYS

Nivan Raman

Printed in India
ISBN: 978-93-5776-430-8
First Printing, 2023
The Write Order

A division of Nasadiya Technologies Private Ltd.
Koramangala, Bangalore
Karnataka-560029
THE WRITE ORDER PUBLICATIONS.
www.thewriteorder.com
Edited by- Yashika
Typeset by- Srishti M
Publishing Consultant- Jayantika Bajpai

I am inspired, and have grown up along with you,
Japanese Animation and Comics.

This is my tribute to you.

This Book is not possible without you my Friend-O; Hem-Anand-O.
Special Thanks,
Shobana Akka,
Christiga
Krithiccs Chechi,
Kums Macha
The Team WRITE ORDER
My Friends and Family

NOTE TO READERS

Dear All,
Many Thanks for picking up my book and giving me the opportunity to write more.
This book is dedicated to all of you and everyone around you.

PLEASE FOLLOW THE BELOW TO PERUSE:

The time-line of the story tends to jump on certain occasions and to differentiate,
the chapter titles are indicates as follows:

Chapter 'Present'
-Chapter- 'Past'
-Chapter* Starts from Past and ends with Present
*Chapter- Starts from Present and ends with Past.

All we need to remember is one thing, "Miracles do happen, and you can't even explain it."

"Life is full of Secrets,
Living is full of Sacrifices,

And choices we make in our life to live are Sorrowful."

Prologue

I am air,
I am nothing but a part of nature,
And even if I get a physical human form, you can't see me.
A human can't see me,
Until I want them to.
I liked to wander around learning about people,
And by mistake, I brought in a disaster.
The natural disaster they say, in the life of two individuals.
A thing done, is done,
even nature can't change it.
I can't change it.
Imagine If I had a magical power in my palm,
The only way left was to manipulate the change
And bring the messed-up pieces back in order.
Few say correction of mistake from nature itself is called
A MIRACLE.
This is the story of those two,
I messed up
And submit a part of magical realism in their life.
Just a part, expecting it throughout is an act of sheer folly.
This is the story of
My Mess, Miracle, and Me.

The AIR...

CHAPTER 1

2019

At dawn, the dark sky started clearing up, the fog turned yellow with the road full of cars and motorbikes moving to and fro. Our protagonist parked her Enfield in front of a hotel for breakfast. Her long straight hair and sharp nose jutted out as she pulled the helmet off her head. The hotel reflected in her shiny eyes as she glared at it.

Her watch was broken straight at 12:00 with both its hands together. She walked past me in the hotel, but I didn't let her see me— *She wouldn't be able to. I am air, you might know already.*

She ordered idli-sambar as she was in a hurry. She was running around from last night in search of someone who stole something from her and in return he gave her something precious. The search was so important— priority number 2— that she ran away from her house, and nothing could stop her except priority number 1— food.

But I must agree, food is very important.

A message popped up on her phone screen as she took her first bite.

"Shalini, a total of five schools are now in a row, many students have applied for theatre acting, I am happy, I can finally start teaching again."

A message from Raghav's dad, Varadarajan. She smiled. She took one more bite and texted back saying, "Congratulations

Uncle, I will be back soon with your son, let's party hard," with a fire and heart emoji and then again, she reverted to priority number 1.

The sun was already out as she paid for the food. She walked out wearing her coolers and sat on her bike— well her brother's to be precise. She borrowed it to commute from Coimbatore to Ernakulam.

She left her house last night from Karnataka and it took her seven hours to travel to Coimbatore. She went to her brother's place, took a small nap, borrowed his bike and then she was ready to begin her journey to Ernakulam.

And to keep you posted she disobeyed her parents and literally ran away from her house hence she was expecting a call from them anytime soon.

"I should have received a call by now, what is dad doing?" Shalini whispered as she started the Enfield.

***

Shalini's father— Dr. Ravichandran woke up with a long yawn, and he looked at the time with a pleasant face which turned serious in an instant.

"Oh! Shit…" he said and rushed out.

He gasped after finding Shalini's mother— Elizabeth, who was cool and cooking breakfast. He went to brush his teeth and a few minutes later, as always, he sat on the veranda and screamed with his bossy voice, "Where is my coffee?" He scratched his trimmed beard awaiting response and picked up the newspaper on the table.

Elizabeth brought his coffee with a bland face, but it should have been Shalini. So, he tried being indifferent and asked, "Where is Shalini?"

"She ran away," Elizabeth said and kept the coffee cup on the table.

"What!" Ravichandran was shocked. "What do you mean?"

Elizabeth raised her eyebrows at him, "You don't know?"

"What! We never gave her permission to leave," he said and slurped.

"I know who gave her permission to leave, and I know what you are both up to."

She walked back to the kitchen, annoyed.

Ravichandran glanced into the kitchen to make sure Elizabeth was unarmed and secretly dialled Shalini's number on his phone from the bedroom.

Shalini answered the call.

"What took you so long?" she asked.

"Your mom…" Ravichandran started but Elizabeth pulled the phone from his hand.

"It's mom," she said.

Shalini took a deep breath as she shifted her imagination to the worst that could've happened over the other side.

"Hey mom," she panicked and ran out of words.

"I don't know why you are giving him so much importance," Elizabeth said and exhaled, "you already left, so I won't stop you now... but you have to get back home safely after meeting him, or else I will murder your father in cold blood."

Her mom's voice was already cold. Elizabeth didn't bother to wait for Shalini's answer, so she gave back the phone to Ravichandran and left.

The call got disconnected and with her mother's threat, she resumed her journey.

The crystal-clear memories she made with Raghav flashed inside her head. It was strange for her to even understand that nobody remembered how she was in those two years until a photograph displayed the past. It took her some time to put the strange feeling aside, she stopped bothering others to remember the past and she only wished if Raghav's memories weren't as cloudy as the others and with that note, she took off.

Because of a simple and small mistake, fate could have turned

upside down affecting the chain of future events and people around it. To get it back straight and in the process of correcting it, the cloudy memories on the chain emerged and it is the so-called after effect.

I wish Raghav would have understood by now that the future is on the way to him. It's been a long time since I visited him.

By the way, is he still playing the keys?

***

The melting melody covered the whole empty auditorium; the pianist played every key with perfection and speed without messing up the tempo. He stopped when he heard the claps. He turned and it was Joel and others.

"It's been two days, and you are still here," Joel said to the pianist— Raghav.

Raghav gasped, "Two days, huh?" And wore his power glasses.

"I found a crumpled piece of paper from your backpack while looking for some clothes," Joel held that crumpled paper, turning it back and forth, "Scribbled Lyrics note?"

Raghav became uneasy, "I didn't expect you to find that,"

Joel said, "Play this for us, the lyrics look good."

Raghav put down the wire attached to the piano in his lap. "Will you leave if I sing it for you?"

Joel smiled and nodded.

"Alright then… get your guitar and match me up," Raghav said and started singing along with Joel's melody.

And then this part came,

"A road which is never-ending and far away,
Take a walk straight crossing the snag in your way.

What is waiting for us is unknown?
Cause the end we're chasing was never shown."

Shalini raised the throttle with excitement and chose the road which was far and mysterious. All she had was Raghav in her mind replaying the past from the beginning.

The past which was submerged in despair.

The past which was a fantasy.

The past where life was a mess.

And the past where she met a boy, who had a more messed up life than herself, two years ago…

-CHAPTER 2-

2016

May 03rd

Finally, Shalini and her family were set off for Karnataka after a long procedure of transfer. It was Elizabeth's dream to work at St. Mary's school— where she herself completed her schooling. She got accepted as a Mathematics teacher and she also wanted Shalini to join the same school for her senior secondary.

They were in a hurry to shift as Ravichandran was scheduled to report to his position by the end of the week. It was not urgent for Elizabeth or Shalini though as it was vacation time but Ravichandran as a doctor had no exceptions, and it was a must for a government employee to visit his respective public hospital so that he could finish the pending paperwork and sit comfortably in his chair. The excitement didn't prolong as Elizabeth had something to be worried about along with it— The tenth grade CBSE Board Results.

During the train commute she was booked with her worries, and she was speechless throughout. Shalini had no idea why her mother was so desperate for her to go to that school. But she was easily brainwashed when witnessed the green-y soccer playground in the school as well as the locality around the area of their stay.

Shalini studied at Kendra Vidyamandir Chennai till the 10th

grade. She wasn't the type of girl who devoted herself to studies; she was more of a tomboy who loves to play football. There were only three things she gave importance to— Football, which she loves more than anything; then her friends and family; and last but not least, the most essential need of every human— food.

Shalini's eyes were stuck outside the window as the train moved forward. She was assorted with her feelings. She was sorry because she had to leave her goody friend Richu, but she was also the type of person who understand the fundamentals of life, so she chose to leave anyway for her mom and Ayesha— Shalini's childhood friend who shifted to Karnataka after 5th grade. She was happy about that and a bit excited too. She kept the transfer from Ayesha to surprise her with a blast.

The excitement didn't last long as she soon slept out of boredom and regained her consciousness only when they reached Mysore railway station for good. They came out of the station with limited luggage and jumped into the taxi.

Ravichandran was on a call with packers and movers throughout the first 10 minutes of the ride. "Our stuff will reach our house by tomorrow," he said to Elizabeth. "Let's decide how to organise things beforehand."

"Seriously!" both Elizabeth and Shalini said in unison. "Don't you want to get some quality sleep before that?" Elizabeth added.

Ravichandran turned off in seconds, and he zipped his mouth shut until they reached their destination— Green River Park. Their house was just above the park's cliff; the main gate was attached to a wide, road bend. The house was 'wow', as both Shalini's and Elizabeth's reactions were conspicuous.

Shalini tried to look down the cliff at the end of the road and found a boy in the gazebo below, writing something in a notebook— tearing off the paper due to lack of satisfaction and tossing it into the river near him.

"Shalini…" Elizabeth yelled. "Let's get in."

***

The house was painted yellow with white edges. It had a veranda with a wooden swing. The surrounding was calm and refreshing as the gap between the house and the main gate had vast space for gardening.

Shalini moved around the house figuring out the way to organise things to make a home. *She did follow her father's call.* She found a wooden sofa placed in the hall which looked old and classy. There were a few more things left behind by the previous owner. She continued her tour throughout until she was exhausted.

She selected a room that was attached with the balcony for herself, whereas Ravichandran and Elizabeth took the other room near the kitchen. The house was single floored with a terrace, but from Shalini's room's balcony, it would be like a room on the first floor because of the high ground-level compared to the other houses around.

Shalini opened the balcony door and walked out to see the surroundings. It was chilly and the park down the cliff was visible. She could even see the gazebo and the boy again continuing with his writing. She couldn't see his face, but she felt something peculiar, and the chilly wind started blowing. Keeping those feelings aside, she got back into her room.

After having lunch, she called Richu and got into a conversation for over an hour. She made a lot of friends after Ayesha left but nobody made her feel the way Ayesha did and because of being in touch nobody could replace the position of Ayesha in Shalini's heart.

Shalini was a picky type of person as she only had two actual friends in her entire life to date and was never desperate as well. She decided to call Ayesha after the next day's war to organise things.

Time flew. After dinner, Shalini and her parents relaxed in the veranda gazing at the clear sparkling sky filled with stars.

"It's beautiful here," Shalini rejoiced.

"Isn't it?" Elizabeth elated, "I am so excited to see my school after this long."

"I am feeling sleepy," Ravichandran yawned.

Elizabeth punched him on the thigh and tittered.

***

"Can I sleep with you?" Elizabeth asked.

Shalini made her bed in her room, "Yeah, you can, but why?"

"We are new here, right? You must be afraid."

"Kidding, right? Hope you are not… a-f-r-a-i-d."

"Yeah…" Elizabeth grinned with embarrassment, "I am afraid of your father's snores."

Both laughed and minutes later they were tight asleep.

***

Ravichandran, who was sleeping peacefully, suddenly got a disturbing vibe. The whole room was silent, and Elizabeth was lying next to him. Around 01:00 a.m. the sound of the banging windows tried to wake him up. Some intruder used the window noise as his decoy and walked noiselessly to Elizabeth with a sharp knife, intending to slash her neck.

"Eliza…" Ravichandran shouted and got up, seeing that she wasn't next to him, he stepped out of his room with shaking hands. He checked the locked main door twice and peered into Shalini's room. When he found his wife there, he sighed peacefully and laid next to her after making his bed.

The peaceful night came to an end, the sunlight dazzled into their faces, and they were slowly processing to get up.

Elizabeth slightly squinted and found someone lying next to her. She flinched and shouted without comprehending that it was

Ravichandran— which made him and Shalini shiver off the bed.

"What happened, Mom?" Shalini sighed with a yawn.

"Your father was sleeping next to me," Elizabeth said. "When did he come here?"

Shalini yawned, "I don't know, but what is a big deal? He is your husband, right?"

Elizabeth muffled something staring at Ravichandran and their day began with a shout and a flinch.

"When did you come here?" Elizabeth asked Ravichandran.

"Didn't see the time? I again had that bad dream."

Elizabeth sighed, "When are you going to stop snoring?"

"A week or two…" Ravichandran said and grinned.

Shalini shook her head and got up from her bed.

Later within a few hours, all the furniture and stuff reached them and the day passed organising it. By the time they were done it was half past six and after a cold shower, Shalini decided to call and surprise Ayesha by inviting her to the house-warming function the next day.

"Shalini!" Ayesha's voice bloomed as she picked the call.

"Yeah, it's me, and guess what? I moved to Karnataka for good."

Ayesha with delight got super excited and laughed, "What?"

She remembered the past she had spent with Shalini, which made her go out of words. Her excitement reached fever pitch when she also got to know Shalini's address— It was just four streets behind her own house.

After a long friendly conversation, Shalini once again invited Ayesha and her family for the house-warming function and hung up.

Ravichandran also got back and cracked his neck sitting on the sofa next to Shalini.

"There is an apartment nearby, sombre and gloomy. I got scared and ran back home," he said.

"Did you invite anyone from that haunted house?" she

asked.

"I tried, the door was open but no response," he sighed and cracked his neck again, "Tough day!"

"Indeed."

***

Only a few people showed up at the house-warming function. The room was filled with silence but with Ayesha's arrival, Shalini's mood uplifted. She gave her a tight hug and welcomed her in.

A glass of warm milk was handed out to everyone and an hour later, everything came to an end with a little interaction with the neighbours.

Ayesha and her father stayed a bit longer than others, she glanced at the house and shot a thumbs up with joy.

They both got seated exhaling hard and Ayesha chuckled, "You have grown up since I last saw you."

"And you gained a little weight," Shalini giggled but Ayesha was an adorable seventeen-year-old. "Did you stop playing football?"

Ayesha turned off for a second and then she answered, "A long time ago, since I got here."

Shalini nodded and continued after a few seconds of silence, "Why don't we join any clubs?"

"I am actually good, so…" Ayesha said without leaving any space and continued, "CBSE results will be out soon."

Shalini's face turned fearful, "Shit! When?"

"By the end of this month."

Shalini started trembling, "Doomsday!"

Ayesha laughed, "You said you did fine."

"Yeah, I did, I guess," Shalini smiled with panic. "Mom might chop me into pieces if I fail in any of the subjects."

"Which school are you trying to join?" Ayesha asked curiously.

"St. Mary's,"

"Your mom will chop you. Pray to God that you should pass all the subjects and a miracle may happen."

Shalini's eyes alone rolled to Ayesha, "What will he ask in return?"

Ayesha shrugged, "I am also trying to get into the same school."

Shalini fell into the lake of confusion and spaced out. Ayesha shook her, "You said you wanna join a football club, right?"

"Yeah"

"Let's go. I know a place less than a mile away."

***

The club was a ten minutes' walk from Shalini's house. On the way she randomly— once again saw the boy down the cliff, writing something. She did get curious about him for a second, but she was more excited about the football club and she was easily diverted.

She witnessed paradise— the football field and enrolled in the club with haste. She was asked to join the club from the next day. Excitement and thrill rose with a good anticipation of new team, new game, and new beginning.

After getting back home, they had their lunch and by 02:00 p.m. both Ayesha and her father left.

The day passed and Shalini got selected in the current roaster for the football club as she was already skilled enough to prove her reliability as an asset to the team. All her teammates were the best and everyone had their clear goal in life.

With the passage of days, Shalini mingled with everyone in her team and even with other age group attendees, finding wide happiness out of it.

May 28- Result knocked on her door. She was so scared to open it, and she started sweating hard.

"Disclaimer don't have high expectations," Shalini said, filling in the details to unlock her academic performance.

BOOM! 8.0 CGPA.

She scored 8.5 in English, Hindi, and Social Science, 7.7 in Mathematics, and 6.9 in science.

"You did great," Ravichandran said and comforted Shalini.

But Elizabeth got quiet and refused to say a thing.

"Aren't you happy? She passed every subject," Ravichandran claimed and looked at Elizabeth.

"She even scored 80 percent, but I am afraid if this wouldn't be enough. I don't know if she will make it to that school," Elizabeth whispered audibly.

"What is the big deal? Isn't there any school available other than this?" Ravichandran yelled with annoyance.

"Why did we come here? For what purpose? I thought at least in her last two academic years she would be focused on studies rather than kicking a ball," Elizabeth yelled back.

"Mom, I am sorry, I didn't mean to hurt you. This is the extent I can go to," Shalini roped in.

"No, you can even do better, you can even score first rank if you show a little bit of seriousness to studies as you do in football." She gasped, "I don't want to say anything anymore."

She walked into the kitchen.

Shalini received a call from Ayesha an hour later. She answered.

"How much?" Ayesha asked curiously with excitement.

"Eight," Shalini said, "You?"

"Nine point six," Ayesha's voice went low. "Did your mom scold you?"

"She didn't kill me at least. A miracle did happen."

"Don't be sad, it doesn't suit you. Let's apply for that school and a few more as a substitute," Ayesha said.

They both applied individually for three different schools and hoped for St. Mary's to be the one.

Shalini in addition was very much eager for the football club announcement— a friendly match with seniors before enrolling in the club tournament.

The match was scheduled for 1st of June, and it also knocked on the door in no time.

While going to the match, Shalini saw the banner of 10th toppers in the whole Karnataka in front of St. Mary's school.

The boy who made it in the second had his picture big enough to attract the passers-by. Nine-point eight percent scored by Raghav Varadarajan— the same boy who spent time in the gazebo alone, scribbling.

Shalini's interest in him went deeper. With the slightest thought about him in her mind, she played the game, and the result was obvious— the club team lost to their seniors.

"Don't worry, you did great. Much better than we expected, we are happy to enrol the team into the tournament," one of the seniors said.

Even after losing, Shalini's team got motivated and they decided to have a small practice— half-field match on 3rd of June— with the same team in two divisions to compete.

The night before the game Elizabeth had a little chat with Shalini and apologised for yelling at her. Shalini became livelier and she decided to give everything she got into the match the next day and decided to have a chat with Mr. Mystery, Raghav out of a strange curiosity.

***

2016

June 03rd

The day I ran into the puppy by mistake.

On the football field, the team of fourteen got split into two groups of seven each and because of Captain's absence the team wanted to try something new and they chose to change their positions. Shalini chose to play defence. The match began, everyone was clumsy, the team did not stick to the game plan and their game turned out to be a mess. After the first 45 minutes of the game, both teams figured out the tactic-less gameplay, so they decided to have one for the other half.

The game resumed, the opponent started with a pass to Rumi— the gigantic girl with a good physique who was ideally a defender played forward and to avoid the main defender on one side, she moved towards Shalini to get past her. Shalini tried hard to outplay her. Rumi took back the ball and shoulder-pushed her to avoid a foul, but Shalini didn't give up. Instead, she tried to stop the momentum of the ball. Shalini and Rumi couldn't control their balance and fell over each other. Rumi on Shalini. Both screamed in pain. Shalini felt dizzy and her vision blurred, her teammates took her to the bleachers and made sure if she was okay.

Rumi wasn't hurt though and the practice game was rescheduled to next week. Team tried hard to get Shalini back to consciousness, and minutes later when she woke up and gazed at her teammates, they had pity looks on their faces.

"I'm fine guys… don't stare at me like I am dead, please…" Shalini smiled with embarrassment.

They nodded their heads, "Yeah, we know. We can play some other time."

"Yeah sure," Shalini said.

After a few seconds of awkward silence, everyone started leaving and Shalini was reminded of her added goal. She was in pain yet she rushed to the gazebo with confidence, but strangely Raghav was not available there. Instead, she could see a diary holding a note preventing it from flying away. She was curious and she didn't know why. She walked down, pulled out the paper and read it. Shalini's face went serious as she continued reading. She staggered.

It was a poem with simple words and complexity and even though she could feel the actual poem, she also figured out the existence of the other meaning to it, which she couldn't understand at that moment.

She kept the paper back into the diary and tried to move away, but later she decided to keep the diary with herself.

As she walked towards her house's main gate, she saw the road wet with splattered blood in the middle of the curved road with thoughts that made no sense.

A shiver ran through her spine and the warm atmosphere turned cold along with the dusk. She walked further to the shop nearby and asked about the bloody road.

"There was an accident." The shopkeeper imparted, "I think the car driver himself took the boy to the hospital. The boy lost too much blood, I don't think he will survive."

Shalini looked at the dairy she had in her hand and whispered, "He committed suicide?"

Meaningless Despair

Born in peace as a flower,
Beautifully colourfully,
At the bank of the river
Now, frozen to death.

Literally, nobody has shown up.
I saw the passing clouds,
And went along.
I waited so long and long,
Should I give up, guess I am wrong.
But, still waited to see where I belong.

A mother bird protected her child,
With her feathers as the shield.
Wow! Hope solaced me to live more,
Started waiting for her to knock on the door.

I became happy a bit, smile,
The sky is clear and full of star.
Loneliness and it has been a while,
Going there would be so far.

Days happened,
Rain happened,
Drops stabbed again and again.
I got no blood to drain,

But deep inside, a glimmer of strength remains,
Resilience whispers, dispelling the chains.
Though darkness surrounds, I'll strive to survive,
Seeking truth and purpose, determined to thrive.

-CHAPTER 3-

Existence made a difference, Awe... the blood kept dripping, and I rushed to the veterinary hospital to get the puppy treated. Everything was messed up. I had no time to think and the only possible thing I could do was a trade-off in the situation. I gambled many lives to link the broken chain of fate in order. The situation was ineffable and the days following— the headache began.

Love heals bruises and gives prerequisite to live more. Twisted days started, but the puppy was saved.

Shalini got in the house with a terrifying look, making Elizabeth curious for the cause.

"What is with that face?" she asked.

Shalini was spaced out and continued walking towards her room. Elizabeth shook her off and brought her back asking, "What happened?"

Shalini scratched her forehead and said, "Nothing…um," she started finding words to explain. "There was an accident down in front of our house…"

Elizabeth closed her eyes and inhaled sharply, "Did you see the accident?"

"No."

Elizabeth sniffled, "The accident might not be that serious, don't let it disturb you."

Shalini nodded, holding the diary tight as she got into her

room.

"You remember what I said, I mean the quotes from Lord Krishna," Elizabeth asked before Shalini could close the door.

Shalini nodded, "I know. 'No one who does good work will ever come to a bad end, either here or in the world to come.'"

Elizabeth beamed and with that Shalini locked her room from inside to read Raghav's poem once again.

Even though she didn't know anything about him, she was worried. Suicide always troubled Shalini.

She got into the shower and washed off her back and sore muscles along with the negative thoughts she had in mind. She took time to realise the bleeding through her nose. She was scared out of her wits yet she pretended to remain as usual.

Elizabeth asked, "What took you so long?" as Shalini walked out of her room.

"I tried to wear out my pain in the shower. I fell on my back once again," Shalini said and sat on the sofa. "Today's practice was so aggressive."

"You have been playing football since childhood, but you still keep attracting your butt to the ground," Elizabeth said and shifted the cauldron in the dining table.

Shalini laughed, "New place, new team. I must get in sync with them first and then… you know…"

"Dinner is ready."

"Why is dad not home yet?"

Elizabeth shrugged and picked up her phone to call Ravichandran.

***

Ravichandran's mobile rang as he took off his white coat. When he was about to answer, the senior doctor got into his cabin.

"There is an emergency patient. You will have to take over my shift for tonight."

Ravichandran wore his overcoat back and nodded.

When he got out of his cabin with the senior doctor, a man with rimless specs got in with a patient on a stretcher bed and blood dripped from point to point as the nurse took the patient to the operation theatre.

The lower part of the man's outfit was covered in blood. The senior doctor approached him to learn about the case. Ravichandran phone kept ringing without a break so he answered the call watching the scene.

"Where are you?" Elizabeth asked.

"I won't be home tonight. My shift got extended. You just close the door and lock it."

"What about dinner?"

"I will have it from the canteen, will call you later. Sorry," he said and hung up the call.

Within minutes Ravichandran got another call from the nurse for immediate blood donation.

The emergency patient with lots of blood loss happened to be B negative and the only registered available blood source at that movement was Ravichandran with the same blood type. Ravichandran was ready to share blood due to an emergency and the operation immediately took place. The boy was saved.

He was wrapped with bandages everywhere and looked similar to a half-unwrapped mummy. And his scans were scheduled for the next day.

All the other procedures were followed and Ravichandran after examining a few patients throughout the night was ready to go back home.

***

As Ravichandran reached home by 5 in the morning he went straight to bed and woke up at 09:00 a.m.

Shalini was watching *Oh My Ghost* in the living room lying on the sofa.

"Why are you down this early in the morning? Did you eat

breakfast?" Ravichandran asked and sat on the dining chair.

"I had breakfast, I am just tired," Shalini said and concentrated on the TV show. She was a bit disturbed and pale.

As the episode ended, Shalini went to Ravichandran and sat beside him on the dining.

"There was an accident in front of our house yesterday," she said.

He was startled for a second and asked doubtfully, "Did you see that accident?"

"Nope, I just happen to know," she said, looking away.

"Then why are you talking about it?" he asked and had another spoonful of oats.

"Just curious if… hmm… any patient showed up at your hospital."

"Yeah, a teenage boy," he said and kept eating, "And I hope he is out of a critical situation by now."

She was relieved and hence, she exhaled.

"Why do you look pale?" He asked her and had the last spoon.

"No no… I am alright, just… fell out of my bed this morning," she said. "Will have a peaceful sleep once again and…"

She went to her bed. When it was lunch time, Ravichandran went to Shalini's room to wake her up. He drew the balcony curtain saying, "Wake up, sweetheart. It's lunch time already."

He turned to her and she was sweating, having trouble breathing. He checked her temperature and she was burning.

"Shalini, you are sick! Get up, let's go to the hospital," he said with panic. "This is no good."

She immediately grabbed his hand, "I don't want to go to the hospital. I will take painkiller after lunch."

When Elizabeth came back home, Shalini was already in bed after having lunch and painkiller.

Ravichandran served Elizabeth lunch saying, "Shalini is

sick."

"What?" Elizabeth panicked. "Then she lied about not seeing the accident."

"I think we should take her to the hospital, she is unusually sick today."

"She will surely refuse."

"Then what can we do?" Ravichandran raised his voice a bit. "We have not taken her to the hospital for the past six years since that incident. This is not Chennai."

"Yeah, I know," her voice dropped.

"She can't stay like this forever. It was us who made her hate hospitals, so we also have the responsibility to make it right." He said with a calm voice and Elizabeth nodded.

Shalini stopped going to hospitals when she witnessed the suicide of one of her father's patients who sliced off his neck. Since then, Ravichandran started seeing nightmares of people getting killed or killing themselves occasionally. As Shalini saw this happening in her childhood, she was kept away from the hospital, and whenever she got sick Ravichandran figured out the problem and helped her accordingly.

This time was different, and she was too sick that going to the hospital was crucial.

"I will wait and check if her fever goes down, if not I have to take her to the hospital," Ravichandran said.

They waited until evening and then checked her temperature again. She was getting sicker.

"Shalini, are you okay?" Ravichandran asked with concern filling in his voice.

"No, I am not," Shalini said. "My neck… argh."

Ravichandran looked at Shalini and his mind concluded otherwise, he made her sit and said, "We are going to the hospital for sure." He went to get the keys.

Shalini looked at him with tear-filled eyes. She started bleeding from her nose again. "Daddy…" She sounded vulnerable.

She tried standing up, but her body failed and suddenly fainted.

Elizabeth panicked and tried to wake Shalini up, but she didn't respond. The situation made Ravichandran shiver and Elizabeth cry.

Ravichandran passed the keys to Elizabeth, carried Shalini to the car and they left for the hospital immediately.

***

With the slightest conjecture, Ravichandran took Shalini to the orthopaedist, but also wanted him to be wrong.

Aarthi— one of Ravichandran's colleagues, took over Shalini's examination. They rushed collecting all the scan reports and performed neurological tests. Even though Ravichandran knew what was going on, he chose not to believe it until the final report.

Elizabeth was seated in the waiting hall with Ravichandran.

Minutes later a man who looked like a klutz with a thick beard and long hair approached Ravichandran asking, "Where is recovery room 106?"

Ravichandran directed him to the boy who met with an accident— the patient who wrote a suicidal poem— the patient who placed second in the Karnataka CBSE board 10th examination.

The klutz was his father, Varadarajan, and he walked into the room scratching his temple with nervousness to meet Raghav.

A nurse was standing beside Raghav and was writing the report as he walked in.

She felt his presence and asked continuing making notes, "Are you his father?"

"Yes," Raghav's father said and looked at his son.

"Name?" she asked.

"Varadarajan," he said.

Raghav was sleeping peacefully. Varadarajan's eyes began to fill with tears when he found his son wrapped in bandages.

He held his son's hand and cried, "I made a mistake, she will never forgive me," his tears dropped. He slapped himself.

"He is fine, within a week he will be discharged." The nurse said, "I want you to buy this prescribed medication from outside. Not to be presumptuous but it is quite expensive and you need to pay the medical bill as well."

"Where do I need to pay?" he asked wiping off his tears.

The nurse guided him to the reception. He used his card to its utmost limit to pay for surgical expenses and went broke before buying the medication.

He was forced to call his father, Raja Ram— craftsman who owned a furniture designing company. When Raja Ram learned about the situation, he first yelled at Varadarajan for minutes for the stubbornness he had had all those years. Then he credited double the money needed in Varadarajan's account for medications and future expenses.

When he went back to Raghav's room, he left the medication on the table near him and got seated next to Raghav and held his hand again. All he could think were the last three years pursuing his broken dream, neglecting his son.

He felt Raghav's sufferings without love and support in that moment of realisation. He regretted every action he took in those years which only brought him misery.

Tears that dropped on Raghav's hands were filled with remorse. He hoped to redeem himself and Raghav opened his eyes slowly. When his blurred vision became normal, he found his father next to him and clenched his fist with anger.

He struggled to say, "Why are you here?"

Varadarajan didn't know what to answer, "I was asked to bring some medicines for you."

"Why did they save me? I am better off dead," Raghav said as his voice cracked.

"Don't say another word like that please."

"Why? Does it hurt you? You never cared all these years, why are you worrying about me all of a sudden?"

"Why did you try committing suicide?"

"I didn't commit suicide, and you answer me first, or else please leave me alone."

"Yes, it hurts. I realised my mistake. Please, please. I am so sorry," he said as he held Raghav's hand as tears kept dripping.

Raghav took his hand out of his father's grasp with a pain on his face.

"I don't know if I can forgive you, but I do have a favour to ask. Please never inform mom about this, I am requesting you. Please do this one thing for me."

Varadarajan nodded and walked out of the room. Raghav's words stabbed him hard, but he himself knew that he could not be forgiven. All he could do was try to be a father at which he failed once.

***

Aarthi walked out from the examination room to Ravichandran and Elizabeth which made them stand up.

"She needs a small surgery," Aarthi said. "The test didn't go well."

"What about her neck pain?" Ravichandran asked.

Aarthi nodded, "Yes, she became paraplegic, as per her statement she hit her lumbar spine while playing football, some organs are not functioning well, but her injury is incomplete."

Elizabeth couldn't understand a thing they were talking about, so she interrupted and asked, "What's going on, why does she need a surgery?"

Ravichandran calmed her down and agreed to proceed with the surgery.

The next day Aarthi took Shalini's parents to her cabinet.

"The functions are improving a bit slower, she may regain

consciousness, but we cannot say for sure," Aarthi said. "She needs to be under our eyes for 11 days of treatment, and because it is traumatic SCI, she needs to attend rehabilitation too."

Ravichandran understood everything, he was sad but as a doctor and a parent he was forced to accept it.

Aarthi looked at Elizabeth who was spaced out. She called her thrice to wake her up.

"Please stay strong, a lot of hardship is in store. You must help your daughter to face it," Aarthi said and held her hand. "Have faith in your daughter."

Shalini's life turned upside down, six months, a year, or more or never. Her life left a big question mark and a wheelchair for her to spend her upcoming days.

I asked a question to myself then, "Will she try giving up her life like others?"

-CHAPTER 4-

Ravichandran and Aarthi had a conversation in private and in end they decided to keep it a secret from Elizabeth and Shalini.

"Every patient with a spine injury has a different grade, and yours is not bad," Aarthi said to Shalini during a regular check-up.

"Will I be able to walk again?" Shalini asked.

Aarthi took a minute to answer and said, "Well, yeah you may but I cannot say when or how," with her gloomy eyes, she continued, "you should come here for the next six months occasionally for a check-up, and if your condition improves, you will have a greater chance to walk again."

Shalini gave a sorrowful smile, "Why aren't you happy then?"

"Because as a doctor I cannot guarantee you," Aarthi said and walked out.

Shalini went into a depressed state, she stopped talking to everyone, refused to answer her calls, and voluntarily tried hard to isolate herself. All she did was fake a smile and repeat, "I am fine."

Without getting deeply engaged with Shalini both Ravichandran and Elizabeth found it hard to comfort her.

***

2016

June 8th

Day 4 of Shalini's hospitalisation

"Your son escaped the worst with minor injuries. We thought he would be dead without getting blood on time," the senior doctor said, putting down Raghav's medical report.

"May I know who donated blood at the last moment?" Varadarajan asked.

The senior doctor— who knew about Ravichandran's current condition, believed a warm gesture from the patient's family would motivate him and lift him up, hence he guided him to the neurological division to introduce him to Ravichandran.

Elizabeth was home and Shalini was resting while Ravichandran was sitting in the waiting hall with his eyes closed. As Varadarajan approached him with the senior doctor they shared their names and Varadarajan showed his gratitude by thanking him repeatedly for saving Raghav. Ravichandran didn't get a word to stop him and eventually he cried. He let those tears out which he had kept hidden for the last few days.

"I heard about your situation, not sure if I can say this but… things will be alright!" Varadarajan consoled him, patting on his shoulder.

Minutes passed and Varadarajan went back to Raghav to take him home. The rest of the pending hospital bill was paid by Varadarajan and together they walked out of the hospital.

Raghav received the clothes he wore the other day, covered with blood. The bandages were taken off, and the wounds he had received from the accident became visible. His hair was long, hiding his arrogant face.

"I was so unlucky," Raghav whispered on the way home.

"I told you numerous times, don't talk about something that you will regret in the future," Varadarajan got angry for his whispering.

"Are you trying to be a dad, once again? Well, good luck."

Raghav taunted. He hated being dependent on his father when he was hospitalised, but he was left with no choice. "Have you ever tried being what you just said?"

Varadarajan was silent.

When they reached home, Raja Ram was already home waiting for them. They sat together on the sofa, staring at the ground with silence.

Raja Ram— instead of asking about the accident or the past, he was more worried about something else and asked, "Raghav, why don't you want your mother to know?"

Raghav— who never disrespected his grandfather, answered with a pause, "Because, she will put up an act as if she cares."

"You know she loves you," Raja Ram sighed as he was speechless.

"I got fed up with expecting things from her, and if she is really working hard, I don't want to disturb her."

Raja Ram exhaled softly, "Then, why did you get hurt, and hurt others?"

"I don't want to talk about it. I am tired, please," Raghav said getting up slowly.

Raja Ram helped him to his bed and when he walked out Varadarajan was spaced out.

He sat beside Varadarajan and said, "See, this is why people say parents' selfishness harms their child. This is not a play that you perform, this is life, and you cannot change the fact that you made a mistake."

"I know," Varadarajan snivelled, "and I want to redeem myself. I will never let this happen again even if it means giving up my self-respect which I was obsessed with."

"What about your wife?"

"I don't know, I am afraid to talk to her. Every small conversation we have through call ends up in a fight. I hate to admit it, but I was wrong all the time."

"But you still love her, don't you?"

"Yeah, I do. Still, I was the one who told her not to give up on her dreams. I promised her that I will take the responsibility, but I messed up everything. All I can do is wait for things to go back to normal. I will stop pursuing theatre acting from now on and will look for a job and wait until my son accepts me first."

Raja Ram hugged Varadarajan and said, "Don't give up on your family at least," and he continued backing off saying, "your son said he is interested in trying Marquetry. I left some of my stuff in his room."

"He won't last long. That shit is hard."

Raja patted Varadarajan's back strongly, "Don't talk vulgarly. I want him to give up on woodcraft and practise the piano again."

Varadarajan nodded and looked into Raghav's room to see if he was sleeping, but he wasn't. He got up when his father started cooking for lunch. He picked the stuff his grandfather left for him. He picked out the instruction paper written by his grandfather to try out carving Pikachu, which was something most of the beginners wouldn't try and the only point of it was to make him give up early.

Reading the instruction shot him with the memory of his poem and diary he left the other day. He figured that his diary and poem were already taken to the trash land, so he gave up on looking for them. His fingers weren't calm, they were shaking and he was in no position to try carving a Pikachu, so he gave up in minutes.

He was very much looking forward to visiting the gazebo, the place where he tended to relax and calm his mind. But with his condition, he couldn't move out of his house. He laid back in his bed covering himself with a blanket and boredom.

***

The remaining seven days of Shalini's hospitalisation were hell. She sometimes suffered pain all over her body and sometimes had a respiratory problem. She couldn't eat what she wanted, she couldn't sleep in peace and all she could do was stare at the doctor's face during the examination. She hated peeing without realising it and cried whenever she did. She wished she could rather die than live like this. ***Arduous gamble.***

At the end of the eleventh post-traumatic day, Shalini was transferred to the department of rehabilitation. By that time her bladder and bowel senses increased compared to the first couple of days. Hopefully, she did show improvement.

She avoided talking to anyone in those eleven days. She was allotted to ten days of rehabilitation in a row and then the subsequent four weeks with weekly intervals. The main aim was to prevent future complications that might prolong for the long term.

Elizabeth informed Ayesha about it. Ayesha became downcast for the moment and remembered the conversation they had when they met after many years.

Shalini spent a whole month in the hospital. Elizabeth occasionally took leave from school to take care of her. Ravichandran did the same. Ayesha visited her twice a week and helped her during Elizabeth's absence.

When Shalini went back home, everything looked different, she couldn't touch her feet to the ground, she was only able to roll here and there with her wheelchair.

Elizabeth could understand Shalini's pain, so she rolled her to the dining and sat on the chair facing her.

"If you act like you are fine, do you really think we will be fooled?" Elizabeth asked.

"Mom, I am okay. Even if I show how I am feeling, will that change anything?" Shalini sighed.

"It may not and look I do not pity you. You are my daughter and stronger compared to me and your father."

Shalini lost character having faced the adversities that had occurred in a haste.

"You can still live your life as you wish. The only thing that is required are not your legs but your willingness to live life to the fullest." Elizabeth said.

Shalini slowly started crying and buried her face in Elizabeth's shoulder. Ravichandran entered Shalini's room and made some changes for comfort.

A physiotherapist was scheduled every morning for Shalini, and her daily ordinary life drastically changed.

A day later, Shalini got a confirmation mail from St. Mary's school along with the notice to attend freshers' function and 11th grade commencement date.

Elizabeth jumped with joy and kissed Shalini on her cheek. But Shalini was too bothered with facing the world with the support of wheels.

Both Elizabeth and Ravichandran did every possible thing to bring back the old Shalini. Even though she accepted her disability, she was still embarrassed to go out in public and it troubled her often.

"What about Ayesha?" Shalini asked curiously just when the phone rang. Ravichandran picked up the mobile and handed it over to Shalini saying, "I think she heard you somehow."

Shalini chuckled.

"Did you receive any mail?" Ayesha asked.

"No." Shalini lied with a smirk.

"Really?" Ayesha's voice dropped.

"No no, I got one," Shalini said and laughed.

"You idiot! My heart stopped for a second," Ayesha said.

Two days passed and the night before freshers' party, Shalini challenged herself to face the outside world with everything she got. She wanted to face everyone in school where she belonged for the next two years.

***

2016

July 1st

Freshers function

Shalini received a lot of cold and pity stares which haunted her. She was afraid of those but she somehow managed to shrug them off and safely reported to the school ground where the stage was set up. The school was exactly the same as Elizabeth showed to her in the picture book. She was in a long red dress hiding her shrunken legs, and with Elizabeth, for the first fifteen minutes she enjoyed a long conversation and then Ayesha joined them. She was wearing a yellow kurti with jeans. Shalini relaxed a bit and Elizabeth left them both to attend the function. She joined other teachers to support her role as one of them.

Ayesha showed the list of students who were selected with the photograph she had clicked from the notice board.

She showed the first picture to Shalini, the list of students selected in the science group and Ayesha's name was fourth among them.

"You chose science?" Shalini asked Ayesha.

"Yeah, you didn't know?" Ayesha asked.

Shalini sighed and said, "When did you ever tell me?"

"You chose to avoid my calls, maybe I forgot to mention, what's the big deal?"

"How can I be in the commerce classroom alone?"

"Won't you make any new friends?" Ayesha sniffled.

Shalini went silent and then checked the other picture, the list of commerce students selected and the first name that popped up was RAGHAV VARADARAJAN.

Ayesha started searching for Shalini's name from that list, whispering, "Where are you?"

"Look from the last, you will find me sooner," Shalini said and remembered the diary and poem she had, which belonged to Raghav.

"I found you. You are at 23," Ayesha said, pointing it out.

"There are two more students like me?" Shalini was amazed. "Where did you click this picture?"

Ayesha pointed out the notice board in the corridor, a bit away from the ground and coincidently Shalini found Raghav in front of the board. He was wearing a black shirt and blue jeans; his right hand was wrapped in a crepe bandage, and he was trying to call someone with an annoyed face and decent haircut.

Ayesha noted Shalini staring at Raghav for too long.

"Ohoo…" she interrupted and lifted her eyebrows to Shalini.

"He is the one who met with an accident in front of our house," Shalini said and changed the mood.

"How did you know?" Ayesha suddenly shot a tough question.

"Well, a long story," Shalini didn't want Ayesha to know about the suicide poem.

"I thought it was love at first sight. He is good-looking."

Shalini blushed and widened her eyes. "He is not that good looking."

"Not for you maybe…"

"Cut the crap and concentrate on the function," Shalini acted annoyed and turned to the stage.

Raghav climbed up to the first floor through the stairs and continued calling someone. But this time the person from the other side answered.

"Where are you, bastard?" Raghav asked with wrath.

"I am in my hometown. I will be there by tomorrow," the person from the other side answered.

"You are not coming today?"

"The answer is obvious."

"Abdul, answer me this then. Why did you choose science?"

"What do you mean I chose? You didn't?" Abdul asked and his voice became hard.

"I chose commerce, and I thought you might go for it too."

"Your mobile was not reachable when I was trying to inform you about it. I thought you would choose science and I went with it."

"You are blaming me now?"

"No, I don't think it is too much to worry about."

"Yeah, I am an idiot," Raghav grew angry.

"I believe there may be a reason for me to choose science, it just happened, and I don't know yet," and this philosophical talk made Raghav irritated and he hung up the call.

Abdul whispered, "He didn't change a bit," he looked at his lock screen— three young boys smiling together putting hands on each other's shoulders. He shook his head and carried on packing his stuff.

***

The stage was set, and the function was about to begin. Many students sat together with their parents in the arranged chair. A man who was wearing a mask sat at the last corner leaving all the empty seats in between. His hair was short, and his beardless face was somewhat visible. Shalini looked for Raghav once again from the same place, but he wasn't anywhere around. She turned 180 degrees and stopped as Ayesha glared at her suspiciously.

"Are you looking for him again?" Ayesha asked.

"No," Shalini beamed with embarrassment and the function began, it was dusk by then.

Someone from the back sniggered after overhearing their conversation unintentionally.

Shalini and Ayesha turned to respond for the snigger with anger, but their faces twitched as it was Raghav himself.

His hands were tied and he looked at both of their miserable faces. He didn't show any interest after looking at their faces even for a second and his concentration shifted to the stage.

The principal began with the welcome speech which made everyone yawn.

After a quarter of an hour, the teachers introduced themselves and announced their respective subjects, and then the vice-principal took over the stage congratulating the 10th passed out students from their school and called Raghav on stage to offer him a shield for his achievement and to appreciate him.

Raghav lurched. He didn't want an achievement shield but peace. He was called again which gave him no choice but to show himself. He stood up and walked to the stage nervously with an annoying face he always held.

He forcefully smiled for a photograph holding the shield, which Shalini understood at a glance and she laughed, when everybody else clapped their hands.

"You asked a question, remember? About making friends?" Shalini reminded Ayesha, looking at Raghav clapping her hands.

"Yeah," Ayesha replied.

"He is going to be my friend; he looks interesting and..." Shalini said.

"And... what is that?"

"It is our secret," Shalini said.

"You never talked to him in person but you both have a secret."

"Yes, we do."

"I don't know, but judging from his behaviour, he is a tough one to flatter."

"Then let's bet, I will make him my friend, and you will have to try a lob haircut."

Ayesha's face changed for a bit, but she agreed. She was happy either way.

Shalini felt something with Raghav, something that they both had in common. She wanted him to be the one to help her out from the darkness she was in because she somehow could hear him screaming for help in the same level of darkness.

'One person can change one's life'. The quote she read years ago flashed through her mind. *Credits to the writer.*

She wanted to change his life and in return, she wanted to escape from the darkness they both were in. She was curious to learn about his intention for committing suicide and she felt something more that she didn't understand at that moment.

Moreover, every student who attended the fresher's function was eager about the first day of the 11th standard.

-CHAPTER 5-

2016

July 4th

The first day of school

The weekend passed within a blink of an eye. As usual all the students were excited about making new friends— meeting new crushes— catch sight of the pre-kg teacher etcetera. The final two years of school had got to be exciting.

White shirt and light sandal colour pants were the school uniform for boys to make them look like a gentleman. For girls, it was similar to salwar-kameez— white top, sandal colour pants along with sandal scarf— a disciplined uniform to make girls look more delightful.

When everyone was excited about one thing or another, Shalini alone found it difficult to accept the fact that she needed help from others even for changing clothes. She was forced to be dependent.

After the lower body numbness, Shalini along with the wheelchair tried so much harder to live the way she used to be, but every small thing reminded her that she was unworthy. She tried so hard to suppress that fact but the more she tried the more she started acting fine in front of others. After a great struggle of fitting into the uniform, Shalini set wheels on the road to school with Elizabeth and Ayesha. The road was Crowded.

"These days I miss your mischief," Ayesha soothed Shalini as they were passing through the crowd.

"You must be grateful for that," Elizabeth smirked patting Shalini's head as they crossed Raghav's house which was between Shalini's and the school.

***

Varadarajan offered Raghav a breakfast of two fried eggs stuffed in bread. "Have it. I Even cooked you lunch, take it before you leave." Varadarajan, with short hair and clean shave, looked pretty decent and exactly opposite from the foolish person he was a few days back.

"Did I ask you to cook? Why are you always bothering me like a rat?" Raghav fumed.

"I just offered you breakfast and made lunch for you, what did I do to provoke you? And I am your dad. Not a rat," Varadarajan gasped, calmly.

"Don't say that."

"Yeah, I gave up on you. I broke the promise I made to your mom. I lost everything. I did, I agree. But I didn't want to hurt you either. I distanced myself to keep you safe. Why don't you understand that?" Varadarajan said and his voice gradually went high, "I want to change. I will never give up on you hereafter even if you hate me or call me a rat."

"People don't change. Even if you try to be a good father hereafter, the scars and bruises you gave will never heal, never forget that and keep regretting the past."

Raghav cursed him, his look was cold as usual and his words stabbed Varadarajan, but Varadarajan smiled and said, "I won't give up on trying," and handed the breakfast plate to him. "Don't waste any of the food and don't forget to take your lunch."

Varadarajan went into the kitchen and slid down on the floor, burying his face in between his thighs. He tried to keep his tears from falling out, but he couldn't manage to hide it long and cried silently. He was embarrassed to show his face to his son.

Raghav had his breakfast and picked up the lunch from the table. Something felt off. Even when he realised that his father was trying hard to make up, he grew angrier and more emotional. The way he talked to his father was cold and he was in no position to express how he felt. He didn't even know what he was feeling. Did he want to cry or scream? When he walked past the doorway, the landline phone rang.

Raghav gasped and picked up, "Hello," he said, in a hurry.

The other side was silent, and Raghav figured out who it might be.

"Hello, Raghav," Raghav's mother said but he hung up the call straight away, stood there for a couple of seconds silently, and left for school, annoyed.

"I want to skip school today," Raghav whispered.

Varadarajan filled a glass with water and drank it, trying to stop the sounds inside his head— the conversation he had with his son. It kept bothering him and he dropped the glass jar he was holding.

"Shit," he said.

The floor became wet with water and glass pieces. While cleaning the floor with bare hands and filling the plastic bag with broken sharp edge glasses, the voice in his head and a telephone call made him flinch and he cut his right palm by mistake.

"Fuck," he yelled and walked to attend the call without prioritising his cut.

The blood kept dripping as he answered.

"Varun!" Raghav's mother said.

"I am not in the mood to talk with you right now. Sorry," he said as calmly as possible with burning pain in his palm.

"I wanted to talk to Raghav, but it seems he is still angry with me."

"Yeah, he is and what did you expect?"

She was silent for a moment. She knew her excuses won't do anything. After a minute she continued, "So, how are you?"

Blood kept dripping down from his finger, "I already said, I am not in a mood to talk."

He didn't allow her to talk or ask any further questions by saying, "I am hanging up." That's what he did. He hated being nuts to his very wife, not for this time but from the very beginning. He was filled with guilt that he couldn't talk to her. He also didn't want his wife to know about the accident Raghav had. By getting stuck in between the curses of his son and failure in keeping the promise he made to his wife, he felt insecure for being such an incompetent person.

But somehow Raghav's mother felt the remorseful voice behind Varadarajan's ignorance and could only make a guess.

***

Raghav's mind was filled with thoughts, he was straight behind Shalini marching towards the school along with the crowd and someone from behind him slid their hands across Raghav's shoulder waking him up from the flooded thoughts. Abdul!

Abdul was same height as Raghav, although he was fit and looked more mature than Raghav. His hair was straight and pushed back unlike Raghav who had bangs in front.

"Zoned out?" Abdul asked.

"I don't want to talk to you," Raghav said and moved two steps ahead of Abdul.

"I know you. I somehow knew you would say that, but mate I swear choosing science or parting away from you doesn't mean our friendship would break. It's up to you and me to decide whether to stay as friends or leave, and I will stay. You know me," Abdul reassured without knowing about the incident that had happened the previous month.

Raghav stayed silent, he understood what Abdul meant and it was a bit comforting.

Shalini's introduction was pending to Elizabeth's colleagues, so she was taken to the staffroom first. Ayesha didn't follow her instead she promised Shalini to save her a seat in the commerce classroom.

The commerce classroom was at the end of the corridor right next to the science classroom, so Abdul stopped in front of his class and waved his hand at Raghav. Abdul got along with other guys around him and Raghav walked further, unfortunately with Ayesha, and they both got into the commerce class together.

All the faces in the classroom were invisible to Raghav and the only visible thing was the last bench at the right corner which was empty. There were three last benches, the middle one was taken by girls, and the left corner was full of guys. So, before letting anyone else capture the precious place Raghav marched towards it, and again, unfortunately, Ayesha also had the same thought. They both tried to capture the same place.

Raghav for the past six years had ruled over the last bench and because of his great academic performance, none of the teachers ever bothered him about changing seats. Hence, it became his obsession. But Ayesha's ideology was different. She didn't want Shalini to sweat and get treated as an outcast. As per her theory, the first bench definition was, all eyes are watching, and she didn't want Shalini to be a gossip subject for being the only special child in the class. Both had their strong reasons not to give up the precious last bench.

"Sorry, but you can share the seat with those girls," Raghav recommended the middle last bench to Ayesha and tried to settle down.

Ayesha stopped Raghav insisting, "I chose this one first." Shalini with her wheelchair would need at least a place for two for comfortable seating so she turned him down.

Raghav became annoyed as didn't know anything about what was swinging inside Ayesha's mind.

"You can sit here, I have no objection, but I can't choose

anywhere else," Ayesha made it clear and sat down.

"No, I don't want to sit beside any girl," Raghav said.

"So, do you want to fight with me for a mere place?" Ayesha taunted.

Raghav became angry and cursed Abdul for leaving him alone in this mess.

"I should have skipped school," Raghav whispered. He didn't want to make a scene on the very first day. He looked around the class and all the places were full except the first bench, which he would never choose.

He sat beside Ayesha in the end without any choice and she chortled.

"Don't let anyone sit in this place, I will bring my friend, she will be sitting here," she said and moved.

"What about you?" he asked with a hard voice.

"I am from the science class you dummy. You want to sit beside me," she smirked. "Don't let anyone, okay. I will kill you if you do," she threatened him and left.

"Stupid bitch," he muffled with anger for messing with him when she was in the doorway. She immediately turned to him, which made him shiver. Then she left for good.

"Who gave her the right to be informal with me?" he said with pride after she left. "I won't let her, or her friend use this whole table," he said abruptly, making the table comfortable enough to use it all by himself.

This was the first time after a long time he talked to someone for this long and he hated it. Raghav was the type of person who don't socialise with his classmates and only focuses on teaching if he was interested, or else he would just sleep. Until last year Abdul was his bench partner, and he never faced any problem as such. He almost made up his mind that he met a crazy half-crack witch on the first day of school and let it pass.

***

Shalini had the ability to make anyone fond of her, supporting this she made all the staff feel her warmth. Ayesha, after ending another war by selecting her own place in the science class, went straight to the staff room to help Shalini, it wasn't necessary, but she chose to do it anyway.

After greeting all the teachers in the Staff room, she rolled Shalini out of the staffroom and on the way, she informed Shalini about the incident happened minutes ago which made them laugh so hard that the staffroom turned frightened.

"I never thought you would pick up a fight with Raghav on the very first day," Shalini delighted.

"I thought maybe you sitting next to him would help you to realise that I am going to win the bet we announced, sooner or later," Ayesha said.

"Ah, so you deliberately want to see me lose this. Maybe you got this wrong and it might work the other way." Shalini empathised.

"Nah, don't think so. You will realise that soon."

"Oh, then this bet will last until I give up."

"Then I might meet my lover before that, and you will still be trying."

"Ahh…I see, girl with romantic need. I hope your lover shuts your mouth with his grace."

"And I hope he does that also with a kiss too."

Both laughed, "Stop being erotic it makes me shiver," Shalini said.

It was almost time for the first period. All the students in commerce class were ready to invite the teacher with a powerful good morning. Raghav didn't care, he made his bed and was already yawning.

Everyone heard the footsteps near the doorway and wished, "GOOD MORRRRR…" They stopped in the middle. They were embarrassed and Shalini became the centre of attention in an instant.

Awkward silence soon followed as it was Shalini and Ayesha who marched in the class.

Shalini smiled at everyone, but Ayesha greeted back, "Good morning." Her voice made Raghav wake up and as he looked at her, their eyes met. His face turned fearful, and he made way for Shalini to avoid an unnecessary fight. He knew it would be a drag.

Ayesha rolled Shalini forward. A few students smiled back at Shalini, some gave a strange look as they had never met a disabled person before, few pitied. Shalini ignored the pity and strange looks and when she reached Raghav with prolonged smile, he was too focused on avoiding Ayesha and her annoyance. His response to Shalini was empty, he didn't smile back neither gave a strange look nor pity; his expression was just bland.

Raghav gave Ayesha a look as he pushed the chair to kiss the wall, making way for Shalini to only use the table. He kept his aggression pent up and made sure it didn't manifest in the form of passive-aggressiveness. But he still exasperated after doing everything in Ayesha's favour.

Anger filled-up inside him and he ignored Shalini's gratitude. He sat beside her and when Ayesha was about to leave, she made one thing clear by soliciting Raghav, "Please get along with Shalini, and help her if she faces any difficulty."

Raghav ignored her too and buried his face in his palm. Ayesha left for her class and minutes later the teacher entered, but nobody was enthusiastic enough to greet her after a hilarious flop of their first try. But they did stand up to greet her normally.

She had already introduced herself on fresher's day, but she did it again. Her name was Vaishali, and she was their mathematics teacher.

Raghav relaxed his back on the chair and folded his arms as if something interesting was going to happen. It rooted Shalini to copy him. When she did Raghav got aware of it but still, he chose to ignore her.

"So, let's start with an introduction. Today is the first day, so

I'll give you time to interact with each other," Vaishali said.

Is this the thing Raghav is interested in? Shalini thought and she turned to him.

THUD! He literally fell over on the table when he heard the word 'introduce'.

Is he dead? Has he passed out? Shalini's mind began to fill with questions and she slowly moved to him to check.

"I am not dead yet, I am just trying to fly into my fantasies," Raghav said with his eyes closed.

"I thought you were a very active person," Shalini said to him, facing the teacher.

"I am the laziest one in the entire world who doesn't socialise with others, so just stay away from me for your own good and tell your friend that-" he opened his eyes, which were red with anger, "-she is annoying,"

Then he started pretending to sleep, snoring all of sudden.

"Raghav," Vaishali called his name from the front. "You start…"

Raghav got up from his place with his tired eyes and introduced himself with just five seconds. Preethi from the middle bench gave Raghav a romantic stare, and with that, introduction continued. Shalini went after Raghav, and one by one introduction carried on, when it reached the first bench's last student, the class bell rang and period got over with peace.

After getting informed that Raghav won't socialise with anyone, Shalini had no idea other than talking with him even after getting ignored. That did hurt a little but giving up was not under her choice.

During the first break, when Raghav was standing in the corridor, Ayesha asked him about Shalini. But he ignored her and moved further.

"I asked you a question?" Ayesha followed him.

"And I ignored it," he stopped, "because I didn't get along with your friend. Ask someone else to babysit her. Not me," he again continued walking.

"What do you mean by babysitting? She is sitting beside you, so you are supposed to know how she is in class."

"Why are you bothering me since morning?" he said and stopped again, "Look I am not coming to school to check on your friend or anyone, and don't think I am acting rude, I just don't like to get along with anyone, I hate this version of me but still I feel comfortable this way," he said and exasperated with annoyance and left.

Raghav meant what he said and he was also not ready to make any newer friends, he believed ignoring was a good thing and nobody would hurt or bother him. As he had already lost hope in life, he believed bringing new friends or foes would be more tiresome.

Was he wrong? If we ignore someone, that person would get a bit insulted and just start staying away from us, well best friends won't do that, they get even closer.

But Ayesha and Shalini were not his best friends, not even a friend, but they kept on bothering him.

The bothering continued. Shalini kept finding a topic to have a conversation on and Raghav tended to end it with just a word or two.

Last period of the day, the teacher wasn't there in the class.

"What is your friend's name?" Raghav asked without looking at Shalini as that he could wish God to keep her away from him.

"Ayesha," Shalini said, looking at him out of surprise.

"Well, she is annoying. Just tell her to stay away from me."

"Is that a threat?"

"Hell no! I can't win your friend. Maybe she will listen to you."

"But why are you ignoring us?"

"Don't ask me anything. I already told you."

The bell rang, period got over without a teacher in the class.

Everyone started walking out.

"Hey," Shalini chimed in while looking at Raghav.

He turned back to face her.

"Can you lend me a hand accompanying me?" She put forth.

"Why should I do that? I believe you got a friend to accompany you."

"Yes, I do, but she can't keep help me every day, right?"

"No, sorry…"

He said and left. As he crossed the doorway. Ayesha walked in ignoring him. She went to Shalini to help her as she knew this was going to happen.

"Well, he is not really good with his words," Shalini whispered.

"Shalini let me tell you something, he is a jerk. He is not worthy to be your friend, let's just break the bet. There are many more good guys and girls in your class, try them."

"You won't allow people that easily in your life too," Shalini hinted to Ayesha.

"Well, that doesn't mean I talk rudely, why are you comparing me with him?" Ayesha raised her voice.

"Because he said you are annoying."

"Well, everyone says that."

"Maybe I like being with annoying people."

Ayesha zipped her mouth saying, "Understood."

Shalini chuckled and looked at Ayesha. "He is just acting tough. It will take time to win his trust."

"How long? Six months?" Ayesha gasped. "I guarantee that you won't be able to win him over before that."

Shalini gazed at Ayesha, and Ayesha pretended to be unaware.

***

Abdul and Raghav were walking together on the road on the way to their houses. Abdul was speechless, aghast thinking about something. Raghav noticed his silence, as it was strange that Abdul was quiet, so he asked him, "What happened?"

"Nothing, you tell me. How was your first day?"

"Galled, tensed up with some girls."

"Ah, you too? Today we witnessed a girl, who fears nothing, who can shoot questions even to the teachers."

"Oh!"

"You don't look surprised? Our whole class was frazzled with that girl," before Abdul finishes, "Ayesha!" they said in unison.

"Expected," Raghav said.

"How?"

"I was talking about the same girl. I have never met a girl like her since birth."

"Well, I have met someone, not exactly but similar to her characteristics."

"Do I know them?"

"You will know on your own someday," Abdul said, and they were near Raghav's house's doorstep.

"See you tomorrow then," Abdul said with a wink and left with his bicycle.

After the first day of school, every student tends to talk about the first day experience with their parents but Raghav and Shalini omitted those steps. Raghav was not on good terms with his parents, so it was expected. But Shalini ignored her parents when they asked, and concluded with, "Nothing special."

After getting out from the suffocating uniform, Shalini killed time watching out the shady red sky from the balcony. She also found Raghav again in the gazebo. Her curiosity towards Raghav increased as she somehow could feel him screaming for help.

But looking into the roots of Raghav's life, he wanted to be selfish because he didn't want to get hurt. As per his definition friendship was for temporary happiness and satisfaction— the kind that individuals indulge in to escape reality by believing in eternal relationship. ***Maybe he is right. Friends are not really meant to travel with you till demise.*** But his definition was definitely an incomplete one. With his understanding he decided not to be in the so-called Friendship line which will give him pain at a later point of time. Though he hated the way he behaved with Shalini and Ayesha, he also wanted to justify his actions.

It was almost dinner time, the river next to the gazebo reflected the moon and when it caught Raghav's attention, he rushed back home to his boring pretentious life.

***

Shalini was having dinner with her parents, "It is bothering me, what does 'nothing special' mean?" Ravichandran asked Shalini in the dining room after keeping the question to himself for a very long time.

"It means, it was, as usual. Introduction and stuff. I was bored," Shalini said and went to wash her hands. "I am tired. I am going to my room to get some stuff to prepare for school tomorrow," she said and rolled to her room.

Ravichandran looked at Elizabeth with a doubtful face.

As usual, both were seated on the veranda after making sure Shalini was occupied.

"I can see Shalini is getting no better, she is just faking and pretending to be okay. Can't we do something for her?" Elizabeth asked Ravichandran. "And about her treatment? I know you have been hiding something from me for a long time."

Ravichandran was shaken up when Elizabeth said that. He replied, "I think I can't keep it forever," he exhaled shortly and said, "you knew about Shalini's condition before this accident. Every doctor needs to check the patient history before complete diagnosis. And the truth is although Shalini has regained consciousness she lost due to the injury, there is only one percent chance she can walk again because of her previous condition," his voice went low in the middle, and he sniffled. "I don't want

Shalini to know that until she is ready. I want to believe in that one percent."

Elizabeth hugged Ravichandran in sorrow as tears slowly fell out of her eyes.

Shalini overheard the conversation. She always believed that she would be cured but after hearing her father— who couldn't be a father or doctor at the same time, made her even more worried. She always made her parents worried about her and burdened them, but at that moment even though she was dependent, she didn't want them to burden them with her darkness and drag them in. So, she decided to be honest about that.

"Dad, mom," she said. They weren't expecting her and were shocked when they heard her. They wiped their tears and looked at her.

Shalini smiled at them, the real one this time as if she is going to cry after this.

"I am sorry, I lied," Shalini said.

-CHAPTER 6-

Shalini had numerous thoughts rolling in her mind. After dinner she got into her room, checked her school schedule, and tried to clear her mind by sitting on the balcony. She was finally ready to take back her words about the first day of school and to tell her parents what had happened. She silently rolled out with the thought of startling her parents from their blind side but unexpectedly she learned the truth about her medical condition. The smile she had in her face because of startling thought went numb and all the hopes she had, vanished. Listening to her parents she decided not to burden them with any more of her misfortune.

"Dad, mom," she said and smiled as if she was going to cry just like that.

"I am sorry, I lied, but I am really fine. You have nothing to worry about. I am just trying to understand what life means, after this," she pointed at her wheelchair. "I am still the same. Well… the first day of school was BORING, as I said earlier. Many pitied me, and I hated that." All three of them laughed, having weepy looks on their faces.

The next day, regular classes started. Every teacher started holding scary looks on their faces. More than making students knowledgeable, that last two years of school teaches how to apply the principles they had learned so far, and that's how it was.

Once again Shalini proved that she didn't inherit her mother's trait, Mathematics. The easiest chapter— the first chapter, and yet she didn't understand it quite well. The teacher who was so soft the other day, wore specs on her nose and taught like a cheetah— completed the first chapter's first exercise in a day. She solved one question from each topic and gave the leftovers as homework. She unleashed the evil within her and Shalini was busted. Not only was mathematics hard, but she also couldn't understand 'ABCD' in accountancy too. "Commerce is easier than science-" she was on the verge of choking the one who said that.

Shalini wanted to persuade Raghav with few new tricks, but something stopped her— maybe his behaviour and moreover the classes didn't give her any space to think about it.

Raghav's principle No. 1 was, stay away, don't get attached to anyone. And as Raghav and Abdul were separated because of their academic groups, they had no time to hang out together. This circumstance brought out more loneliness in Raghav's life, and instead of worrying about it, he simply wanted to cut off the ties with his only remaining friend.

Abdul was a type of person, whose principle was *#EverythingHappensForGood.* He didn't like to bother anyone's business or to confuse them any further. Instead, he consoled them on how far he could go and how far it had to be— drawing a line to stop himself from crossing it. He knew everything about Raghav, and the only thing he could do for him was to stay with him. Abdul didn't know the depth of darkness Raghav was stuck into, and without knowing that, he knew talking or consoling with rubbish wouldn't work.

***

Science group students were troubled with the syllabus. The teaching was vague, boring, and lacked interaction. Ayesha did the same thing she did in her previous school, she simply raised her voice and without any trepidation, which every student goes through, she openly admitted that the teaching was not clear.

The whole class was flabbergasted by her confidence. Ayesha was asked to talk with the teachers' in-person to share her thoughts and she did. Some admired her and others loathed her for being too bold, but it was just the starting. With her suggestions and complaints, she became worthy of being the class representative.

***

A week passed, both Science and Commerce were combined for mathematics class. And it became a hassle for commerce students to daily shifting their asses in science classroom on every mathematics periods. Shalini took a seat next to Ayesha, and Raghav next to Abdul. With enough time and space, Shalini caught up with the mathematics teacher and Ayesha enjoyed Mrs. Vaishali's classes compared to other teachers. Shalini sometimes glanced at Raghav during the combined class and, she tried to talk and get along— with talking about academics and stuff, but Raghav was a well-prepared mama's boy. Nothing worked for her to get close to him.

But they did get along indirectly. They were always together, and in other students' perspective, they were already friends.

Shalini then was to attend rehabilitation a whole week after that. Note: She was asked to attend rehabilitation for four more weeks with weekly intervals and it which indirectly affected Shalini's academics.

School:Home:Hospital:Books:Raghav:Food:Feeling:Insecure:

Exams— her days were in the loop and two months later the rehab came to an end with the depressing result of no improvement, although Shalini mentally accepted the facts and her internal organs improved just fine.

Days passed and months passed. The first term exam was done and the cycle test-3 was on the way. Maths class still held like fire and more than half the syllabus was done. Mrs. Vaishali was teaching trigonometry in class and Ayesha couldn't follow her. When she was done, still Ayesha couldn't comprehend and she raised request to teach again. After being taught one more time, Ayesha picked it up but the others from the class remained dull. To make sure if everyone understood, Vaishali wrote down the question on the board from RD Sharma's text and asked for a volunteer to solve it. Many didn't understand and refused, some understood but were not sure, nobody stood up to volunteer.

Raghav yawned and looked around. Nobody showed any enthusiasm and he picked this movement to show some heroism. He was bored, so he stood up as a volunteer and walked to the board. He folded his hands analysing the question.

Thirty seconds passed and there was no movement in him. Everyone was curious and eyes were on him to respond. Unexpectedly his response showed up with a yawn and curiosity turned comedy.

"Why are you waiting?" Vaishali asked when everyone started laughing.

"The question is wrong," Raghav said. And now the class started booing.

Vaishali played all the students, Raghav played her. He corrected the question without looking at the textbook and solved it. He had already solved all these sums in his free time as after school all his time was free time indeed. ***Sorry Raghav.***

"Correct," Vaishali said and clapped for him. She looked at others. "At least you should have noticed if the question is wrong? I am disappointed," she sighed.

"I did ma'am, that's why I didn't volunteer," a boy from science class said and his buddies started laughing at him.

"Cut the crap, I know you," Vaishali said and raised another question to others, "Is there anyone who still doesn't understand this?"

Among 50 students only 10 understood and the rest 40

simply stayed silent. Nobody raised their hands, everyone looked around at others.

Shalini also looked around and it was her time to heroinism, she raised her hands saying, "I didn't…"

"Only one student didn't understand. Hmm…," Vaishali said and nodded. "Raghav, you are her best friend, right? Help her out."

"Ma'am," Raghav blurted out and simultaneously the bell rang. Vaishali left. Raghav looked at Shalini, who in return gave a panicked smile as he frowned.

***

Lunch break

Ayesha and Shalini sat under the tree to have lunch. Raghav looked for them, and when he found them, he approached with his notebook.

"Here you are. Let me teach you that sum now."

"Are you kidding? We hardly get time to chit chat with each other, and you want to ruin it with another sum," Ayesha said.

"Well, she asked for it."

"She had a doubt, and you are supposed to teach her when she is ready to understand it." Ayesha didn't let Shalini answer any of his questions.

"Raghav, why don't you join us for lunch?" Shalini asked with a timid smile. Raghav, who had hardened his heart to get away from others, felt light. Shalini did something which made his heart flutter at that movement. His cheeks were turning red, but he shook his head, "When should I teach you?"

"Well, after school?" Shalini made sure.

"Done. I am leaving now, you carry on." Well, he said that but not with his complete presence. Shalini's word didn't reach his head and with the red cheeks, he hurried back to class.

After the lunch break, classes resumed and got over. When everyone started to leave, Raghav forgot about the promise he had made and was ready to egress.

"You said, you will teach me after school," Shalini volumed up.

Raghav jolted. He closed his eyes, took in a deep breath, and turned around to show disagreement. But when he did that, he couldn't reject her. He decided to end the task as soon as possible asking, "Shall we go somewhere else?"

Shalini happily nodded with a "hmm". She made a guess where it would be.

He took her to the gazebo and sat on the chair.

"Let's hurry then," Raghav said and took out his book.

"This place is good."

"Isn't it? I love to spend my time here all alone and this is my first time bringing someone here."

Shalini looked at him out of surprise, "Really?"

"Yes. Okay, let's begin," he ended the conversation.

He taught her the sum and she also got into it. As they were sitting close together, Raghav's attention got diverted and he stopped in between. He gave her the textbook and maintained some gap in between. He hated himself for his fluttering heart at that movement. He wanted to end that feeling there itself. He had no idea what to do for her to hate him and his mind was constantly thinking of a solution.

"Did you understand?" he asked.

"Yeah, I will try this one more time, and all done," Shalini said, again with a timid smile and this time it annoyed him.

"Okay, then you can leave. I will stay here for some more time."

"Let me stay here too."

"No, I want some quality time here. Alone."

Shalini shrugged. Raghav looked in the other direction for her to leave. But she kept looking at him, without delivering a word. She pouted and kept staring until the annoyance reached to point and Raghav turned back to her with "What?"

She looked down. She wanted help to climb up to the road. She made a pitiful face. Raghav never actually realised her as a disabled person before even though he rolled her to the gazebo, without actually giving any thoughts in his mind.

He wanted to help her and got up but his mind formulated a plan out of nowhere to break all strings attached. He laughed—he fake-laughed, but he did.

"You can't even move on your own?" he asked. She had no answer and opened her eyes wider as she wasn't expecting it.

"Can I ask you something? How are you living like this? It's like you can't even do anything on your own." Raghav asked.

"Raghav, stop it. That's enough." Shalini said. "If you don't wanna help, don't do it," Shalini tried to move on her own.

"Are you planning to cling on everyone's shoulder until you die? I am just curious."

"I… I can't be blamed for my disability, and I don't like to cling as you said."

"I, too, don't want to bring others into my mess. If I were you, I would just die."

"Wait… What?" Shalini turned, "Who are you to suggest someone to die? I thought you would understand," she yelled, and her tears were about to break out.

He knew this would happen. He went cracked.

Raghav chuckled but he didn't have any answers. The moment irked Shalini. She picked out something from her bag and his reaction drastically changed, his fake laugh turned into terror. He became silent.

"How can you possibly understand the value of life? If you don't even consider yours as one," Shalini said.

"How did you get that?" Raghav into absolute puzzlement.

Shalini threw down the diary along with the suicide poem in front of him. "I didn't read your diary. I wanted to learn about you from you. Unfortunately, I read the poem and perhaps that's what made me show interest in you, foolish me. I don't know why but I wanted to help you. Not any more. I know, you want me to stay away from you and probably that's why you barked all this crap to me, but seriously. I will never try to talk with you again. We can never be good friends as I expected. We are done here."

She tried to climb back up once again on her own. Raghav packed his diary and poem in his backpack and tried to help her, rolling her to the road.

"Don't, I can on my own." Shalini yelled and tried to make him back off, but he continued climbing up without paying attention to her words. She hit him on his hands, but still, he didn't react. When they reached the road, they met Ayesha who was on the way home. Ayesha found Shalini a little upset, so she rushed to give her a hand. Raghav backed off and let Ayesha help her. With the bland face he carried on to the other side.

After reaching Shalini's house Ayesha helped her change. Shalini tightened her jaw with anger as she had no other options other than being clingy to work out things. She became even more concerned with her disability.

Ayesha noticed everything but she stayed silent. She stayed with her until Elizabeth got home.

Raghav was so sorry for what he did. He hit his head on the wall for doing something so stupid and childish and moreover Shalini figured out the reason for his action made him more sorrowful. He understood why Shalini was so into him. He decided to apologise right away but he didn't have her number or know anything about her.

***

The next day Shalini was on leave. Raghav didn't understand if she was absent because of him. Half-day went just like that until Ayesha showed up during the lunch break. They both went to the corner of the corridor to have a chat in private.

"What did you do yesterday?" she asked. "Why was Shalini

upset?"

"I hurt her feelings, maybe," he said. "I barked unwanted words at her."

"What did you say to her?"

"I bad-mouthed about her disability."

"And why the fuck did you do that? Do you know anything about her? She just wanted to be your friend."

Raghav went silent. He couldn't say a word after that. Ayesha was heated up and ready to punch him in the face.

"I didn't mean what I said. Okay, I know I did something stupid… and an apology won't work but…"

"But, what?" Ayesha asked. Raghav couldn't say anything and after a minute of silence, Ayesha left.

Time fled; a day passed without Shalini. Next day and to put it clearer, the second day of Shalini's absence made Raghav worry.

Raghav's mind began to fill with questions. *How did my diary and poem reach her? How could she possibly understand my poem? And why was she absent the other day?*

During the lunch break, Raghav looked for Ayesha to enquire about Shalini, but she was nowhere to be found. Later he had a protein bar, instead of lunch, sitting on the steps near the playground. He saw Abdul dashing, here and there, disturbed with a piece of paper in his hands.

"Abdul," Raghav shouted but his voice didn't reach him.

Everyone was tense about something. While watching the football game, somebody from behind startled Raghav by talking so suddenly.

"Don't fill your mind with weird, garbage thoughts," the girl said with a hard voice. "Shalini is okay."

Raghav jolted and got up. It was Ayesha.

"I was never thinking about her," Raghav said.

"Then why were you spaced out?" Ayesha asked.

Raghav couldn't talk more, and he looked at the ground floor out of guilt.

"Why are you embarrassed to face me? Are you in love, with me?" she asked.

"Hell no," he said and looked directly into Ayesha's eyes. She was different from the other day. She was pale.

"Ayesha," someone from the corridor shouted. It was Abdul. Ayesha turned back at him as he marched forward.

"I am sick," Ayesha said.

"Your father will be here anytime soon, let's go," Abdul said to Ayesha and looked at Raghav. "Hey, Raghav."

Raghav waved his hands. For the last few months, Abdul had been a bit busy and the conversation between them slowed down. *Well, it was all because of Raghav himself.*

"Bye, Raghav," Ayesha said, and her steps became uneven. She was on the verge of fainting. Raghav tried to hold her but before that could happen, Abdul was already there for her. He took her to the nurse's room.

Raghav never had an idea about Abdul and Ayesha being friends. He became sad and when suddenly somebody's voice from behind startled him once again.

"What happened to Ayesha?" again the familiar voice of a girl asked— a familiar and the most expected one.

It was Shalini, rolling on the way to class with the help of a boy from the 8th grade.

"She is sick," Raghav said. "Well, what about you?"

"I don't want to talk to you," Shalini said and asked the 8th grader to move.

"I will help her, you can leave," Raghav said to the boy and held the wheelchair. When the boy left, he continued, "I have a lot of questions in my mind. And I am sorry,"

"Where do you want to go?"

"Ladies toilet. Will you take me there?"

"You were about to go with that 8th grader? This is not funny."

"Yeah, not funny. I am just angry." Shalini made her

annoyed face.

Raghav sighed, "I am sorry for the other day."

"Prove how really sorry you are. Take me to the staffroom."

Raghav's mind popped with another question. *Does she want to file a complaint about me now?*

When they got to the Staffroom only three teachers were there, and the rest of the tables were empty.

"Mom," Shalini said and waved at Elizabeth.

Mom? Raghav panicked; he never knew that her mother was a teacher.

"He is the Raghav, I told you about," Shalini said. "And don't ask me about him ever again. We are not friends anymore, we never were."

Elizabeth couldn't understand what she meant, so she kept it aside and looked at Raghav. Another staff member called Shalini for help and she left him with her mother.

"Raghav?" Elizabeth asked.

"Yes ma'am," he panicked.

"Shalini talked a lot about you, and she said you don't like to get along with others."

"Well…"

"Don't bother answering that, leave it. Let me ask you another question."

"Yes ma'am."

"Did she tell you anything about her past? Or about the night on the first day of school?" Elizabeth asked.

Raghav turned puzzled. He couldn't figure out what she was expecting from him or what Shalini had talked about him to her parents. He blinked twice without answers. He was nervous and his mind filled with a question once again.

Does anything happening here have something to do with my suicide poem?

Does it have something to do with my arrogance or my behaviour the other day?

Or something I need to know but I don't?

Shalini was helping the teacher. The break still had 20 more minutes to end and Raghav, standing in front of a teacher— well in front of Shalini's mother to be precise— to answer the question which was not opaque.

-CHAPTER 7-

The night of the first day of school

When Shalini overheard everything, she decided to inform her parents about the thoughts she was hiding.

"Dad, mom," she said and smiled as if she was going to cry just like that.

"I am sorry, I lied but I am really fine. You have nothing to worry about. I am just trying to understand what life means after this," she pointed at her wheelchair. "But I am still the same. Well, the first day of school was boring. Many pitied me, and I hated that." All three of them laughed, having weepy looks on their faces.

"You heard everything?" Ravichandran asked to make sure.

"Yeah, and you didn't have to keep it a secret. I knew it from the beginning. I was ready for this from day one," Shalini said and started sobbing. "Well, I am afraid that I can't play football any more and I must be dependent on others. I will get used to it over time, but I don't want to burden you both any more. I want someone who can see me in the darkness that I am in."

"And why are we called parents if we aren't able to understand your depth?" Ravichandran asked as he couldn't follow Shalini's words.

"I think she found someone to share her burden," Elizabeth

said and calmed Ravichandran down. Shalini nodded with her watery cheeks.

***

In the staffroom, Elizabeth cleared Raghav's flooded thoughts by briefing the night of the first day of school.

Her face went low as she continued, "I think it was you, she never talked about the person she wanted to share her burden with after that, but she always spoke about you. I don't know why, but she believed that you could help her out by sharing her burden with you as a friend. There might be lots of secrets and disagreements between you and her, but I am glad that Shalini is changing."

Raghav was out of words, but he knew that Shalini wasn't changing. He still had lots of questions unanswered, and he decided to figure it out on the same day. He looked at his watch and the break was about to end. He looked at Shalini laughing and having fun with the other staff while helping them out.

"I will take care of her," Raghav said and turned to Elizabeth blushing. "Well, Shalini!" he called out loud and showed her his watch alerting her about time.

When they both left, Elizabeth smirked about Raghav's response, and the bell rang simultaneously.

As they were on the way to class, Shalini said "I took you to the staffroom only because of my mother, don't misunderstand. I am still angry with you."

"Yeah, I know. I know that you won't forgive me that easily, but…"

"I may forgive you, if you…"

"What is it?" Raghav asked as they reached their class.

They were five minutes late, and the accountancy sir was already in the class.

"May I come in sir?" both Shalini and Raghav asked in unison from the doorway.

"You are late, where were you?" the accountancy staff said.

Raghav in an instant figured out a way to get into the class.

"We were helping Anita ma'am with her pending stuff," Raghav said.

"Oh! You were with Anita ma'am, get in, get in. Don't waste any more of my time standing outside."

Subash— the accountancy staff with muscular arms and serial killer looks turned into a lover boy whenever he heard anything about Anita ma'am. The whole class knew about it and everyone snickered.

The class started with a yawn and ended with drools. The last three periods were also quite the same.

After all the classes ended, Raghav helped Shalini and rolled her out.

"Are you sick? Why do I feel you are erratic today?" Shalini asked as they were getting out from the school campus. .

"No, I have many questions to ask you. Can we talk?" Raghav asked.

***

"Did my mom?" Shalini asked when they reached the gazebo as she wanted to confirm the change in Raghav.

"Yeah, your mom," Raghav chuckled and sat on the chair to face Shalini. "Tell me what to do? I want you to forgive me first."

"Yeah, you must kneel and say sorrys. I will look into your eyes to see if you really are," Shalini said. She thought Raghav would never do that, but he did. He looked her in the eyes, her cheeks turned red. "Why are you doing this? I was just playing. I forgave you a long time ago, now get up, please."

"I am a fool. I didn't value or understand what you were trying to do. I'm sorry… I am sorry for real…"

Shalini pulled Raghav up and made him sit in the chair once again. "You are definitely sick."

Raghav grinned and asked, "Now, tell me how did you get

my diary? How can you possibly understand my poem?"

He didn't know about Shalini being aware of his suicide and stuff and so, he loaded stupid questions.

"I saw you here every day when I moved to this neighbourhood, you were writing something on a piece of paper and tossing it in the river. I grew curious. I wanted to know what you were writing all the time and when I decided to talk to you, I found your diary and poem alone in the gazebo. I read your poem. It was dark and stupid at first, but later when I couldn't feel the warmth for my own, I read it again. I could somehow feel that you were crying for help, crying for a hand to lift you up…"

Raghav was silent, and all his past replayed at once.

"I thought comforting you would bring me comfort, and we could both, together, come up to the light," she said and looked at him. "I am selfish, right?"

"I always thought about myself and myself alone. I thought I was the only one who was suffering the most but when I talked to your mom, I wanted to know more about you," he said, and with a pause, he continued. "No, I want to know you."

Shalini twinkled, "Promise me, you will do the same. We are not close to becoming friends anyway. Still let's trade each other's secrets."

Raghav nodded. "We are definitely not friends."

Both wore laughter on their faces.

***

Shalini speaks

My birth was the happiest moment for my parents; they used to tell this to me every day until they got to know I was born with a physical impairment. They figured it out when I was three years old and started walking. My right side was slower than the left. It was a nervous disorder.

As a doctor, my father was the first one who noted the disability and he took me to the specialist. As I was born with it, the only way to get it treated was to rely on Physiotherapy. It was the treatment to bring both my left and right-side work in conjunction. Just because my parents figured it out early, I got treated and learned to sync both my sides when I was seven.

My father was a football freak, and I spent more time with him than my mother. We always watched football on the TV together, and because of that football became one of my things. I started kicking my toys and running here and there. My father figured my interest in it and started teaching me football at home, from there on my weakness turned into my strength. I joined coaching, life became stunning again.

Playing football made me behave more like a boy than a girl and it created a scene in my family and my grandparents were against it. Both mom and dad fought for me and, looking at them, I grew up into a cheerful and strong person.

Everything has a downside. Even though playing football made me a strong and bold person, it also made an impression on my academic report card. My mom, who was a teacher in the same school I studied in, started emitting a wild and monstrous aura. She was the type of person who got corrupted with naysayers and she forced me into studies. To pull me into the interest of studies my father brought me story books and novels, but this pushed me behind and both my father and I stood in front of my mom like criminals.

One time, I failed in all the subjects and brought huge embarrassment to my mother that she couldn't even go to school. She was on the verge of killing me, but again my father saved me, as always, and started an argument with the two-horned, red devil.

"She will do her best in the upcoming exams, and she will make her papa happy," my father said and looked at me.

"Yes, I will make you happy papa," I said. I didn't know that he had tricked me at that time, but I made progress in academics and that made me happy. My mother also stopped bothering me with my studies from then on. I became an average student in academics, and the vice-captain for the under 15 junior school team at the age of 12, which was an unprecedented feat. I was proud, happy. I played against many schools and won. But when I was about to turn into a captain on my senior secondary, when it was my time, I had to come here. I also thought there was no other person in this world to be this unlucky. Football was not my actual goal— instead, being happy was my only greed, and because of that football became my first priority.

After coming here, within a month I lost my happiness.

My 3Fs, football, food, and friends were completely crushed. Food never tasted good after that and I started being dependent on others which made me cry all the time. Football turned, obviously, impossible.

***

"What you said was true the other day, but I won't die just like that," Shalini said. "No matter how painful it is, I still have my life and my priorities will change."

She cried without realising and her tears were rushing out.

"Why did you choose me to share your burden with?" Raghav asked.

"Because… because… I don't know. You are the way out of darkness… maybe. And… and I don't want to leave you behind as I know you are somewhere next to me in this depth," she stuttered.

One more drop of tear was sliding down her cheeks, Raghav wiped it for her and in an instant, Shalini's skin heated up from his touch.

"Why are you burning up?" he asked.

Shalini became embarrassed and shook her head fast. Raghav sat on his knees once again and held her hands saying, "You feel, okay? If sharing the burden helps in lowering the pain, I want to try it too…"

Shalini smiled.

"Uff… I can't believe this. You let your tears out, but still, you can smile with little comfort. I also want to cry, laugh, smile, but even if I feel it, it is deep inside. I couldn't just let it out…" he said as he was feeling the warmth in Shalini's hands.

"Because you lost trust, you decided nothing can make you happy or sad anymore. I don't know how… but I felt this in your poem too."

"I never knew that someone could actually realise that I-" Raghav said. "The poem I wrote was for my mother."

She nodded.

"I was too angry with you earlier but now I feel okay." She said and sniffled, she wiped her cheeks. Raghav got up from his knees and sat on the chair.

"Now tell me, why did you decide to end your life?" she asked.

"Why didn't you read my diary?" he asked.

"What for? I thought it would be personal," she said and looked at him. "No way, the answer is in your diary?"

"3 June," Raghav said.

"Don't you want to tell me in person?" Shalini asked.

"I may not be truthful, I may lie to make myself sound righteous, but what I wrote down in that diary was how I really felt back then… it's the truth," he said.

Shalini turned the pages and from May onwards many pages were scribbled in black ink and every third page had the same heading— Who to blame? June 3rd was the last part that started with the same heading. "You wrote a short story!" she got excited.

CHAPTER 7.5

Who is to blame?

Life wasn't easy for me from the start. I hated the crowd—they said I'm an introvert. I don't know if I was, but I had a smile on my face, I slept peacefully, everything in my life was fine.

I had two friends. Joel, Abdul, and I, put together, we were called 3-idiots. We weren't serious enough to understand what life was. It took time for me to figure out that the meaning of life tends to change in every phase of life. Before that my life was a boomerang flying between school, playtime and piano.

School was sick, play time was fun (maybe only because of Joel and Abdul) and piano— which was my mother's charm and made my mom happy, was my light.

Everything was good until I realised my doomsday was approaching. A job approval to my mother who wanted to be a writer. She was accepted in one of the famous writers' associations as a member to work in their art. And she was lucky enough to team up with her favourite writer Rahul Batt. My family and I were excited. We didn't realise the after effects it will have.

My mom was happy and when she found me beside her, she turned sad instantly.

I didn't know that she had to work for five years straight in Mumbai. I was in 7th standard then. She couldn't miss this opportunity which she had craved for over the years, and she also didn't want to leave me behind.

She came and hugged me tight saying, "I want to go badly, but how can I stay without you?"

I was silent and had no idea about anything other than the news which should have been a happy one.

She backed off and looked me in the eyes and asked, "Can you take care of yourself until I get back?"

She sounded sad. I didn't want her to be.

I blinked twice, I smiled. "I am not a kid anymore, mom," I said but I was a kid living in fantasy. "I got daddy by my side, and I can take care of me on my own, you have nothing to worry about."

I meant every word I said, but I didn't know the depth of it.

"I will become the best and come back to you. I will miss you badly," she hugged me. "And I will earn for the hardship I am going to face."

She backed off again and kissed me on the forehead.

Even after that, she was confused, she couldn't decide whether to leave. My father was my mom's darling. He never decided anything without asking my mom, and I never saw him disrespecting her, not up to my knowledge. He persuaded her and made her leave.

"I promised that I will support you with your dreams to make them come true. Remember?" he said. I didn't know when he promised that, probably when they were dating.

"I do remember," my mom said. "But…"

"No… no… don't confuse yourself. You wanted to go, so you applied. Now that you have been accepted, don't take a step back. You may regret it if you do."

I didn't know the meaning of the word regret and I just stood between them playing snakes in Nokia.

And then she left. I wasn't sad. I was used to spending most of the day with my dad rather than mom. My mother has a disorder when she writes she forgot everything. She stayed locked for days and occasionally showed her face. I thought I was used to it.

Days passed, I was attending music school with Joel and taking piano classes for my mom. I decided to complete the grade exams one by one and make my mom happy. That much I could do.

A year passed, but my relationship with my mom was fine. She never missed a day to call and talk. I also cleared the 3rd grade music exam by then.

Days without mom were a bit cold, but I had my dad's and Joel's shoulder to lean on. Joel was my best friend. Having friends was a blessing according to me back then.

The second year without mom was quite hard. Her phone calls swiftly stopped. Every day became once a week, the long conversation got short. Small fights got bigger and with that, the problems finally started to show up, one by one.

My dad's theatre school got suddenly shut down due to the lack of students and maybe more issues which I didn't know about. He became tense. He was a bit of a short-tempered person to begin with, and he couldn't handle the pressure during those days. He was sometimes sweet and sometimes scary too. He worked in a weekly theatre drama show as an artist along with the school but when his school got shut, income declined. His regular audience from theatre shows also steadily decreased and he turned furious. He started to have alcohol every Monday after his theatre acting, and it was his practice. He never drank on any other days but at that time he changed and slowly started drinking every day. Was it because of his failure in school or declining audience rate? I don't know but he got wasted.

When he was drunk his temper got worse and due to which I, too, practised to stay away from him on Mondays. Who knew that in my mom's absence everything would fall apart and everyday would become a Monday.

He made no mistake other than searching for comfort in alcohol and as days passed, he became addicted.

The failure reached my mom's ears. She started calling whenever she found time and dad got a bit comforted too, or maybe not. He didn't like to be a loser and his habit of drinking didn't stop. He sometimes faked to mom as being sober, but he never was.

He was afraid that he would become a bad example in my life, so he tried hard to deal with problems alone in hiding but nothing worked, and getting drunk became his only escape. So, to raise me without corrupting, he started staying away from me.

The second year which started quite badly, turned worse as time passed. Even my birthday was forgotten.

In the third year, once again mom couldn't reach us. Her phone calls were reduced to once a week, or sometimes once in two weeks.

One day I tried to make my father sober, hiding all his bottles and had a chat.

"Why are you drinking every day? You aren't my dad. He never crosses the limit in anything."

"Sorry. But I am sad. I want your mother to come back. I am the one who always starts fights with her. I am the one who troubles her whenever she calls, but I couldn't ask her to come back and I don't want to do that. I don't want to spoil your mother's dream too, at least I don't want her to fail," he said with tear-filled eyes.

"What is your dream dad?"

"I was given this theatre art and asked to bequeath the same to the next generation. Now that my school has closed. I cannot think of anything. I feel betrayed. I have become nothing but an example of failure. I don't want you to become like me. Everything I choose to do turns out to be a mess. I am afraid that you'll end up becoming like me— a failure. I am drinking every day to forget my sorrow, to get out of character which I am not."

"Still, dad, I don't want you to drink again," I said. He agreed but wasn't faithful.

He was okay for a few days, but I didn't know he was secretly drinking every night, and one day mom figured it out and that night was a huge mess. He started drinking more.

He forgot about me.

Joel's shoulder was the only thing left but that didn't stay long either. He went far away from me, he changed all of a sudden. He slowly stopped talking to me, and sooner that year his father was transferred and he left with him.

He could have stayed with his mom if he wanted to. But he chose to leave and I was left behind. I slowly got angrier at everything. Everything I had was taken away. I had Abdul but he was Jovial and could not possibly understand my pain. He was always happy in his own company and I was jealous of him.

My father started looking for a Job, so we shifted to another house owned by my grandfather, just two buildings away from the previous house. My father wanted to use the old house as collateral to bring back his theatre but again his plans went unsuccessful.

He gambled with his house without my mother's knowledge and it worsened the entire situation. My mom stopped talking to my dad.

I stopped playing the piano. I started hating everything I did. I hated making friends after feeling betrayed by Joel. Abdul was the only friend I had and had no idea how many days he would last.

Time passed. My birthday showed up, and that same day my father again failed an interview. Of course, he was sad, but I was naïve and was angry with him for not remembering my birthday.

But surprisingly, he remembered and brought dinner from my favourite restaurant.

"I got your favourite biryani and see… Happy birthday. Sorry, I forgot." He said and he looked sober, but I could still smell alcohol. His "Happy birthday" and biryani didn't make me happy, and I was furious at him for breaking our promise.

I ignored him and continued doing my homework. He brought the plate full of biryani and grinned.

"I am not hungry…" I said.

"Don't lie, I am sorry. Got rejected in my interview today, was upset and you know," he said and again persuaded me. "Come eat with me."

He put the plate over my book and touched my shoulder. I pushed him and threw the plate out of my room. I acted aggressively and didn't realise the consequences in that instance.

My father nurtured some principles with his living, and it had to be followed in his house. I broke one of them and his eyes went red with anger and a nerve above both the eyes became visible.

I had never seen this version of him before. He was just another man and I was scared as hell.

He picked the hockey stick near him with teary eyes. He hit the thrown plate over the ground with anger and stood silently. I was fearful so I ran out of my house screaming and neighbours were alerted. I didn't realise that if they were not around, I would have been already dead.

They brought my father back to senses, holding him tight. They made him bite his teeth strongly when they realised, he was having a seizure. I was hiding behind the neighbour checking on my father without knowing anything happened at that moment. My father realised what he did seconds later and started repeating my name with sorry. He knelt and cried when I started hating my mom. I regretted promising her that I would take care of myself. Maybe if I hadn't let her go all of this wouldn't have happened.

I started hating both my dad and mom, but I still tried to change for them. I once again wanted to accept them and started concentrating on my studies. The neighbours taught me how to cook, and sometimes I made food for my dad and myself. But we never talked to each other after that incident.

I reached 10th standard. I was all alone even with Abdul by my side. Rumours about my mom and dad abruptly started spreading in the neighbourhood and at school. I didn't care and concentrated on my studies to make everyone astound.

I did. I made the list of all India toppers, and I was so excited to watch my parent's reaction.

"I am happy for you, I mean it," my father said. He was bland and he didn't even look at me. I waited for my mother to call and she did an hour later after the result.

"Congrats, Raghav! I wish I was there," she said and her voice broke. She started talking to someone out there. She was busy, "I will call you later, sorry," she said and hung up.

I felt broken and I was probably still naive, all my efforts seemed like nothing. I started seeing things with a narrow-minded perspective and nothing could make me happy any more.

Maybe I am seeking their attention and the only possible thing stuck in my mind is to give up everything, even my life. I don't know how people actually get the guts to kill themselves.

I was weak and biding for my time to come. Obviously, I was afraid but still I wanted to cover it up by my message to my mother. A poem.

It took nearly half a month now and I got to complete my poem yesterday.

I don't know why I am writing this, a stupid story, an incomplete story. Maybe I want to prove myself right. Maybe I want to justify my actions, maybe I don't want my parents to stay clueless about my death.

I don't know whom to blame, should I blame the situation? Should I blame my mom? Or blame me for believing in something which was a big fat lie?

I don't want to find the answers anymore, I am sick of it. I am sick. I am still a kid and probably I am still stuck in those days. Those days when I was happy.

Maybe today I will be dead. **03.06.16.**

-CHAPTER 8-

Raghav was leaning over the post of the gazebo with his eyes fixated on the river as he replayed his past.

Shalini closed the dairy and looked at him, whispering, "You are still alive."

He chuckled.

"I don't know what to say," she said and looked at him again.

He turned to her, "You don't have to. I was a coward. I wrote this as an excuse to commit suicide but couldn't even do that."

"What do you mean?" she asked.

He gasped, "That accident was actually an accident, and I didn't jump in front of any car."

"What?"

He nodded smirking.

"Is it alright if I say something?" she asked.

"Yeah," he said.

"I don't know anything about your father, mother, and your best friend. I could only understand that you suffered a lot and your head is filled with craps. Throw it out even if it is true, don't let it bother you. Lie to yourself to feel better. Tell yourself that your mom loves you for real, that your dad is trying hard to avoid repeating his regretful actions and chose to stay away from you;

tell yourself that your friend Joel had his reason to leave and it is not because you."

"What if it isn't true?"

"What if it is?"

Raghav became silent.

"Remove all the scum floating in your thoughts. Even if the happiness is temporary, we may find another reason to move on later, just like my change in priorities."

"You are talking like an old woman like you have had lots of experience in it."

"That's not true. I was the happiest girl, you know," she said, "I am a bibliolater."

Raghav blew out with laughter.

"What?" she asked.

"You are funny, I thought you were the immature type earlier, but now I can see an old granny in you," he teased trying hard to stop his laughter.

Shalini made him sit on the bench. She pulled his face to her and looked into his eyes, "But you are, you are still a kid," she said and poked him on his forehead.

"Ouch," he backed off. Shalini imitated his laugh.

"We are friends now. Aren't we?" She asked.

Raghav smiled a little and nodded.

"Both of us are afraid about engaging in certain activities due to our negative past experiences. We must change that and make good new pleasant memories, don't we?" She gasped.

"I am not afraid of anything."

"You clearly wrote you are afraid of making new friends. Tell me honestly, are you considering me to be your friend?" she asked stiffly.

Raghav was silent again for a few seconds and then said, "How are we going to create new, good memories together?"

Shalini smirked, "How about a bucket list?"

"Of what?"

Shalini grinned.

***

Streetlights turned on and Raghav helped Shalini to her house. When he stood in front of her house, he became utterly shocked and rendered speechless.

"What happened?" she asked.

"Do you live here?" Raghav turned to her with a muddled expression.

She nodded and asked, "Why?"

"This was… this was my house," he said.

She was surprised and said, "Really? Want to come in?"

Raghav shook his head and tears burst out from his eyes.

"I am afraid," he said, wiping his eyes and Elizabeth showed up opening the main gate.

"Why are you late?" Elizabeth asked Shalini and turned to Raghav.

"Hello, ma'am," he said with hesitation.

"Hello. Raghav," she said. "Don't be too formal outside the school, call me Elize…" she smiled and then frowned at Shalini.

"What?" Shalini asked Elizabeth, "You are the reason I got late."

"I am leaving then," Raghav said and took a step back.

"Why were you crying, though?" Elizabeth asked.

"Our house made him cry," Shalini said.

"What does that mean?"

"This is where he used to live. He is the previous owner." Shalini gasped.

Elizabeth was surprised. "Oh, seriously! why are you standing outside? How about a cup of tea?"

Raghav strongly refused and shook his head, "I Can't," he whispered. "Perhaps later," he said.

"He will only jump off the fence to see me. Directly getting into the house is outdated," Shalini smirked.

Raghav smiled with a teary face and left waving his hands.

***

Elizabeth stopped rolling Shalini into the house instead she sat on the veranda steps.

"Why was Raghav crying?" Elizabeth asked, looking at Shalini. "Why does he hesitate to come in?"

"How would I know, maybe he has trauma or something."

"What does that mean?" Elizabeth was even more confused with Shalini's improper way of answering.

"He thinks his mother abandoned him, and this house reminds him of her," Shalini exhaled and shook her head. "It's my assumption, I am not sure."

"I don't think any mother can abandon their child, forsooth," Elizabeth dropped her opinion.

Shalini grinned, "I have got the best mother," she messed up Elizabeth's hair with a smile.

Elizabeth got up with the messy hair and rolled Shalini into the house, "indeed,"

"Mom, Raghav said I talk like an old woman, is it true?" Shalini asked.

"Nope. You are immature as hell. Raghav might have candied the truth."

"Momma…" Shalini yelled. Elizabeth laughed and helped Shalini change.

***

After dinner Raghav was studying with a distracted mind. He remembered an old granny's conversation and tried to recall every word she had said but for not so long as a call woke him up. He answered the call with bossy voice, "Hello, who is this?"

"What? You didn't even save my number," the caller from the other side yelled.

"Shalini?" Raghav relaxed his back on the chair.

"What are you doing?" Shalini asked.

"Nothing much, trying to study," he said.

"I made the bucket list," Shalini said.

"Congratulations," he showed no interest.

"Are you trying to mess with me, at least fake some interest?"

"Oh great! What have you got?"

Shalini shook her head with annoyance and said, "Well, how about a trip to the aquarium tomorrow?"

"This idea is fine, but timing is not, are you crazy? We got exams coming up in two days, and you want to go for an outing in between."

"What? Exams?" she freaked. "When did they make an announcement?"

"A week ago, and you were sleeping in the class I guess."

She gulped, "How about next week then?" she hesitated.

"How about a challenge on back of it?"

"Wow, now you are showing some interest. What is the Challenge?"

He smirked, "If you fail in any of the subjects, the trip is off."

Shalini bowled over, "Seriously?"

"Yup, I don't like to work hard alone," he said.

"Seriously!" she smiled back.

-CHAPTER 9-

English, economics, and business studies— Shalini was confident with those subjects, but accountancy and mathematics were scary and moreover they were the first and last exams respectively. There was no peace until the exams were over.

Shalini had not once opened her textbooks since the end of the first term. The only thing that could save her from failing was the attention she had paid in those classes in the past months. Accepting the challenge turned into a pain.

Raghav, on the other hand was carving a big piece of rectangular wood chunk. He was trying to carve out a big maple leaf from wood, but every attempt failed. He had ruined more than 10 blocks by that time.

"This shit is hard. I can't do it any more," he said and his hands were shaking.

Raghav refused to touch his book, doing unwanted things to pass time though he had exams from the next day.

***

Shalini called Ayesha through a mobile lying on her bed.

"What got into you?" Shalini asked Ayesha when the call was answered.

"What do you mean?" Ayesha closed her book and paid more attention to the call.

"You were the one who always called me first. These days no calls or messages. Is there any problem?"

Ayesha gasped, "Actually…" she said and stopped.

"What?"

"Nothing. I was preparing for my exams, it's a bit tough, you know…"

"What do you mean by tough? You never say that."

"I couldn't attend all the classes and missed important lectures…"

"Oh! I thought you were still sick."

"I heard you are getting along with Raghav?" Ayesha asked.

"Yeah, I won my bet. Your prediction was accurate. It really took us exactly six months to get along."

Ayesha chuckled, "See, I was never wrong."

"Okay, we are planning for a small trip after exams. I hope you will come along with us. Abdul is also coming."

"Abdul won't come, and neither will I. You don't know about our timetable?"

"No," Shalini turned quizzical.

"Our exams are from Wednesday, and it will end exactly on the seventh day from that."

"Holy shit. But it's okay we can go a week later then."

"Sorry Shalini, but the coming two to three weeks are toilsome for us. You go with Raghav and enjoy, we will all go later some other time."

Shalini sighed, then they talked about academics for a few more minutes, and the call ended.

Both Shalini and Raghav were back to square one, as both Ayesha and Abdul refused to join them for the trip.

***

Exam day

Ayesha wished luck to both Shalini and Raghav with a smile and deadly stare respectively, Raghav ignored the stare and thanked her for her wishes. He rolled Shalini into the class, most of the students were into the books and some were murmuring prayers. Raghav didn't belong to any of the categories.

Preethi, who was preparing for her exams got distracted by Raghav's presence and she found something different in him. She saw something which she had never witnessed in the past few years. She started emitting an envious aura as she knew the change was because of Shalini and there would be no other way. The atmosphere in the class, which was already dark, grew colder.

It was rainy outside, and with a rumble of loud thunder, the exams started. Shalini somehow managed to write the exam with chapters she covered hoping for pass marks, and the exam ended. Raghav had a bland expression, so it was hard to figure out his performance, unlike Shalini.

But exam seasons were best for Preethi to find an opening to look up for Raghav. She had had a crush on him since the 8th standard but couldn't approach him because of his cold behaviour. But looking at him melting down because of Shalini, she started regretting that she couldn't be the one. She was happy, but sad.

The next day, the next exam went on and got over in no time.

The English exam was the third for commerce students and first one for science.

The seating arrangements constituted two students sitting on a bench, commerce student and science student across. Raghav wished for a less annoying someone by his side and he was very unlucky to have Ayesha beside him. Both felt uncomfortable, but they had to follow the same order for the mathematics exam too. Ayesha was different compared to their first encounter, she was silent and somehow it bothered Raghav.

Shalini, Raghav and Ayesha managed to finish the exam expecting to pass in all the subjects.

The results were expected the next day, that was Saturday.

Raghav and Shalini asked Ayesha and Abdul about the trip one more time, but they continued to refuse, listing out the things they got to do after exams. Raghav felt kind of uneasy to go alone with Shalini but Shalini didn't.

"Raghav there is no more hope in expecting anyone anymore. We are going alone," Shalini said.

Raghav hesitated, "But… Shalini,"

"What?"

Raghav shook his head, stopped what he was about to say, and changed the topic, "Did you forget, we have to pass all the exams to go?"

Shalini shrugged, "I remember, and I am going to rock it."

The exam results in each subject were distributed. Raghav never paid attention to anyone, but Preethi was desperate to make him acknowledge her. So, she tried so hard to score more marks than him.

In accountancy, Preethi scored 38/50.

Raghav scored 35 and Shalini scored 35. Her mission to make Raghav acknowledge failed as both Shalini and Raghav scored the same.

In economics Preethi couldn't beat Shalini, Shalini was the topper. Raghav just passed.

In English all scored around 35 to 45, so it was no big deal. Business studies was also the same.

Even though Shalini pretended to be confident in passing all the exams, she wasn't ready to see mathematics marks yet. Shalini was lucky though, the paper wasn't corrected.

Preethi screamed because of her frequent defeat and all class turned to her. She turned red and hid herself.

Shalini and Raghav's plans for the trip the next day were ruined because of rain and the whole Sunday passed with annoyance. The plan was shifted to next week and, once again, persuading Ayesha and Abdul ended up in failure as their eyes were submerged in fear and that was how the suffering of science students became obvious to Shalini and Raghav.

Mathematics results were also out in that week and the teacher distributed the paper in reverse.

Shalini hardly passed with 23 marks and received her paper before Preethi and Raghav.

Raghav got a 47 and he checked for his mistake.

Then Preethi was called, and she got 50/50. The whole class went, "Woah!"

Raghav now lifted his head to look at her and both of their eyes met. Preethi, who was expecting him to acknowledge her, broke the eye contact in seconds as her heart fluttered.

Shalini noticed Preethi's reaction and had a hunch. Everyone clapped their hands and encouraged her.

***

During lunch

Raghav turned page to page to figure out why he was wrong in a particular sum, and he started whining about it to Shalini.

"Why don't you ask Preethi? She got full marks," Shalini planned a favourable situation for Preethi with her hunch.

"I feel awkward. I have known her for years, but I never talked to her," Raghav said.

"You are stupid, always overreacting," Shalini said. "Call her here."

Raghav looked at Preethi and waited for her to turn towards him. Shalini had no patience, so she hit Raghav on his head and asked him to scream her name.

"Preethi," Raghav asserted. Preethi jolted and turned to him slowly with surprise. He changed his tune, "Come here, please." He was shy.

When Preethi got there, Shalini made her sit in their chair, and then Raghav cleared his doubt but Shalini couldn't follow Preethi and yawned. Shalini concentrated more on Preethi's hesitation and trembling.

"Thank you," Raghav said after learning the answer.

"Preethi, are you free this coming Sunday? We are going on a small trip," Shalini asked Preethi.

"Um…yes. I am free I guess… but…" Preethi dragged.

"But what? You are coming, okay?"

Preethi hesitated first but then she nodded.

Shalini gave her number along with Raghav's and asked her to call any of them to discuss it further. There were four more days until Sunday and Preethi's nervousness was at its peak from day one.

When she got home Shalini made a call to her and briefed her on the details about the trip.

"Do you have feelings for Raghav?" Shalini asked with the flow. Preethi was thrilled and she couldn't answer it. "Okay, no need to tell me, but if you do have feelings for him, you should have the guts to tell him yourself."

Preethi shook her head and said, "No, I don't have any feelings for him. You must have misunderstood."

"Yeah, I might have. Okay as planned, come to my house we will be leaving from there."

"Okay," Preethi said and sighed. She hit her forehead with the phone out of embarrassment.

Preethi considered Shalini's advice, but she couldn't decide what to do. Even though she lied to Shalini, she also wanted Raghav to know about her feelings as soon as possible.

She asked her older sister for a solution, and it was relatively the same as Shalini's. In the end, Preethi decided to propose to Raghav before the day of the trip, so that she can decide whether to go on a trip or to pass depending on his answer.

Three days passed and her three years of hesitation came to an end.

She called Raghav for the first time on her own.

He answered with,"Who is this?"

"This is Preethi," she said. "I think you didn't save my

number, it's a bit embarrassing."

"I didn't have anyone's number, sorry. I will save it now," he said and started to save her number by putting the call on speaker.

"Ok… Ok…" she said and couldn't talk more. Her hesitation, once again, started dragging her down.

"So, are you coming tomorrow?" he asked.

"Yeah, and before that I want to tell you something," she said with everything she got with closed eyes.

"Hmm, what is it?" he asked her while typing her name in the contacts.

"Believe it or not, I have had a crush on you since 8th standard, and I think I love you," Preethi said and tightened her jaw.

Raghav, who was about to press the save button stopped and didn't respond.

"I love you," she said one more time to make it clear.

-CHAPTER 10-

Sunday showed up and the trip was on. Varadarajan was happy considering Raghav's change in behaviour. He didn't want to ruin his son's glow and remained silent.

Raghav walked to Shalini's house. His hair was combed, and he was wearing an orange shirt tucked into his navy-blue pants, as if he was going for an interview, and Shalini freaked out when she witnessed Uncle Raghav. Shalini was wearing a pink dress in which she looked cute along with her ponytail, which she always held even in school.

Ravichandran who was beside Shalini had a pleasant look on his face because of Raghav's dressing, both father and daughter showed different reactions which made Raghav anxious.

"Hello, uncle," Raghav greeted Ravichandran first.

"Hi, so only you two are going?" Ravichandran asked Raghav.

"No," Raghav said, "Yes," Shalini said. In unison.

"Preethi isn't coming?" Raghav asked and he started sweating.

"She said, some sudden work showed up," Shalini cleared Raghav's confusion.

Raghav demented out of worry and scratched his forehead.

"Okay then, have a safe trip, get back home before dusk," Ravichandran said and left.

"Let's go on a date then," Shalini said with excitement.

"What… you want to go on a date…" Raghav widened his eyes.

"Yeah, but what happened to your hair, why is it combed?" she pointed.

"Oh! This." Raghav chuckled. "I wanted to look good."

"You look like an builder uncle, come here."

He bent down a bit and looked at Shalini's face from close. She was pretty and his temperature rose.

Shalini styled his hair asking, "Were you trying to impress my dad with it?"

"No, why would I?" he slurped.

"I kind of felt like asking it, never mind," She said and looked at his face with the hair she styled, "Okay all set, let's go."

"Did Preethi say anything else?" he asked as he stood up.

"No, like what? Did you do anything to her?"

"No, no. I would have brought my scooter, if only we two are going," he said.

"And you are kidding now," Shalini said. Once again, he forgot to realise about the wheelchair.

"Ah… my words are getting twisted today, let's get moving then," Raghav grinned with a burst of panic laughter and he rolled her to the bus stand.

They boarded the bus on time. Raghav bought the tickets for both and stood next to Shalini. In the first five minutes of travel both were speechless and they were glancing out from the window. As the time passed, Shalini got annoyed and started talking instead.

"Do you know? I am here with you," Shalini said.

Raghav turned to Shalini and said, "Of course, I know. Why? What happened? Any problem?"

"Don't add onto the question, I cannot handle any more silence, talk about something. I am bored."

"Hmm," Raghav thought of many things, but he couldn't

figure out what to ask or talk about. "I don't know, you ask something."

"Okay, how dare you say you would have brought the scooter to pick me up."

"Is there any problem with that?" he said and sniffled, "To be frank whenever I look at you, I keep forgetting about your wheelchair."

Shalini's heart fluttered, "I like that." She said blushing.

"Ahaan," Raghav's voice broke out.

She shook her head and yelled, "I am asking, why are you riding a vehicle without a licence? You dummy."

"Who said I don't have a licence?"

He waited to see Shalini's reaction and then continued. "I don't have a licence…"

She punched him for his humourless gag.

"I like riding bikes," he clicked his tongue, "but to be frank, I had a hunch that I would be dead or won't be able to ride a bike by then, when the time come. That's why I tend to use my father's old scooter often."

"You and your shitty thoughts. Throw them away and try to be more mature," she said in a bossy voice.

"Yes madam," Raghav said and bowed down. Shalini laughed.

***

Shalini and Raghav stepped down from the bus when they reached their destination. The dried leaves which were withering down from the tree flew as the bus carried on. Some of the leaves got stuck into Shalini's hair and Raghav plucked them out as they were approaching the aquarium.

The aquarium looked dead without a crowd, lacking the usual Sunday atmosphere. Raghav bought the tickets and walked in. Few couples were seen inside the aquarium as they marched forward, but Raghav and Shalini were more into all sorts of exotic fish and facts. It was peaceful.

"Why did you want to come here?" Raghav asked rolling her in.

"I was expecting this question for a long time. I will tell you while getting back home, but you should not overreact or make fun of me," Shalini said and observed the fish swimming in the big fish tank which kept extending to the exit.

"Okay," Raghav said delving into reading intriguing facts about each sea creature showcased in every section and Shalini provided insightful comments on each fish she encountered with "Cute!" *They were scary too. Was she blind?*

The peaceful surrounding turned noisy at once, and a bunch of annoying kids marched towards Shalini and Raghav in three lines with three teachers in-charge. The kids were wearing Saraswathi Vidyachalam uniforms as they were on a school trip. Their lines were imperfect, and the aquarium became lively.

Raghav exhaled hard and concentrated on avoiding the crowd, Shalini rolled forward on her own and glanced at the Betta Fish and its movement. The three imperfect lines of annoying kids passed Shalini but a girl from the last continued gazing the wheelchair and approached Shalini, parting from her classmates. She was the tallest of all and looked sad as she approached.

"Why are you using this chair? Are you sick like my mom?" the schoolgirl asked, looking at the chair intensely. "Or you don't like to walk?"

"I would love to walk, but I can't. Sad, isn't it?" Shalini pursed her lips sadly. "And what happened to your mom?"

"My mom was also using this chair, she was sick… and she told me that she was forced to be on this chair. Like a fish taken out from the sea as if they are not allowed to swim again,"

"Yeah, your mom is indeed right. it feels exactly as she mentioned."

"Then, can I also leave the sea? Can I also sit in this chair?"

"Why? What makes you say that?" Shalini's refreshing face turned low.

"How long can I stay without my mom in this sea? My father said my mum died."

Shalini wasn't expecting that, and her looks turned sullen. The girl waited for Shalini to answer.

"I will tell you a secret which only the fish from the land can see. Your mom is right next to you, protecting you," Shalini made up things to change the perspective of the girl and patted her head.

"Can I see her too?" The girl got excited.

"Yes of course you can see, but you must meet your mum's expectations first. Don't you? You need to become happy. You need to become strong and bold to face challenges. You need to become a good successful girl by making your mom proud. If you do that, gradually, she will emerge into view. You will find her happy, proud and then you can swim along with her, the only thing you should have, is patience and the spirit to keep going."

"Really?" The girl's mood lifted.

"Yes. You should just believe in yourself and keep moving happily."

The girl delighted. "Then I will make her see me instead."

"That's the spirit, keep going on," Shalini smiled and bumped thumbs up with the kid.

"Bye, sis." The girl said and ran silently to her classmates. Shalini with a smile on her face turned around to see Raghav, but he wasn't there.

Raghav was a bit far from her, taking pictures of baby sharks secretly breaking the rules of the aquarium community. Shalini gave a cosy stare and whispered, "The girl earlier was more mature than him, I guess."

***

After passing the exit of the aquarium, the sunlight fell directly onto Shalini and Raghav's faces. It took a few seconds for them to clearly find the exit and they found the small food stall with tables around it.

"I am hungry," Shalini said, keeping her hands on her stomach. It was past lunchtime.

Raghav ordered lunch from the menu and sat beside Shalini at a table.

"Mangalorean biryani and Halbai? That's new to me," Shalini said, waiting for her order to arrive.

"Are you a spice-loving person? The biryani is going to be very spicy," he said.

"Hell yes," She was excited.

The food reached their table. Shalini served the biryani on a plate and offered it to Raghav. They shared the biryani and kept Halbai aside for a final touch. Shalini was fast, she ate more than half of the biryani before Raghav could finish his first serve.

"It's good," Shalini said. "Feed that sweet to me," she asked Raghav with her burning mouth.

Raghav dragged along "Whaaaat?"

"If you don't want to, then pass the plate to me," She was in a hurry to calm her burning mouth.

"Oh! I thought you were asking for real."

"I am asking for real if you want to."

Shalini opened her mouth Ahh, Raghav's heart fluttered hard. He fed her fast and avoid looking at her.

"Why are you anxious? Think of me as your sister and everything will be easy," Shalini promoted Raghav as her brother.

Raghav's heart shredded into pieces, and his red face turned pale within seconds. The lovely heart-warming situation turned into a hilarious tragedy.

"I wish Preethi, Ayesha, and Abdul were here, it would be fun," Shalini said and had the whole bowl of biryani until she made it empty. She completely forgot about Raghav to share the biryani after the first serve.

Raghav's pale face became paler when he heard Preethi's name. Shalini sensed something was wrong. She fed the Halbai to Raghav, but all his excitement was gone.

When they reached the bus stop, Shalini asked Raghav, "Did you and Preethi fight?"

Raghav answered, "No…No… We didn't fight, we…"

"What?" she asked. "I knew something was off. What happened between you and Preethi?"

He struggled to open but minutes later he admitted, "Yesterday she proposed to me."

***

"I love you," Preethi said over the phone call. "I…"

"Wait Preethi, please don't tell me anything more, I didn't expect this… umm… and I don't know how to respond. I never had any idea about this," Raghav said calmly.

"I, too, don't know how to continue talking after this. To be honest, I was afraid you were already in love with Shalini, that's why I wanted to tell you as soon as possible."

"Shalini and I are friends and nothing more than that. You sure, had the wrong idea."

"Yeah, I guess so, but I did confess my feelings to you."

"Yeah… and sorry, but I must reject them. I think you deserve better, and if you think I changed from my past that's because I am trying to, but I haven't yet. I still have the cold side of me."

"Don't be sorry, it doesn't suit you," Preethi chuckled as she wiped her tears. "Sorry… I couldn't do anything for you because of my cowardliness…"

"No… No… it's okay…" he said. The situation was awkward. "But we can still be friends?"

"No. I don't know… I don't know if anything is okay now. Maybe later?"

Raghav nodded and said, "Yeah, later…"

***

Raghav informed Shalini about the conversation that had taken place between him and Preethi.

"Preethi is pretty..." Shalini whispered after hearing him out.

"Yeah, she is..."

Shalini tried to hit Raghav, but he backed off. "Then why did you reject her?"

"I know... I said something cringe, but I am not really in the mood to date someone. I have never thought about it."

"You were on a date with me the whole day, what about that?" she asked.

"This isn't a date," he insisted.

"I will label it as a date."

"No."

"Yes."

Both laughed together. "So, you rejected her. She might be hurt," she said.

"I know."

"I was also rejected once, and it was painful," she said and nodded her head. "But maybe she is destined to be with someone else."

"What do you mean? I am not ready yet. Maybe I will ask her out in the future."

"No... No... she deserves someone better," she said and laughed and with that, the bus arrived.

***

When Raghav rolled Shalini past the main gate of her house, he asked, "Now tell me, what was your reason for wanting to visit the aquarium?

"If you had stayed by my side all the time, you would have known."

"Don't tell me you were talking about it to that little girl and I missed it?"

"Yeah, that's exactly what happened."

"Shit, okay. Tell me now."

"Hmm, it's like a human being turning into a fish…"

"A mermaid?"

"Yeah, I am a mermaid," she said and nodded her head with a smirk.

He pouted as he couldn't follow her and Elizabeth walked out of the house.

"How was the day? Did you guys make good memories?" she asked.

"Yes, we did," Shalini said as she turned to Raghav and continued, "I guess…"

"Why are you silent, Raghav?" Elizabeth asked.

"This is the first time I went out for a trip after a long time," Raghav said.

"Hmm, everything has got a first time, which would eventually turn into unforgettable memories, isn't it?" Elizabeth smiled.

***

Raghav went back to his house. The day was over, the happy good memories were made, but something was incomplete at the end for both.

Shalini called Preethi after dinner three times but she couldn't reach her, so she decided to have a face-to-face conversation the next day.

Raghav shared the photos they took at the aquarium with Shalini. The selfie they took with the empty bowl of Mangalorean biryani and his pallid face made her laugh.

"The little Shark is cute though," Shalini texted Raghav after checking out all the pictures he sent.

-CHAPTER 11*

There was no unusual behaviour with Preethi the next day, and Raghav was relieved. After school Raghav went to Abdul and Ayesha to talk about their exams, in the meantime Shalini took the opportunity to talk with Preethi in person.

The staff from the last period continued using the class so Shalini asked Preethi to take her to the end of the corridor where most of the students talked in private.

"Why weren't you answering my call yesterday?" Shalini asked when they reached out there.

"Sorry, I was very busy and didn't even check my call logs. Very sorry," she apologised.

"Raghav told me yesterday that you proposed to him. Don't tell me your distance has to do something with that."

Preethi was silent and her fake bright face turned dull, "So he told you. Well, yes. That's why I couldn't talk to anyone. I was sad, I cried all day. I didn't want to ruin your day as well. So, I pretended to be busy."

"Yeah, I can understand how you feel, but don't burden your heart. He is just confused with everything if you really love him you can keep on trying."

"But… but what I keep thinking is that both of you look good together. You did something to him that he changed. You made him realise something that I never tried to. I envy you."

"We are just friends, Preethi, don't get the wrong idea," Shalini said.

Preethi grinned, "Yeah you are friends but that doesn't

mean that you will remain the same. I have been studying with Raghav since kindergarten and I know what he lost when his mother left and what he has now with you is the same thing. None of you realise it yet but either of you will soon do. I am really angry with myself for giving up this early, however I guess you deserve him more than I do. I don't want to bother Raghav again, but I will beat both of you in the 12th board exams."

Shalini beamed, "I am glad. But you don't have to challenge me, I am really, *really,* weak in academics."

Both of them laughed.

"Have you ever been rejected by someone? You said you understand how I feel," Preethi asked.

"Hmm, well not exactly rejected, I had a crush on the boy's football team captain, Aaqil from my old school. I literally stalked him, gave him hints, and in the end, he ignored me completely. I was never a girly girl in my previous school, so my friends' made fun of me. Then I realised he was more into football than anything, so I challenged him to a game."

"Did you win?"

"Of course, I lost! But you know what? I actually learned a lot from it," Shalini exclaimed with a smile, but then it slowly faded as she continued, "You see, sometimes rejection can be the best thing that happens to us." As she uttered those words, Preethi noticed tears streaming down her face, catching her off guard. "I... I fell in love with football," she choked on her words, overcome with emotion, not even realizing she had started to cry.

Preethi didn't comfort her, instead she asked one more question, "How are you holding up now?"

Shalini chuckled, "I am trying to get over it, rearranging my priorities," she wiped her tears.

"SHALINI!" Raghav shouted and found them at the end of the corridor, "What are you both doing here?"

"Just a little chat," Shalini said. Preethi looked at Raghav and smiled.

"Shalini told me about her crush," Preethi said.

"Whoa, really?" Raghav asked looking at Shalini and then turned to Preethi again, "And, are you okay?"

"No, I am not. But I will be, you got nothing to worry about.

Worry about the 12th board, and I will be your rival from today," Preethi said and walked out from there with a smile.

"She is cute but not that sad," Raghav said.

"She cried a lot yesterday," Shalini mentioned.

***

2019

APRIL 5th

10:37am

The loud honking sound brought Shalini back from her past. She was waiting for Richu in a tea shop. When he arrived, the journey to meet Raghav resumed. As per planning, Shalini headed to Richu's house in Thrissur. Richu, Shalini's school friend from Chennai, ended up being in the same college as Shalini.

It took nearly ten whole minutes to reach his house which was behind the mountains. Richu took Shalini to his empty room and gave her space and time to shower and change.

"I have reached safe and sound to Richu's house and from here on he will guide me. Shalini texted a message to her father after changing her clothes and went into a deep sleep for two hours straight.

Later Richu took her to his parents' and introduced her.

"You came here looking for your friend?" Richu's father asked.

"Yes uncle, he is studying in Waves Music and Fine Arts College," Shalini said with a smile.

"Getting admission in that college is a pain in the neck, your friend must be someone tough," Richu's mother praised Raghav.

"Yeah, he is, but he is stupid too. He arrived here surreptitiously, keeping it a secret from me, and made me worried sick," Shalini said and clenched her fist. "I am going there to teach him a lesson."

Richu's mother laughed at Shalini's determination and asked, "It looks like he means a lot to you."

Shalini pouted *'I don't know'* as she was confused on it from the very beginning.

Then they had lunch together, which included a traditional

Kerala fish fry. Shalini was out of hands and enjoyed three servings, like she was in home.

Richu's mother talked with Shalini for over an hour about Richu, college, and stuff.

When the clock hit 03:00 p.m., Shalini and Richu were on the veranda and many were middle-aged boys; around 15 years old. In the empty field in front of their house with a volleyball.

Shalini was excited to watch the game but when she realised the game was going to be a football match she ran over to the empty field and volunteered to play.

Most of the boys were the same height as Shalini, and she was placed into the weakest team assuming her to be a weak player. Richu was also teamed up with Shalini and he chose to remain as a goalkeeper.

The game began.

The barefoot street football with volleyball gave quite a different vibe than the actual game. It was the same as Shalini playing with Ayesha and her friend during childhood. Shalini's team started the game and within seconds she scored the goal and made the opponent startled.

The next set began with the opponent and they tried their best to keep the ball away from Shalini, but she was so fast that she didn't let them throw the ball over Richu who was half asleep.

It was a 20-20-minute game. So, the first 20 minutes the score was 1-0 as the opponent couldn't make a goal.

The next 20 minutes, the game started with the opponent and this time Shalini gave space for the other players on her team to shine but unfortunately, it didn't turned out well and became an advantage to the opponent. Still, Shalini enjoyed the game and continued giving instructions to her team mates to try different things so that they could win. The game turned into an interesting one as the other players from Shalini's team tried to show their best. The first fifteen minutes were 1-1 and in the last five minutes Shalini scored another goal and made her team win.

"Never look down on anyone, we never know what they are good at," She gave advice to everyone on the empty field, and Richu was totally asleep in the standing position.

The clock hit 04:25 p.m., when Shalini got ready to resume her journey towards Raghav, towards Ernakulum, the last stop.

***

The sky was cloudy, which was good for travel. Shalini thanked Richu's parents for letting her stay and kick-started her bike, whereas Richu was lazy enough to press the starter, which made his parents embarrassed.

"Few more minutes to go, then I can see my long-lost friend," Shalini said riding the bike.

"Are you prepared to see him?" Richu asked as he was riding the bike parallel to her, passing through the greenwoods.

"I want to, but I also get shivers thinking about it," she said and shivered in real life while riding the bike.

"This is my first time seeing a girl in search of her lost friend," Richu said and smiled a little, which made Shalini remember all the first times Raghav went through with her.

"I am stupid, aren't I?" she asked, looking at Richu. The road was empty enough for a safe ride.

"You don't need to ask," Richu grinned and said, "But what I am thinking is, if he left you without any goodbye, that means he never wanted to leave you in the first place."

Shalini pressed the brake hard and jolted. "Wait!" she said.

Richu went a bit far and stopped, "What happened?"

"I remember the same line you just said from somewhere else," She started thinking, over and over again.

"It's from *No Matter How Far,* the novel," he himself admitted.

"Did you read that book?" she asked with excitement.

"Yeah, just a few days back I completed it. It was good. I am waiting for the sequel."

"Wow, but how can you use that precious dialogue without copyrights?" Shalini yelled.

"My bad, okay," he said. "We are getting late, shall we proceed?"

When once again they caught up the speed, Richu himself started a conversation out of boredom.

"So, how has your trip been so far?" he asked.

"Exhausting, but fun. I was replaying the past in my mind, thinking about Raghav, Ayesha, and Abdul."

"Ayesha and Abdul? You mean those love birds?"

"They are love dragons," she raved.

"I wish I had the same love story as them," he whispered and raced his throttle.

Shalini's mind filled with various thoughts, nervousness as she was just a few kilometres away from Raghav, and talking about Ayesha and Abdul made her remember the things that happened a week before the 11th grade final exam and the following days.

-CHAPTER 12-

2017

-April mid-

A week before the 11th grade final exams

The last period was Physical education. The boys were playing football, girls were in the volleyball court and without disturbing them Shalini and Ayesha spent that period in the staffroom helping Elizabeth and her colleagues with their stuff.

The football teams of boys didn't include Abdul and Raghav as they were very much interested in skipping the PE period and preferred jogging around the field.

"Hey, Raghav, did you notice any change in me?" Abdul asked jogging behind Raghav.

"Hmm, I don't know you've lost some weight I guess," Raghav said.

"Does losing weight look good on me?" Abdul asked with a pile of excitement, in the afternoon sunbath.

"What are you trying to say now?" Raghav stopped jogging and looked at Abdul seriously. "I am feeling so baked here already, just don't tell me you are in love."

"Shit," Abdul jogged again. "Well, then the convo ends here."

"You are in love? You stud muffin," Raghav got surprised and followed him. "Is that a girl or a boy?"

"Fuck you, Raghav. It is a girl and a very familiar one," Abdul said firmly.

Raghav once again stopped in the middle of the track and started panicking little by little, "Who is this familiar 'she'?"

"Ayesha, of course," Abdul whispered in a way only Raghav could hear and started blushing.

Raghav got chills when he heard and shirked, "W-H-A-T?" and at that very moment a football hit him, hard enough to make him faint, saving him from losing his mind.

***

In the infirmary, Raghav got up with a shock.

"Nothing serious. Wash your face and take a painkiller if it hurts," the nurse said to him.

He gazed at Abdul who was standing beside him with a terrified look and both walked out.

"Have you gone crazy?!" Raghav exclaimed, aiding his head with bare hands. "Ayesha? Seriously?"

"Why? What's wrong with Ayesha?" Abdul murmured with tension.

"Don't say her name. It's a trigger to doom. You just saw what happened minutes ago."

"Does it have anything to do with her? Stop this nonsense. I know you don't like her, but you will soon," Abdul said with disappointment. "I will be waiting at the school main gate come fast."

"What about Shalini and Ayesha?"

"They already left. Shalini said that she had some business to attend to." Abdul made it clear as he walked into his class.

Once Raghav freshened up by washing his face, he retrieved his backpack from the classroom and joined Abdul on their way back home.

Abdul was silent which made Raghav annoyed but that was the first time Abdul looked serious about something. So, without any hesitation, Raghav apologised bowing down.

"You don't need to do that," Abdul said. "You have changed a lot."

"You too," Raghav said and asked. "So, when did you figure out you were in love with her?"

"When she suddenly stopped messing with others, I started

missing the funny, brave Ayesha a lot. That's when I realised, from that time on. I couldn't talk to her as usual," Abdul shrugged.

"So, how are you going to propose to her?"

Abdul stopped walking as he realised that one day or another, he had to do it. He started sweating and said, "Never thought of that," and looked at Raghav with a sweaty face.

"Seize the moment and propose to her without delay, or else your own feelings may start to waver," he urged insistently.

"How do you know that?"

"Well… I just happen to know that" Raghav grinned.

"What if I get rejected?"

"She might bury you alive if she didn't feel the same."

"Do you have any idea on how to propose to her without getting doomed?"

Raghav stopped grinning and started to think, "Umm, I don't know, but I want to help you with this."

"Really?" Abdul's face turned bright.

"Yes," Raghav smirked. "But remember love doesn't always give you happiness. It sometime brings misery with it."

"You talk like a very experienced pro," Abdul said.

"Pro, my foot," Raghav said as they reached his house and stopped. His face turned sad on spot, "I pity you my friend," he held Abdul's hands and shook with closed eyes, like a church father.

"For what?" Abdul got confused.

"Soon you will realise," Raghav grinned out of pity.

***

"Is there something you are hiding from me?" Shalini asked Ayesha in her room after getting changed.

"No. I am just nervous about the upcoming exams."

"Are you sure that, that's what is bothering you?" Shalini asked, "You said the same thing last time."

"I don't think I have to answer that," Ayesha said without looking into Shalini's eyes.

"It's already been months since you started acting weird," Shalini said boldly. "You are not the Ayesha that I know, she fears nothing and I admire her for that."

"Time changes people. I just stopped being noisy. Isn't that what everyone wanted in the first place?" Ayesha said and looked her in the eyes with annoyance.

"No," Shalini immediately answered and became uneasy. She went silent.

"How is your exam preparation going?" Ayesha changed the topic and started another conversation.

"It's fine," Shalini said and nodded. "Raghav is helping me out with it."

"Good to hear that you actually made him your friend."

"And you took the bet seriously," Shalini looked at Ayesha's lob hairstyle, "I told you, it will suit you well."

"Yeah, I love it."

Both giggled.

The week and the exams passed faster than the Indian government bus. The month of May was graced as a summer holiday and the bucket list was on.

This time Ayesha and Abdul lacked excuses and they couldn't help but to join and strike down the list one by one.

They enjoyed the beach on Shalini's birthday. Raghav made sure all of her wishes were met and they presented her with a well-packed gift, which would take at least a day to unpack.

Then they enjoyed the movie *Meri Pyaari Bindu* in theatres on the first day of release, and surprisingly Abdul sobbed during the climax.

Lastly, a dinner night at the Waterfall Chinese restaurant was announced. It was almost like a double date for Shalini and Abdul and they waited for the day to come.

***

The Date Night

An hour before sunset, Raghav, Shalini, and Ayesha, all three, got ready in their respective houses, but Abdul with his unclear mind wasted the whole day deciding what to wear to impress Ayesha.

Raghav, who had some past experiences, knew how to get dressed and style his hair, so he worked on it and was a bit happy that the darkness in him slowly tended to walk out. Making good memories helped both Raghav and Shalini to overcome their depressed minds.

Shalini wore a dress— a white and pink Patiala salwar kameez, presented by Raghav on her birthday. Elizabeth was out of breath when she found Shalini glowing in that dress and was impressed with Raghav's selection.

Even after taking hours of preparation, Abdul finally wore a kurta with jeans and somehow, he was the first one to set foot from his house. He rode on his activa to Raghav's.

When he reached, the first person he met was Varadarajan.

"It's been a long time since I saw you last," Varadarajan said and invited Abdul in. "So, how many of you are going for dinner tonight?"

"Four of us. Raghav, Shalini, Ayesha and I," Abdul settled on the sofa, eagerly anticipating Raghav's emergence from his room.

"Hmm, just don't hang out till late," Varadarajan said and relaxed.

"Sure uncle," Abdul said, shaking his legs with no patience.

"You know, Raghav is still not talking to me. But I feel like he is changing and will talk to me soon."

"Everything that was missing is finding its way back home. He is indeed changing," Abdul nodded.

Their conversation ended when Raghav walked out of his room.

"Shall we leave?" Raghav asked and both of them walked out.

"Have a great evening and get back home safe," Varadarajan said.

"Sure, uncle." Abdul said.

"Sure," Raghav said, nodding.

Varadarajan didn't expect that and he was frozen with happiness. Raghav climbed on the activa behind Abdul and they left for just 500 metres to hit Shalini's house, who had been ready for a long time.

Shalini waved her hands from the veranda to Raghav and Abdul when she found them outside the gate.

Elizabeth helped Shalini to the gate, saying, "Raghav is looking damn hot."

"Mom, behave," Shalini said and Elizabeth walked back home after saying hi to them.

"You like my gift?" Raghav asked when he found Shalini wearing it.

"Your outfit is fabulous, and you look absolutely stunning today," Shalini complimented with genuine admiration.

"What about me?" Abdul asked and grabbed her attention.

"Don't tell me, you are trying to flatter Ayesha with it," Shalini asked.

"How did you know that?" Abdul spilled without realising it.

"I was just trying to kid you, but wait? Really?" Shalini asked and busted with surprise.

"I will pick Ayesha up and come," Abdul scooter-ed away.

"I will tell you about it on the bus," Raghav said and started rolling Shalini to the bus stand.

Raghav revealed everything about Abdul's feelings, everything from the beginning. Abdul's one-sided love story made Shalini excited.

***

When Abdul reached Ayesha's house for the first time, she was already waiting for him. She was wearing a mayo-mustard, yellow kurta with white leggings. Abdul's heart fluttered as she walked towards him.

"You look fabulous," Abdul said and fell in love even more as she started blushing and was embarrassed to make eye contact.

Abdul, noticing Ayesha's delight, generously offered the chance to ride the Activa, bringing a smile to her face.

For the first five minutes they were silent. Abdul fell on her at every speed breaker, not intentionally, but he did love it.

Ayesha continued to stay silent, which was unlike her. She was so focused on the road that she forgot to react. It bothered Abdul for a long time so he started a conversation, "Shall I ask you something?"

"Yeah, go ahead," Ayesha said and let out a long breath.

"What happened to you? Why are you trying so hard to avoid being yourself?"

"What! Umm, what do you mean by that?" Ayesha asked.

"I kind of feel like you started hating yourself and I don't know why. I think something is bothering you and you don't want to talk about it."

"Yeah, you are right. I don't want to talk about it, so please…" Ayesha admitted.

"Okay, I won't force it out of you, but do you know, the first day, the first time we spoke— I mean, we fought," he chuckled. "It was annoying, but I liked it. I really can't stop laughing at those stupid and meaningless arguments we had gone through. I want to be frank, the Ayesha now, who is possessed by something— I don't like her. I prefer the annoying one more."

He looked at the sky which was covered with clouds and then in the mirror of the Activa. Ayesha was crying.

He felt concerned but decided to respect her boundaries and not bother her. They arrived at the hotel, and as they walked towards the entrance, they noticed Raghav and Shalini approaching from the opposite side.

All four of them got into the hotel together and got seated.

Ayesha and Abdul sat next to each other, facing Shalini and Raghav. They clicked selfies for their Instagram stories and later sometime the waiter showed up to get their orders, giving them enough time to decide.

"Two Shoyu Ramen, two Schezwan fried noodles, and spring rolls," Shalini ordered for all.

When the order arrived at their table, Raghav hesitated to dig into the Ramen. The other dishes were still comparatively familiar. He looked at Shalini, worried that he had made a mistake by letting her choose, but when he tasted the Ramen, it was like discovering a taste of heaven.

"It's good," Raghav said after slurping.

"It has to be. We are paying for it," Ayesha said, digging in too.

"I don't think she changed," Raghav whispered in Shalini's ears.

Ayesha nodded her head, as she heard his whispering. Abdul

was strangely silent, eating without interacting.

Shalini looked at Abdul to provoke him.

But he gave her a bland smile.

"You didn't like it," Shalini asked.

"No, no, it's good," Abdul slurped the noodles.

"To lift up your spirits, we are going to talk about each other's crush today," Shalini said.

"Interesting," Ayesha barged in.

Abdul struggled to breathe at once and Ayesha passed him a glass of water, patting his back.

"Okay, let's start from Raghav then," Ayesha initiated. Abdul started sweating in the air-conditioned room.

"There was once a girl who held me captive with 88 keys. I can't provide any further details or explanations," Raghav remarked mysteriously and dug into the Ramen.

"But it is bland. I don't understand. Can you rephrase it better, for us to show some interest?" Ayesha complained.

"There is nothing interesting in it. This is it and rephrasing it would be tiresome," Raghav insisted.

Shalini felt a bit jealous, but she suppressed it.

"Now, Abdul, tell us about yours?" Ayesha asked, looking at him; she was so close to him that his temperature rose.

He couldn't find his words and was afraid to expose himself.

"Hmm, spill it out," Ayesha kept digging in.

"You were waiting for this situation dude, tell her," Raghav said, smirking.

"You were waiting for what?" Ayesha's mind muddled with thoughts. "Who is your crush?"

"You are," Abdul exposed.

The atmosphere turned too awkward to eat peacefully, but Shalini enjoyed her Ramen regardless of the situation. She drank the broth and emptied the bowl, and then asked, "Are you okay Ayesha?"

"Yeah, but you aren't surprised?" Ayesha asked and nodded her head. She turned to Abdul, "You have something more to say?"

"I'm not sure how to put it into words," he stammered, mustering up the courage to express his feelings. "But if the

Ayesha I used to know, the one full of life and laughter, still exists, I need to tell you something. I've been missing you so deeply, and that's when I finally understood—I'm in love with you."

Ayesha nodded and had the last piece of the spring roll.

"Shall we leave?" Ayesha asked, and then turned to Abdul saying, "I don't have to answer that immediately, right?"

Dinner night turned unpleasant as Abdul predicted. Raghav went to Ayesha and asked. "Why are you not responding to him?"

"Because I have nothing to say and I want some time."

"You became more annoying," he said, "I always had respect for you for your quick, sincere response."

"You know nothing. What do you think made me more annoying?"

Raghav simply shook his head slowly and shrugged.

Ayesha simply walked to Abdul's Activa and waited for him.

The dinner night, which was supposed to be the funny and memorable one, turned into a tragic event, leaving behind a deep rift that strained their once-strong bonds.

-CHAPTER 13-

After the messy dinner night, some kind of barrier, an embarrassment, stood between Abdul and others. He turned silent and the pending bucket list planned, met its end.

Ayesha was not reachable throughout and exactly 14 days after the night, the school reopened and they got promoted to 12th standard.

One more year of school life before it ended, so the students were not exactly happy with their promotion. The promotion was more like a nightmare to them than a blessing.

With the incomplete feeling, Abdul went to school and found Ayesha, but she ignored him. The answer for the proposal was pending but he had already concluded losing her as a friend. More than Abdul, Shalini and Raghav were very much interested in the answer, so both invited Abdul and Ayesha to the gazebo. Answer was the solution for the discomfort they were in.

As the four of them settled in the gazebo, a sudden chill filled the air, causing Shalini to shiver in response to the cold breeze that swept through.

"So, what is this meeting for?" Ayesha asked, sitting beside Abdul.

"You don't know?" Shalini asked while her arms crossed. "Why are you drifting away from us? I don't know if I am right, but something about you is known to my father but not me."

"Why? Let's consider you are right, but why do you want to know? You must have realised that I don't have any intention of sharing any of it with you all. Sorry, if I am being harsh but…"

Ayesha said and shook her head.

"Okay, keep it to yourself, but how long do you plan to keep Abdul waiting for your answer?" Raghav asked.

"The great Raghav, who doesn't socialise with others, is talking now…" Ayesha was harsh. "I don't have any excuse. I simply never thought about it."

"Ayesha said that she found Abdul cute last year," Shalini added.

Ayesha frowned at Shalini, "Why are you bringing that up?"

"Are you a lesbian?" Raghav interrupted in the middle, making everyone say, "What!" in unison.

Ayesha got a bit embarrassed to be there and said, "I am leaving," and got up.

"Ayesha, there is no way out now. Since when did you start lying? I have always admired you for being yourself, and I also thought we were all friends and meant to share each other's happiness and sorrows," Shalini said and looked at the river being stabbed by rain droplets. Ayesha couldn't leave as the rain got severe.

Abdul continued, "It hurts to think that you keep burdening yourself, hurting yourself while keeping something from all of us. Do you really think we will leave you to suffer all alone? As Shalini said, we are friends and we are meant to laugh and cry together. We are here to share each other's burden. Even if you don't like me back, it's not a problem but I, who never dared to get into other's business, am worried. I don't want to give up on you. I want to know what's bothering you."

Ayesha's eyes were glued to the floor. She didn't respond to any of them. She clenched her fist hard and tried to suppress her feelings to keep them hidden. She sat back.

Abdul asked for her hand to calm her down, and although she did give her hand to him, she refused to show her feelings.

Her hand was warm as she said, "I don't want to talk about it, please. I don't want to hurt you all, and talking about it won't change anything." She took her hand off from Abdul. She hid her eyes. Her lips were trembling to tell the truth and her heart was as hard as a rock.

Abdul's eyes were also turning watery, but he smiled, "I feel a bit awkward here," he hid his lips. "I am leaving, let's meet at the school tomorrow."

Ayesha's heart sprinted when she heard him.

"It's raining," Ayesha said as she wanted him to stay longer. She wanted him to stop. But still he walked out in the downpour. "It's raining," she repeated. Shalini and Raghav kept watching them. Abdul didn't stop. Ayesha relaxed her clenched fist and ran to him. She hugged him from behind to make him stop.

"Don't go, I want you to stay. I love you too," Ayesha started weeping, "And that's why I don't want to hurt you with my secret."

"Aren't we thinking the same thing?"

Abdul turned to her and wiped her tears which were hard to distinguish because of the rain.

"Which one are your tears?" he asked and they both chuckled.

Shalini gazed at them and Raghav scratched his scalp. When he looked at Shalini, the rain, the surrounding, which was so romantic, made him blush and his eyes stuck on her. When she turned and looked at him, both of their eyes met.

"What are you looking at?" she asked.

Raghav shook his head. "They will need a towel, or else again Ayesha will escape."

Shalini nodded, "Yes."

Raghav ran out and pulled them both into the gazebo to save them from getting drenched completely.

"What is this that my father knows but I don't?" Shalini asked Ayesha.

"Your father knows that I don't have a guaranteed life," Ayesha said and nodded. "I have RHD. Rheumatic heart disease."

***

Ayesha speaks

I think four months ago, I fainted in Abdul's arms at the school and I think it all started from there. I had a fever and went to a small clinic for a check-up. I believed it was just a fever and ignored it, but the fever got severe and it was the same as the one I had in Chennai. I went to the hospital then and got diagnosed with Rheumatic fever. The same fever which took football away from me was now seeking out my life.

I was with my father and after the check-up, I was asked to consult a cardiologist and that's when I met your father in the hospital.

He guided me to the doctor, checking my case file and his face changed all of a sudden. I realised something was wrong with me.

I was asked to take a certain test, and after a few days, I learned it was too late…

"You are affected with RHD," the cardiologist said.

I went to the hospital alone that day and Ravichandran uncle was the one who stood by my side.

"You might have had the same fever years ago and didn't get treated. It's late now. Your heart valve is growing weaker. You need surgery." The cardiologist said, his face wasn't that serious. And he started asking about the family history, which I wasn't sure about.

My surgery was scheduled for this month, so the doctor went through my family history and performed certain tests as a precaution. I was disturbed and confused, and I was bothered about my studies back then more than my condition.

I was doomed when my grandfather was diagnosed with Brugada Syndrome. It was a genetic disorder, and because of that my surgery got rescheduled.

"If you also get diagnosed with Brugada Syndrome, your surgery might go wrong," the cardiologist said.

I didn't understand the complication, but uncle comforted me and made me understand.

It all happened just a week ago. Brugada syndrome is a potentially life-threatening heart rhythm disorder and nobody can say when or how it is triggered.

My current situation did not start from the day I fainted in Abdul's arm or the day when I was a kid with a severe fever. It all started from my birth.

"It has no cure, and proceeding with surgery without

treating the syndrome first could potentially be life-threatening," uncle said with a tone of concern and humility. "There is nothing to be afraid of. Many specialists are there, don't let any of this harm you mentally, stay strong."

His comforting words sounded as if he was comforting himself with it. My grandfather was lucky enough to live his life to the fullest without any triggers.

"Don't let Shalini know about it," I said.

***

"Why?" Shalini asked sadly.

"When my parents got to know about it, they cried a lot because my life was turning into a question mark. I started looking for the answer," Ayesha said. "And all I could do was to get ready for the worst."

"Don't say a word more…" Shalini became angry. "You can still be saved. I believe in my father's words."

"I know… but…" Ayesha said.

"But, what? Will keeping it away from us make you a good person? You thought getting away from us will make your death less painful?" Abdul asked.

Ayesha was out of words.

"I feel like slapping you hard," he said. "I hate you now… I really…"

"Ayesha, friends are there to share each other's happiness and sorrow like I said before. If we can't do that, we will regret it our whole life, which will be more painful than anything," Shalini said.

"I don't want to die," Ayesha said and cried. "I am afraid, I am afraid of it more than anything."

Shalini rolled to her and hugged her.

Raghav was unexpectedly worried and his eyes were on the verge of tearing up when Ayesha noticed him. She backed off from Shalini, wiped her tears saying, "This is my first time seeing you on the verge of crying."

Raghav immediately wiped his tears and said, "No, I just stayed long without blinking and that made my eyes irritated."

Ayesha laughed, "I see."

"Did they confirm that you have that syndrome?" Shalini asked.

'No. I have an appointment next week. I will get tested," Ayesha said.

"This may sound stupid and familiar, but don't worry a miracle will happen," Shalini said.

Ayesha giggled, "You remember that?"

Shalini nodded.

Then Ayesha turned to Abdul and said, "Let's not do it. I don't want to get into a relationship with no certainty."

Abdul nodded and said, "Why can't you believe that we are all going to age and grow old together? Why can't you be optimistic for once and believe that there is no doubt and you will be okay," Abdul was half dead when he said. "Why?"

Ayesha couldn't answer that. She couldn't say a word to defend herself.

"I want to take you to the positive side. I want to grow old with you. I want to make you happy until my last breath. I want to be by your side. I am your answer."

Abdul offered his hands once again, this time with a real smile, without any nervousness.

"Do you mean it?" Ayesha asked with a pleasing look. Abdul nodded and with that, she held his hand tight and hugged him, crying out loud.

"I thought of many reasons to reject your proposal all this time," Ayesha said. "But I couldn't find any," she blushed.

Abdul couldn't understand what she really meant by that, but Raghav caught it right away.

"Bro, she just proposed you," Raghav asserted.

"Really?" Abdul said and tried to look at Ayesha's face, which was red.

"Stop making her heart flutter, you idiot," Raghav once again bumped in. "Now I get why she is concerned about not letting the truth out."

Ayesha laughed, "Were you trying to mock me?"

"Oh! The old Ayesha is back," Raghav said.

"See how easy it is to share your burden," Shalini said.

Ayesha and Abdul were still hugging.

"And you can stop hugging each other now. It looks a bit odd," Shalini said.

Ayesha and Abdul moved away from each other in a different direction out of embarrassment.

"I am getting jealous now," Shalini said and looked at Raghav. "Shall we date too?"

Raghav flinched and said, "I am more into sexy girls."

Shalini punched Raghav for that and all of them laughed.

"I am feeling good after a long time," Ayesha said. "I am happy that you didn't give up on me."

"And I am happy that I met Shalini," Raghav said with a smile.

Even though everything turned out good at that moment, they weren't aware of the upcoming challenges. And Abdul was a little half-witted to gamble his feelings when he had no idea how much burden he had promised to shoulder.

Although we both were even in that case.

Everyone in the world is looking out for a miracle to happen.

-CHAPTER 14-

I didn't know how many more days it would take to happen what I expected. Waiting wasn't my thing. My Question back then was, "Did he forget our conversation or was he still a selfish arrogant boy putting on an act?"

Ayesha and Abdul started dating. The love they shared, helped them to move-on from despair. Soon they got approval from their parents and dated for real.

The hangout got shunned by both Shalini and Raghav as the board exams were nearing. The portions for exams were divided into parts and the management targeted to get it done before three or four months from the board.

With the busy schedule, Shalini's parents became carefree as she started spending more time with Raghav and others. Raghav grew closer to Shalini day by day. And the mocking Ayesha's comeback had him busy with debates.

When things were getting back to normal— when Shalini's lower organs improved up to 80 percent, when Ayesha began to take medication to control her syndrome, when Raghav started to understand things and when Abdul acknowledged his misguided thinking— the surrounding got more complicated and was in the urge to somehow put them on a crisis or a state of super excitement.

That day, during the last period was mathematics and the teacher didn't make it to the class. It was also a miracle and the surroundings offered them excitement. When the other students used the free period to have fun, Shalini and Ayesha were summoned to the staffroom for some registry work. As time crawled, the period passed and school got over, but they were still at work and it was nowhere near done. Abdul and Raghav wanted to wait, but they were forced to leave with each other.

***

Raghav and Abdul, together, walked out of school after a long time. They crossed the main gate and Abdul asked, "Do you remember the day when you screamed at me for choosing science instead of commerce?"

"Yeah, and I am still mad at you for that," Raghav said and gave him a frown.

"Sorry, sorry," Abdul sighed. "I really didn't have any slightest motive to choose science."

"Yeah, I know that. You mentioned it earlier," Raghav shrugged.

"So, you may also remember me saying that something good might show up from the choice I made without any idea, and something might give me the courage to move forward without making me regret it."

"Yeah, you said and I know what you are going to say next," Raghav said.

"Maybe not," Abdul smiled, "I am planning to study medicine."

"You wanna be a doctor? Where is this coming from?" Raghav's prediction was a flop, and he was shocked.

"Here," Abdul said, pointing at his heart.

"Chest?" Raghav asked and Abdul punched him in his. Raghav continued, "It was cliché. I can't stop myself from poking fun at you."

"I got happy when Ayesha smiled, and it felt so good that I wanted more and more of it. I met Shalini's father the other day, and after having a little chat with him, I understood that saving lives gives warmth to the heart… and I want that."

Raghav nodded. He understood what Abdul was trying to

say and he thought of himself and his future. Nothing popped in his head other than Shalini's smile.

When Abdul realised Raghav was zoned out, he shook him and asked, "What happened?"

"Nothing… I… uh…" Raghav said and shook his head. He reached his house. "Okay then, let's meet up tomorrow."

Raghav walked backward, slowly waving his hands at Abdul.

Abdul's mind was at something and he said, "Stop."

"What?" Raghav stopped.

"There is one more thing I was trying to tell you all this time."

"What is it?" Raghav walked to him.

Abdul swallowed, cleared the blockers and said, "I wanted to apologise…"

Raghav was confused and waited to understand what for.

Abdul said, "I was and still am with you. But, for all these years I couldn't be a good friend. I always drew a line between you and I, thinking that I shouldn't cross it, or I didn't have the right to. But I was wrong all the time. My way of thinking about friendship itself was wrong… I never tried to understand the pain you have been going through all these years. Shalini proved that my thinking was wrong when she forced Ayesha to spill her secret, making her share the burden. The rights of a friend, a dear friend, she grabbed them. I couldn't do that… Good things take time. I wasn't good enough. That's why God sent Shalini to you," He hugged Raghav when the tears were about to roll down Raghav's cheeks. "I am sorry. I understood that I cannot be right all the time, I thought I have never made a wrong decision till date, but I was wrong. I regret leaving you alone."

Raghav nodded with tears and sniffed, stepping back, "I was the one who pushed you whenever you tried to make me talk, but you are right. I didn't want you to give up on me but to keep trying…" he laughed. "You are going to be a doc, but please do scare your future patients with your advice." He laughed again, "I hugged you with watery eyes… EWW… let's not do that again."

Abdul blurted, "You bastard," with a punch and they hugged again.

***

Shalini and Ayesha were bustling with excitement as they worked in the staffroom. This year's annual day was in full swing, unlike the disappointment of the previous year's cancellation. The planning and organizing were in full swing, filled with energy and determination.

There was a list of students voted for certain event management and Ayesha was stunned when she found her name was in the list next to Raghav, as overall in-charge.

"My final medical check-up is also around the annual day," she whispered.

Shalini patted her shoulder and gave a wide smile. She was already drenched with happiness, looking forward to the day.

The work they were doing was just the beginning. The main groundwork was still pending but they were done for the day.

When Ayesha got home, the first thing she did was to inform Abdul about the exciting, upcoming annual day. Whereas when Shalini tried to inform Raghav, Varadarajan was the one who attended her call.

"He is sleeping, Shalini. Call back after two hours. He might be up by that time," Varadarajan said.

"Sure, uncle, and how are you doing?" Shalini asked. It was the first time that she was talking to Raghav's father, Varadarajan.

"I am fine, ma. Doing a lot better, thank you for asking," he smiled.

"I will call back after two hours then, bye..." she said and hung up.

She waited for two hours to pass, but the whole night passed unspoken as she dozed off.

***

"Why do you have a mobile if you are not going to use it?" Shalini yelled at Raghav in the classroom.

All the students awaited staff to arrive, but Raghav on the other hand, was annoyed and lazy. He wanted to hear the last period dispersal bell. He ignored Shalini's yelling.

"I wanted to tell you something very important, but you are

not interested, right?" Shalini provoked him. "I won't tell you. That's your punishment."

But he was so weary. "The punishment is okay, I just want peace. I don't want to be involved in any important topic today."

Her mission failed, and Shalini turned her face away with a sound of annoyance.

Everyone stood up when the teacher entered the class, but Shalini and Raghav were sitting. Shalini was excused but Raghav got sniped with the chalk for sleeping during the first period.

He stood up steadily but when his blurry vision went off, and when he found Mrs. Vaishali in front of him, he flinched, "Woah!".

"Why are you flinching?" Vaishali asked.

"I saw a blood-sucking devil when I just woke up."

Everyone laughed.

"You are not talking about me, right?" she asked.

"No, ma'am. It was just a vision," he shook his head. The mathematics portions were pending so without any delay, she forgave Raghav and started the class.

In the middle of an ongoing lecture, the security guard came to the doorway to pass the notice from the principal's office.

"Ah, annual day," Vaishali gasped. "So, guys, the annual day is in three months."

Everyone started talking and the class turned noisy.

"Silence!" Vaishali shouted and checked the notice completely.

"You were planning to inform me about this?" Raghav asked Shalini.

"Yes, sort off," Shalini said.

"I told you, it was going to be a boring topic," he said and kept his head on the table, closing his eyes for the moment.

"Raghav and Ayesha will be conducting the first half of the main program," Vaishali announced.

Raghav flinched again, "Raghav…WHAT?"

"Is it still boring?" Shalini smirked.

"What happened to you again? Did you hit your head somewhere?" Vaishali asked Raghav. She signed the register the security guard was holding and as he left, she came back to her place expecting Raghav's answer.

"Ma'am, I wasn't informed that I would be presenting the event and stuff."

"Yeah, this is a management decision. Nobody is going to ask for your permission for this, you must obey the decision and work for it. Now sit down," Vaishali said. "The second half will be conducted by Preethi and Draswin." Everyone from the class cheered them up.

"You should have told me earlier," Raghav sighed to Shalini.

"I tried to," she snarled. He scratched his forehead.

"And Raghav is also requested to play piano on the annual day," Vaishali added.

He flinched again and said, "What?"

The bell rang and with an annoying look towards Raghav, Vaishali left.

The remaining seven periods passed in the blink of an eye, giving no place to think about the annual day.

Raghav murmured with the last period dispersed bell.

"What are you?" Shalini asked.

"Did you recommend me to the management for this piano thing?" Raghav frowned.

"It wasn't me, but maybe someone I know," Shalini said.

"Who is it?" Raghav asked, rolling Shalini to her house after school.

"MY MOM," she replied.

"Ah, I can't do this. I want to remove my name from the list," he said, annoyed.

"Why? Even if it was not my plan, I want you to do it. I want to hear you playing the piano. I want to see how good you are."

"No, I am no good. The piano is the absolute trigger to my trauma, no."

"And that's why I want you to play so badly," Shalini insisted.

"No, I can't do this. Please don't force me into this, please," he looked frightened.

"You promised to make new memories with me, to overcome the past. Now is your chance to break free from your trauma and triumph over it."

Raghav didn't respond back and they reached Shalini's house.

"Say something," Shalini insisted.

"Let's complete the exams for now, and then we can discuss," Raghav said with little disappointment in him.

"Exams, huh? Exams always save your ass," she shook her head.

***

The exam days knocked on everyone's door. All subjects were tough but the initiatives they took for it helped them a lot. One by one the exams got over, and one by one the result papers were distributed.

Raghav and Shalini scored more than 40 out of 50 in all the subjects. Ayesha and Abdul were also at the same level. A month passed just like that.

After school, Shalini and co, sat together in the school ground over the green grass and inhaled fresh air to let go of the stress they had because of the exams. ***I am the stress buster! How funny!!***

Ayesha brought up the annual day and the discussion resumed.

"So, is anyone planning to do something on the annual day?" she asked, leaning on Abdul's shoulder.

"No," Abdul said. "I will be busy being in the audience."

Shalini chortled, "Me. I am going to sing… and Raghav will be my accompanist."

"We never talked about it before?" Raghav said.

"We need not to. I have made up my mind. It will be only a matter of time to coax you into this."

"This is unfair," he said. "God why are you always on her side?" he asked looking up at the sky.

"I am on Shalini's side too. It will be nostalgic. It has been years since Raghav played piano on Annual day," Abdul said.

"What?" Shalini and Ayesha said in unison. "Now, there are no excuses," Shalini added.

Raghav frowned at Abdul and nodded. "I am not sure. I will try though."

"And I want you to write your own lyrics," Shalini blinked twice. "We have to own the spotlight."

"I am getting used to it," Raghav said, pretending to cry.

Everyone laughed.

And then they headed home.

***

Abdul's home

"Oh god, why do I have to study this much?" Abdul whispered, sitting on the chair. His room was tiny and his father was behind him reading a newspaper.

"Think about the smile you want to see in the future," his father tried to motivate him.

"Easy for you to say," Abdul said and dropped his head over the book.

"You chose to pursue medicine, don't take a step back now. Be a man," his father added.

***

Raghav's home

Raghav attended Shalini's call while scribbling in the notebook.

"When are you planning to take a nap?" she asked.

"I am already sleeping," he snored.

"I wanna come to your house next week. We can study and practise for the annual day?" she suggested.

"Hmm, okay. You can come anytime," he said. Then they talked for few minutes regarding the exams they were done with, comparing the mistakes they made.

When they hung up the call, Raghav dropped his mobile over the answer paper on the table and turned to his left. The white screen was covered with dust sealing the entire space behind it, and particularly that part of his room, looked eerie and depressing.

***

Time 6:04pm

Raghav was walking to the gazebo, and before crossing the road, a bike passed by him at max speed and he was forced to jump behind in terror. He was saved, but the bike ran over a puppy near him. The bike's tire crushed the puppy's legs and it was bleeding. The blood rushed out. Raghav was afraid to get up and help it. Suddenly from the opposite side a big car with horns accelerated towards him. He immediately got up, and had no time to think, so he jumped off the road, mistakenly down the cliff.

Raghav flinched and got up from his bed. The time was 06:05 p.m. It was a dream ***and a reminder.***

"Not again," he said with his tired eyes.

-CHAPTER 15-

Raghav died again and again; woke up again and again. Every day was the same, but again, one day he became a coward. He hung up the call he received on his house landline and went to school.

Subject teachers walked in and out, time fled. Raghav who was lost in his thoughts throughout the whole day, was finally brought back to his senses in the last period by the Economics teacher. With her yelling, Raghav started to breathe again in real and with consciousness.

"Give me the gist of today's class?" she asked Raghav, putting down the book on the table.

Raghav got up from the bench with confusion and blabbered, "Well… hmm…" he struggled to answer which made Shalini help him. She opened the first page of the chapter and pointed at the heading.

"Foreign exchange," he said just when the bell rang, and the classes got over. He was lucky enough to escape from the economics teacher who knew Shalini had helped him out. She glared at both and gave up her questioning. Instead, she said, "You have to take a seminar tomorrow on this very topic," and left.

"Busted," Shalini sniggered packing her bag to leave.

But Raghav showed no response. His emotions were frozen and he was in a deep disturbing thought.

"What is it about? What happened to you today?" Shalini asked after putting the bag on her lap.

"Nothing, just… um…" Raghav said, wearing his bag on his

shoulders, ready to leave. "Actually… um, my mom called."

"Really?" Shalini was surprised. "What did you do then?"

"I hung up when I realised it was her," Raghav said.

"What?"

"I don't know. I have done this many times before, but strangely I feel bad for hanging up today."

Shalini rolled herself out from the class saying, "You have done that many times? You are such a coward. You don't hate her, but you want to."

"What do you mean by that?" he followed her.

"You tell me, what was different today from earlier times?"

"She was crying with joy. She screamed 'I did it!' She was happy. She was so happy, and it made me sick. I didn't want her to be happy because she abandoned me and gave me a tough time."

"Shh, don't say that. I have already told you, she didn't abandon you, and even if she did, she is living in hell as well. Take it in a positive way, dummy."

"I couldn't. All I could think was that she left me alone, and now she is happy somehow."

"You said that she was crying, too. What do you think that means?"

They stopped in the corridor midway. He tried to make up an excuse to blame his mother and said, "Yes, I am trying to hate her. I am trying to blame her for something which I don't understand but, even after doing it, I don't feel comfortable at all. I am suffocated by complexity."

"You feel the pain because you still love her and you still want her back," she said and looked at him. "See, you might say the old granny is back, but I have to say this. You may try to hate her, you may try to resent her, you may not want to talk to her at all, but everything will eventually wash away when you meet her in person," she gasped and continued. "I was so angry with you when you tried to badmouth me and my disability. I believed you did it to avoid me at that moment. I was angry, too, and decided to not talk with you, but look what happened in the end? Do I look like a fool?"

Raghav shook his head. "No, no. You were formidable."

"I was a fool, you duffer. My mind went blank when I saw you. All my anger faded because I believed your reasons. I want you to do the same for your mother, even if it is a lie. There is always a possibility that your positive thoughts might be right in the end and it will give you a chance to contemplate that you never gave up believing it."

Raghav nodded, "I love you." He shook his head, "I mean, I love what you said."

Shalini squinted, "I too prefer sexy boys."

Raghav snickered.

Suddenly someone rested their hand on Raghav's shoulder.

"Long day," Ayesha said. "It's hard to find you both these days."

"It would be easy if you were single," Raghav said, with his arm locked into her arm.

Shalini giggled.

"Where to?" Ayesha asked Shalini.

"Raghav's house," Shalini said.

"Let's go then," Ayesha said and took a few steps ahead.

"Abdul?" Raghav asked.

"He is in the library with Vaishali ma'am," Ayesha said and stopped, "is he cheating on me?"

"With that old school?" Raghav asked and nodded, "Hmm…better than you, of course." He got punched.

***

Raghav opened the door wide and rolled Shalini into his house.

"Get in, what are you waiting for?" Raghav asked Ayesha, who was standing outside.

Ayesha shook her head and said, "Something popped up in my mind all of a sudden. I am busy, you both carry on."

"Ayesha, really?" Shalini asked.

"Yes, bye bye," Ayesha waved, stepping back. "Take care of her. If you hurt her, I will kill you with my bare hands."

Raghav smiled, "Of course, you will. I know."

Ayesha left and Shalini looked around the dark and depressed house. She rolled on her own and found Varadarajan in the kitchen. She was startled at first as Varadarajan was neat with a young handsome face. She never imagined him to look like that.

He looked at Shalini and said, "Hi Shalini, I'm Varadarajan. Nice to meet you!"

"Hi, uncle. You know me?" she asked.

"I guessed, it would be you…" he chuckled.

Raghav opened his room door loudly; loud enough to call her without yelling her name.

Shalini gave an uncomfortable laugh to him and rolled to Raghav saying, "Nice to meet you too."

Raghav gave her an annoyed smile as he never wanted to introduce her to his father, "This is my room," he said.

The room was clumsy but spacious. Raghav worked hard to make his room neat; he worked to some extent even though it wasn't organised well.

The corner of the room, the left side, made Shalini more curious than the main area.

"What is behind that white curtain?" she asked although she didn't expect an answer. Instead, she rolled forward and opened the curtain, allowing the dust to float all over. She coughed and closed her eyes. The first thing she saw was the bookshelf, which wasn't dusty at all compared to the other things around. She approached the books first and found the novels and self-development books of her taste.

"I have the same collection of books at my house," Shalini said out of surprise.

"It's my mum's," Raghav said. "My mum used to keep this shelf, particularly this one, clean all the time. She doesn't like dust on her books. My dad is following her legacy now, and he bought some new books last month. I don't know why he is doing that when the person itself is not here."

Shalini turned to the other side and found something similar to a table, covered with a shiny dark blue cloth. The big object that looked like a table was easy to predict. "A piano," she held her breath to avoid inhaling dust. "I always wanted to have one in my house."

She removed the blue cloth halfway and opened the keys.

She played the C minor note from the corner. She looked at him as the piano was working fine.

She breathed in with a smile and sneezed.

Raghav chuckled at her sneeze and he sneezed back with it. The chuckling and sneezing continued as Shalini counted the keys one by one to the end.

"Eighty-eight! I knew it. This is your girl?" she asked.

"It was my girl. Was. First love is always a failure, 99 percent of the time at least."

"Your first love is not a failure or going to be. I am not going to let it fail." She said and pointed at Raghav's heart. "You will play it and show me how to love."

Again, the sneezes and laughter continued, and both of them rushed out from behind the curtain.

Minutes later after all the fun, Shalini took out her Economics book and taught Raghav for his seminar. When they were done, they both relaxed in the living room.

"So, shall we start practising for the annual day from tomorrow?" Shalini asked.

"Yes," Raghav nodded with hesitation.

"I am not forcing you, am I?" Shalini asked.

"No. I want to give it a try too, at least don't want to resign after being pushed to this extend," he said.

"You are mean! Are you sure?" she asked.

He also didn't want to disappoint Shalini. He didn't know how many more days they were going to be together, but he always wished it could be forever. The thing which he feared the most was back. His life changed, he smiled again, he cried again. He was willing to live more but without Shalini, he couldn't have imagined it. He was sure enough to choose darkness over light for Shalini; for her to stay by his side even if it was for some time.

"I want to live more without any fear," he said. "I will try. I will try to do it. I will win you the spotlight."

Shalini nodded.

Varadarajan overheard everything from his room. He was happy.

Raghav stood up and said, "It's getting late, I will help you get back home."

"I will inform uncle and come. You wait for me," she said and Raghav walked out.

When she rolled to Varadarajan he was already at the doorway, "Thank you, Shalini…"

"For what?" she asked.

"For coming here. Please, visit often," he said.

"Sure, uncle, I would love to," she smiled.

"Shalini, you coming?" Raghav called her out loudly.

"I am coming, wait." She said back loudly and waved at Varadarajan before leaving.

***

The next day as Varadarajan learned that Raghav was going to play piano. He knew that practising in a small and enclosed area won't be enough, so he moved the piano next door to his theatre. When Raghav came back from school, he saw the piano in the theatre room which made him happy. Happy enough to want to go and hug his father for helping him out without being asked. But his ego held him back.

On that very day Varadarajan had started working in an advertising company as a scriptwriter a year ago. To celebrate his one year of working experience he decided to take Raghav for dinner.

Raghav was practising alone in the theatre room, literally struggling to start over his relationship with his first love but Varadarajan interrupted. "We are going out for dinner tonight, be ready."

Raghav couldn't ask why. But Varadarajan himself answered. "I have been working for an advertising company for almost a year now. I couldn't inform you earlier. I am sorry, but today it's my treat. So be ready."

Raghav nodded with a smile. He realised something was changing. The past flashed his mind and he remembered how his father and mother had been there for him when he was young. He tried playing the piano again and this time he felt a bit more comfortable.

***

After the dinner night, days flew by. The practice turned severe, but it was like meditating underwater. Raghav struggled but Shalini believed in him and kept pushing harder. Ayesha and Abdul also joined the practice whenever they had time.

When Raghav was slowly getting along with the piano and was turning comfortable focusing on the flow, they wrote two songs that came out perfectly as expected. One was a happy motivational song and the other was about a sad farewell. The main themes were friendship, memories, and hard work.

The practice days itself turned memorable and funny. Raghav's and Shalini's friendship grew stronger. Raghav composed the song he wrote and Shalini helped with his melody. In their free time, they even concentrated on their studies, not always, but whenever they remembered the oncoming board exams.

They smiled and laughed together. They even practised during the power cuts with a candle which provided a romantic beam of light. They were attracted to each other and awkwardness gave them a hard time to practise.

Too much happiness was bad, so God decided to bring in a crisis, a headache— a timetable for the upcoming exam with three-fourth portions from the syllabus.

Shalini and Raghav, Abdul and Ayesha gave equal importance to both practice and studies, as well as, to both romance and studies respectively. ***Ha ha.***

Ayesha's medical check-up came around the corner and she became busy with a lot of stuff to prepare.

Twenty days before the annual day, the official invitation was distributed to the students, requesting parents to attend the event. Everyone was happy but not happy enough to laugh boldly due to the exams.

Raghav didn't give too much importance to anything other than perfecting piano keys. Shalini's presence was an advantage which made Raghav improve to a great extent.

"You can do better," Shalini said. "Remember the good memories you made with your mom."

Good memories with Raghav's mom were going round and round in Raghav's mind. At first, he was interrupted and lost focus because of it, but practising hard made Raghav turn it into an upper hand.

-CHAPTER 16-

2017

November 12th

Ayesha was checking her phone in the waiting hall at the hospital. She was asked to undergo certain tests like Echocardiogram, Electrocardiogram, Electrophysiology, chest X-ray, Cardiac MRI, and a blood test. Most of the tests were done since she had been in the hospital from the previous day.

She was scrolling down the syllabus, checking the portions which had been covered and pending as the board exams were nearing, day by day. English and chemistry were the only subjects whose syllabus was completed on time whereas physics, biology, and mathematics were pending. Ayesha gasped when she was done checking. Unlike science, commerce classes were way ahead and only mathematics' syllabus was pending for them. Ayesha gasped again after acknowledging it.

When she was the next registered person for the Cardiac MRI, she found Ravichandran on the way to his cabin.

"Hey, uncle," she said and stopped him.

"Oh! Ayesha, aren't you done yet?" he asked surprisingly. "And where is your father?"

"He went out to have a cup of coffee. After this MRI, there will be a blood test and I'll be done," she said.

"Good, you look much better than the last time," he said and smiled.

"Yeah, somewhat," she said, holding a nervous smile on her

face.

He nodded and his face turned sad, "I don't know if Shalini is doing well. Nowadays, she is not sharing anything with me or with Eliza. It's been months since I last saw her smiling brightly."

"She is doing fine, uncle. She is in fact doing well. You don't have to worry about it," she comforted him, holding hands.

He gave a wide smile, patting her head when Ayesha was called to get ready for the scan.

"Go," he said. When she left, he received a call from Elizabeth.

"I'm heading to school now. I won't be home this afternoon," Elizabeth said walking on the way to school.

"What about Shalini?" he asked.

"She is at Raghav's house, preparing for exams and the annual day."

"Oh! So, why did you call?"

"Your shift is until noon, right? Shalini will be back for lunch. LOOK AFTER HER!" she said in a bossy voice and hung up.

***

Raghav let Shalini into the house with a pondering face. Shalini rolled in with a paper bag on her lap. She greeted Varadarajan, who was working on his laptop in the living room with utter concentration. She felt a little uncomfortable in that gloomy atmosphere and turned to Raghav, but he marched into his room without paying any attention to any of them.

Varadarajan closed his laptop and greeted Shalini back saying, "He is studying seriously, and he didn't even realise that you were here."

"Oh!" She nodded with a smile and rolled to Raghav.

"Won't you say anything, like 'come in'? Let's study together?" she asked when she reached his table.

"Oh! Shalini, when did you come?" he asked, closing his economics book.

"What? You opened the damn door for me minutes ago. I can't believe this," she scoffed.

"Hmm, I see. I got too much into economics, forcefully," he groaned. "This shit is exhausting!"

"Anyway, Let's do Maths. We got one more chapter that's pending. Let's end it for good."

"Yeah, I want to relax my mind too," he said and emptied his table. He took out the mathematics sample questions from his bag.

"You are going to relax by doing maths?" she asked with her eyes wide open.

"Yeah," he said and started turning pages.

She shook her head and they started solving the question papers. Shalini was stuck at the very first sum, which gave him no choice but to help her out.

When he was done, he found her paper bag on the table and asked, "What's in that bag?"

"Oh! I totally forgot," she said. "Do you have a tray?"

He nodded and brought her one. She spread out the contents inside the bag on the tray. She put the bag aside and the tray on the table, which was full of chocolates and Raghav who was curious at the beginning became annoyed.

"What is it?" he asked.

"Chocolates," she said with super excitement.

"What is it for?" he asked.

"Hmm, my mom used to tell me that having chocolate while studying improves focus and memory."

"Oh! Wow! And since when have you been following this practice?" His face was still annoyed but tough to predict.

"Since 5th Standard, I guess," she said and had a bite from the chocolate bar.

"But even after all this, you couldn't score decent marks," he smirked.

She gazed at him for his comment with annoyance saying, "Damn, I concentrate on one thing at a time. When I have chocolate, I concentrate on it."

"Okay, I understand... let me ask you the same question again, what is it for?" he asked.

Shalini's mind was muddled and she blinked with no answers. She became embarrassed after understanding his question with one more bite and she dropped the chocolates back in the bag. "Sorry, these are for annoying you."

"You are the one who focuses on one thing at a time, not me," he said and picked the chocolate from the bag.

She, with a sharp annoyed evil stare pulled out the chocolates from Raghav's hands saying, "If I can't eat the chocolates, nobody can."

He snickered and stared back at her. For a moment, they were both on the verge of killing each other but later they started studying for real.

After two hours, Shalini rolled out from Raghav's house to leave.

"Let's practise piano in the evening. We only have a few more days left," she said.

"You can give me a chocolate now," he asked.

"You want one," she said and picked one out from the bag, "Think before you trash me hereafter."

Ravichandran got home at the same time, and he found Shalini and Raghav laughing and having fun on the way home. He smiled and remembered Ayesha's words— *"She is doing fine uncle. She is in fact doing well, you don't have to worry about it."*

"She is really fine," he whispered and Shalini found Ravichandran beside his Jeep.

"Daddy," she shouted and hurried to him. "You are late."

Ravichandran walked to them and held the wheelchair to help her get home.

Raghav gleamed at Ravichandran and said, "It's good to meet you, uncle."

"Yeah, me too," Ravichandran replied. "Lunch?"

"Sorry, uncle. My father is waiting for me. I will come some other time," he said.

"Liar," Shalini interrupted. "You will come one day," and her stomach growled.

Shalini blushed with embarrassment and made a panicked smile.

"See ya," Raghav grinned and walked out.

Shalini and Ravichandran went back home and had lunch together. Ravichandran became rest assured after he witnessed his daughter back to her original form with a smiling face. They both spent their time together having fun over conversations and later that evening Elizabeth came back home. Shalini changed her clothes and went to Raghav's house again for the practice. She found various reasons to pass time with Raghav and seek his company.

***

"Why are you making the same mistake again and again?" Shalini yelled at Raghav in the theatre room. They had both been practising for the last 10 minutes and Raghav couldn't keep up with Shalini's tempo.

"It's been years since I last played it, sorry. I will try again," he gave the same excuses again and again, sweating in the cold room.

She sang again and matched the melody with Raghav, but the interruption continued, "What happened? Not feeling well?"

"I am losing myself, I don't know but I want my mom to see me playing the piano," he said and looked at his fingers.

"Then call your mother and ask her to come," she said.

"It is kind of complicated. Even if I were to risk my life calling her, I won't be able to ask her to come."

She shook her head, "Whatever I wanted to tell you, I already did. I cannot repeat again and again to make you do things. I'm just trying to show you the way, but you have to decide whether to go by or not."

"I tried calling her, a few days ago," he said and breathed hard. "Her mobile was not reachable…"

"Try one more time and another time, until you reach her there is nothing wrong in it."

"I don't want to. She said she did it, which means she is making her dream come true and finally earning for her hard work. I will wait for her to come back on her own."

Shalini smiled, "Are you good now? I am sure someday or the other your mother is surely going to see you play the piano."

"Yeah. Let's go again." He played the first key and gave the lead for her to start and he was almost at the part where he kept making mistakes and this time he was focused too, but unfortunately, the phone call interrupted them.

"Raghav," Shalini yelled. "I am leaving."

"It was not me, this time. Somebody called," he said and picked up his phone. "It's Ayesha."

He called back.

"Hey, Ayesha. How are you doing?" he asked.

"Wow! Raghav Varadarajan asking, 'how are you doing?' I'm touched," Ayesha said.

"Don't be," Shalini pulled the phone from him.

He frowned and took the lyrics paper from her hand to cross-check with his music notes.

"How was your test? Did you reach home?" Shalini asked.

"Yeah. I even had a long sleep before calling you," Ayesha said. "Test results will arrive soon."

"Hang in tight, worry not," Raghav interrupted them.

"Is he sick?" Ayesha asked Shalini out of curiosity.

"He totally is," Shalini said gazing at Raghav.

"Are you practising? I learned a few moves to dance while you sing," Ayesha tee-heed.

"I thought Raghav was a piano genius, but we were deceived," Shalini said.

"I never said I was a genius," he whispered.

"Whatever," Shalini said to Raghav and replied to Ayesha. "We are struggling here, until last week and before, he was good. I don't know what happened to him now," Shalini shrugged.

Ayesha laughed, "No worries, you will do well." And was alerted with the second line. "Okay, practise well. I am hanging up, Abdul is calling."

"Yeah, bye," Shalini said and hung up the call.

"Let's practise," Raghav said. Shalini stared at him with annoyance.

***

"Hey," Ayesha said to Abdul overcall.

"I was thinking about you the whole day," Abdul said.

"I know you would do that," she said and invited him over. "Come home tomorrow, let's prepare for the upcoming exams."

Abdul gave a sarcastic smile and said, "Yeah."

"What's with that sound?"

"This is the first time you have called me to your house."

"So, what about that?" she asked, smiling.

"Nothing, just saying," he smirked.

"Don't have any dirty thoughts in your mind. My father will be here too."

"Okay, but when will I get my first kiss," he asked whispering.

"I am going to hang up now," she muttered in shyness.

"Wait, wait! Okay, fine then," he said, his face changed. "My ass is not cooperating and sitting in one place. Please help me with my studies. I want to get into the same college as you."

"Okay, let's score the highest in the class then."

"No, no. I want to beat Shalini and Raghav too. Let's top the school,"

"What about your ass? Is it okay with it?"

"Things are going to get interesting, it will eventually cooperate," he said.

Both sniggered.

Then they started studying together, day by day, and with a blink of an eye, the most awaited day showed up.

***

2017

November 17th

Annual day

Ayesha and Raghav were asked to report at school for anchoring rehearsal along with Preethi and Draswin at 04:00 p.m., two hours before the program was scheduled to start.

Raghav and Ayesha reached there a little early. They were asked to wait for some time. The work for the annual day was going on in every direction they turned. Juniors were rushing here and there with tension, performing the work allotted to them.

Shalini was waiting nervously for the clock to hit 06:00 p.m. A lot was going on in her mind at that time. She, who was afraid to face the people who pitied her, got along with the environment. She, who was afraid to attend the fresher's day previously, got ready to climb up the stage to sing along with Raghav.

She had the lyrics papers in her hand, so she started rehearsing while waiting for her father to arrive. She was singing when Ravichandran got home. He stayed outside until Shalini finished to surprise her.

"Wow!" he said and entered the house, clapping. Shalini flinched.

"When did you come?" Shalini asked, blushing.

"I came just a few minutes ago, maybe when you started singing," he said proudly.

"Oh," she said and buried her face into her palm.

"It was good. I swear," he said.

"Really?" she asked. She was wearing a red shirt and a beige long skirt.

"Yeah, and you look dashing," he said.

Shalini lifted her face and smirked.

Then they both left for school on the crowded road. When Shalini reached the school, it was already 06:00 p.m. When Elizabeth found them approaching the stage, she rushed to them and hugged Ravichandran, looking at Shalini.

"You look gorgeous," Elizabeth said to Shalini with a wink.

"What about me?" Ravichandran asked and took a step back.

Elizabeth tugged him close to her and said, "You look like a hero, Ravi. I am flattered."

The piano was already on the stage at the corner.

"When are Raghav and I supposed to climb up to the stage?" Shalini asked.

"Hmm, let's see," Elizabeth said and looked at the agenda sheet in her hands. "Second from the last," she looked at Shalini. "Do well, okay. I am going to the front," she said, kissing Shalini's forehead.

The program started, and all the seats were occupied with audiences. Only Raghav's and Ayesha's parents didn't show up. They climbed up the stage, wearing school uniforms, and welcomed everyone gathered there. They talked about the school for some time, praised the teachers, asked the principal to talk for a few minutes and as usual, it took longer. It was quite boring.

Then the 12th board toppers of the year 2017 were called to the stage to collect their medals and honours. That part was a bit motivational. Ayesha and Raghav conducted the first half of the program perfectly fine.

Shalini's eyes were on them throughout.

"Raghav looks good, right?" Ravichandran asked Shalini.

"Does he?" Shalini questioned with a smile. For anchoring the next half of the program, Preethi and Draswin climbed up the stage and without any interruptions the program continued.

Shalini rolled alone to the changing room to meet Ayesha and Raghav. Abdul found Shalini on her way, he rushed to her, and together they approached the changing room.

Raghav walked out of the room with the maroon shirt and grey pants.

"Are you ready for the stage?" Shalini asked on the way to him.

"I am tired, just a few minutes ago I got off the stage. Now again I have to go through that shit," he whispered.

"Yeah," Ayesha walked out from the next room, wearing a denim shirt and black pants. "I am safe though."

Abdul walked to her and hugged her tight. He was wearing a denim jacket over a white tee and black pants. Both were dressed nearly the same, literal couple goals.

Raghav and Shalini exhaled, looked at each other and shrugged.

"You did great, I don't know why, but I missed you very much," Abdul snivelled.

"Okay," Ayesha grinned. "This is school, and if anybody sees us like this, we will be in trouble."

Abdul took a few steps back blushing and looked at both Shalini and Raghav.

"Have you two kissed already?" Shalini asked Abdul.

"Yes," Abdul said happily.

Ayesha hit him in the head, "Tell them the truth."

Raghav and Shalini laughed.

"Let's sing the happy song," Raghav suggested and Shalini gave him a thumbs up.

Then together, they went back to the ground to check the

junior events.

The event started with a short mime act. A rap song with the beat-box was next, and the next and the next, and people cheered, clapping hands with a joyous face.

"We have exams after this!" Raghav reminded them, sitting in the corner seat along with others.

"Here we go again. Raghav, please don't take your mind to academics for today," Shalini said and Abdul frowned at Raghav for that.

"But what he said was true, right?" Ayesha added, supporting Raghav.

"Since when did you both join forces?" Abdul asked.

"From a very long time," Ayesha said.

The audience clapped their hands loud.

Ayesha received a call from her cardiologist in the middle of the event. She walked out from there to attend the call, smiling nervously at others.

She reached the corridor and answered.

"Sir," she said.

"Why didn't you come to the hospital today?" he asked but his voice was normal.

"Today I had to attend a school function, and to be frank I was afraid, so I decided to come tomorrow…" she imparted with sorrow. "I didn't expect you to call."

"Sorry if I disturbed you. It wasn't an urgent call or something. We can talk later if you want."

"No… No… No… I'm not busy. Now that you have called me, please tell me… what happened?" her eyes were already watery.

"Your results are good," he said and she exhaled as a drop of tear slid down. "Your valve damage is sustained and there is not much difference from the last test."

"So, I'm good now, I don't need surgery?" Ayesha asked.

"Of course, you do. Your valve must be treated, as soon as possible," he said.

"Is there any other problem?" she asked and kept her hand on her chest.

"Yeah, your syndrome gets triggered with certain

medication," he said.

"You mean?"

"I mean, you have two options. Either you have to wait until we find a solution to control your syndrome, or the best alternative is to take the risk and get the surgery done. If everything goes fine your syndrome-related treatment will be next. Now it is up to you to decide,"

"What will happen if the surgery goes wrong?" she asked.

"Ayesha, you have nothing to worry about. The medical system is improving. You have to trust us, and if you ask me, I will vote for the alternative."

"Yeah, I know you are ready to take a risk, but I need to know everything before deciding. Do my parents know about it?"

"I asked your father to meet me tomorrow."

Ayesha nodded and she clenched her hand on the chest. "Tell me, what will happen if the operation goes wrong?"

"The worst you could possibly expect…" he said. Her heart broke down into pieces. "If you choose to wait, we cannot predict the future complications. Either way it is risky. That's why…"

"Yeah, either way it is risky… I know, but if I choose to wait. I may live longer," she said.

"Take your time to decide, but you shouldn't lose hope."

But she had already lost her way. She was staggering in search of her way out, in search of hope.

The call got disconnected. Tears burst out, and she started sobbing alone in the corridor when everyone was on the ground, clapping their hands and enjoying themselves.

Raghav and Shalini were ready for their turn to climb up the stage. Abdul looked for Ayesha from his chair but couldn't find her.

"Where is this, Ayesha?" he asked Shalini.

"She got a call, she went to the corridor I guess," Raghav said. "We are next, go and bring her to the ground. She said she will dance. I wanna see it."

"Yeah, me too," Abdul said and smiled before leaving to the corridor.

Abdul's *'I miss you'* echoed in Ayesha's mind as she sobbed.

She couldn't dare to choose either.

"Ayesha?" Abdul shouted when he found her in the corridor and approached running.

Her cheeks were wet, but she tried to wipe them before Abdul reached her. No matter what she tried, he figured it out and asked, "Did you cry?" He took a few steps to her slowly, "What happened?"

He touched her cheeks and wiped them for her, "Our strong girl is crying," he tried to comfort her, but her face didn't change. "Was it a call from the hospital?"

She nodded; he hugged her. "I don't care if someone sees."

Minutes later Raghav also went looking for them, but when he found Ayesha crying, he backed off.

"Ayesha is crying," he informed Shalini when they were near the stage.

"What?" she tried to move.

"Don't. Abdul is there for her."

"Was it the call from the hospital?"

Raghav shook his head, "I don't know, maybe…"

"Let's change the song," she whispered.

He nodded.

The dance got over, the audience clapped their hands and waited for the next. Ravichandran and Elizabeth were eagerly waiting for Shalini and Raghav's performance, and again a person with a mask on got ready with the camera to record their performance.

Preethi announced the names and gave them an opening.

Elizabeth saw that both of their faces had worn off, but she was clueless on sudden change.

Raghav pressed the first key and gave a lead to Shalini, who started by humming along note. It started with an awkward look on the audience's face but when the song touched the sad phrase the audience started lending their ears to it. Shalini started singing and the strong feeling of the lyrics hit the audience deeper and deeper. The senior students who were living life after school heard that song and were mesmerised. Some of them were left in tears and other faces turned depressed.

As the song gently weaved its melody, it resonated deeply

with Ayesha, embracing her with a profound sense of sorrow. Its lyrics held a concealed message, one that only Ayesha and Abdul could truly comprehend, forging a silent bond between them.

A nostalgic atmosphere was created, everyone ran back to their past and reminisced how happy they were during school days.

Ayesha couldn't bear to stay there anymore. She backed off from Abdul and started running out from the school. Abdul followed her.

Shalini cried while singing, Raghav made no mistake; it was sharp as a double-edged sword, peaceful and painful. As everyone was recalling their past, Raghav also went through it. The love of his mother flashed in front of him. He played it beautifully and showed his real strength as promised, but the situation was not favourable to them, they were also crying.

As Ayesha crossed the main gate, Abdul held her hand and stopped her from behind.

"Look, as I promised… I won't leave you to suffer alone. I may not save you, or change the way things are, but I love you… I love you… I will be with you in every situation holding your hands. I will stand beside you until your last breath…" he smiled sadly with tears in his eyes, "It may sound cliché as always, but this is how I really feel…"

She took away her hands and screamed, "Please stop it, I don't want any of you in my mess, and this is why… this is why I kept it from you all."

"You kept it from us because you cared for us and you still do. Your life isn't a mess, your life is how you live and I want to be a part of it…"

Ayesha remained silent for some time, "Don't talk nonsense. As if you are going to die with me, you have a family."

"And you are one among them."

Ayesha went silent again.

"Here look, it happened to me before. Raghav was the same as you. He, too, deliberately pushed everyone from his life. I was a fool back then and gave up on him. I can't do that to you— the person I care for the most."

Ayesha shed tears and Abdul again wiped her teary cheeks

saying, "Now I can see your tears." Ayesha tittered sobbing. He continued, "Don't worry, I will be with you. I don't know what happened, but I hope that everything will be okay in the end."

As Abdul comforted Ayesha at the main gate, Shalini and Raghav made the audience cry with their song.

The audience took a long pause to realise that the song ended and started clapping hard.

The next performance was a dance, the same rocking and cheerful one. Shalini and Raghav rushed to find Ayesha and Abdul. When they did, they too gave their warm words to comfort one another.

"Everything will be okay," Abdul whispered and comforted himself.

The most awaited annual day came to an end with another challenge for everyone to face.

CHAPTER 17

2019
April 5th

6:30pm

Shalini reached Waves' college campus with Richu and waited for Joel to show up. It took 10 minutes for Joel to reach the main gate.

"I'm Joel," he said and offered a handshake.

Shalini shook her hands with him and they introduced themselves.

With the greeting, "Nice to meet you," they entered the campus.

"Are you sure you wanna meet him today?" Joel asked.

"Why is there anything wrong?" Shalini added.

"No, actually he is a mess right now. He hasn't come home for the past two days and he is stubbornly working on pieces."

"And why is that?"

"After a week we have a competition and many musicians will show up. If any of us steal the show, they might recruit us for a lifetime."

"Wow, it might be a wonderful opportunity then," Richu said with surprise.

"Yeah, but you should know overworking is not healthy," Joel replied to him in disappointment and by that time they reached the Opulence Hotel, which had a large auditorium in it.

Joel asked both to wait at the reception, and he went to

Raghav to bring him out.

Waiting was not fun when excitement was at its peak. Shalini started scrolling through her phone just when she received a call from Abdul.

"Hey Abdul," Shalini said as she attended the call.

"Shalini, did you meet that bastard?" he asked half-heartedly.

"No. Not yet, but soon. I will meet him today and break his face. You have nothing to worry about," she said and smiled. She knew something was wrong with Abdul's voice. He sounded troubled.

"Did you get any calls from Ayesha?" Shalini asked.

He took too long to say, "Yeah. She reached Delhi just an hour ago. I spoke to her, and she sounded just fine, but I can't help but worry."

"When is her surgery?"

"In a week."

"I was hoping to ask you this. Why didn't you go with her? You promised to stay by her side, holding her hands."

"She didn't want me to. She asked me to trust her that she will be back," Abdul said. "I trust her more than myself."

His voice was still wrapped with sorrow. Shalini couldn't comfort him as she herself needed to be comforted.

"I, too, trust her," Shalini said before hanging up. "She will keep her promise."

She was sitting on the couch facing Richu. She was pensive and nervous at the same time. Even after crossing miles to meet Raghav, she didn't feel right. Her thoughts were muddled.

"Why are they taking so long?" Richu asked, scrolling through Instagram.

"How would I know?" Shalini jumped out from her thoughts. "Did you inform your parents that we have reached?"

"No," Richu said.

"Do that first."

"Huh," he scoffed. "How about you?"

She gasped and said, "I already did."

"What did your father say?" he asked curiously.

"He asked me to be safe," she said and slowly became scared. She imagined Richu being horny and creepy, even though he was totally innocent. She looked at him and asked irrationally with wide eyes, "I doubt something will happen now, but am I safe with you? Can I trust you?"

"What's gotten into you?" he laughed with all nostrils.

"See, you look minacious," she pointed at him with panic.

"In what way do I look like that? You were fine all this time," his weird, fearful face continued to stay put.

Shalini smirked and laughed hard, "Awe, how cute. I was just kidding. I am okay now." She played him to let go of her own nervousness and it worked.

Joel was alone when he came back to the reception. When Shalini and Richu found him, they understood something was wrong with Joel. "What happened?" Richu asked. "You don't look so good. And where is Raghav?"

"He is… Can you meet him tomorrow? I will do something to bring him out," Joel asked.

"Why? Why not today? I have waited too long for this," Shalini said. Her words were shaken up.

"He is very much, into the piano thing and all he said is that he is not ready to meet you yet," Joel said.

"And why is that?" she asked.

Joel shook his head with no answers.

***

Minutes ago

When Joel went to Raghav to inform him about Shalini, Raghav was sleeping over the piano, drooling. He looked stressed with dark circles.

Joel woke him up and said, "Guess what? Someone is waiting for you at the reception."

"What?" Raghav yawned, "Who? How can I meet them like this? It's been two days since I took a bath."

"Who asked you to send the nurse back home? Never mind, they won't bother you looking crap, come out."

"Who is it? Has Shalini found me or what?" Raghav asked and yawned again believing his thoughts were fictitious.

"Yes, she is waiting for you," Joel sneered with too much excitement.

"What?" Raghav was fully awake, "But how did she track me out?" he asked with confusion and started frowning at Joel furiously.

"It wasn't me," Joel confirmed. "I promise you."

Raghav looked down at his black and white piano keys, "Do me a favour. Just send her back, tell her I am not ready to meet her yet."

"What? Until yesterday you were so much into her, what happened now?"

"Nothing, I just don't want to meet her. Disappointing her like this would be better than showing up to her."

"How long are you planning to hide? She came down to Kerala only to meet you and you want me to send her back?"

"Because I haven't had any contact with her for the past year. If I meet her today, all I have done would be for nothing,"

"But I don't think she will leave without slapping you."

"Joel, please make her go. I have no intention to leave the auditorium until the competition ends."

***

Joel did what Raghav asked him to. He couldn't betray his friend and he also didn't want Shalini and Richu to leave. He wanted to help Shalini without betraying his friend, and he only had one choice left.

"I can't leave like this, mom would kill me. I must meet him no matter what," Shalini whispered.

"Did something happen between you and Raghav?" Richu asked with a sigh.

Shalini frowned, "Nothing happened, up to my knowledge."

She looked at Joel and asked, "He is refusing to come out, so why don't we go there?"

"You want me dead, right? I will lose his trust, don't you think?" Joel said and looked out through the glass wall, "It's already dark, he wants me to send you back home. Well, it is up to you to decide whether to stay as stubborn as he is or go back."

"I will stay, there is no way out until I kick his ass," she said. "I will persuade my father."

"Hmm, I will take you somewhere, come with me," Joel said.

Shalini stretched and walked out of the hotel along with him.

"Where are we going?" Shalini asked, climbing on her bike.

"To my friend's."

***

"This is Tanzeela, she is crazy, so beware," Joel said pointing to his friend in her house.

"What kind of introduction is that," Tanzeela said with an annoyed face, and then she looked at Shalini and Richu with a smile.

Shalini and Richu smiled back nervously.

"Nice to meet you, get in," Tanzeela said and let them in.

"I have some work to do, I will come back after 08:00 p.m., and you can stay here tonight," Joel said to Shalini. "Is that okay for you?"

Shalini nodded.

"And you Richu, I will take you to my house after coming back."

Shalini laughed silently.

"Nah bro, I am leaving, my house is just nearby." Richu said.

Joel nodded and patted his back. Shalini didn't persuade Richu to stay, as it was already uncomfortable for her to stay in some stranger's house.

Tanzeela made them sit on the sofa and she sat beside Shalini.

"Thank you for helping us out," Shalini delighted.

"Never mind," Tanzeela shrugs. "So, you are Raghav's girlfriend?"

Shalini said, "No…" while dragging the 'Os,' looking confused.

"Relax, I can see you are confused with your feelings," Tanzeela beamed.

"Do you think so?" Shalini asked and laughed nervously.

"Yeah. You came all the way here just to meet him, that shows how desperate you are. And Raghav never missed a day talking about you," Tanzeela said, Shalini sighed without believing her. "Well today he didn't, but usually he does."

Shalini blushed silently.

"See, you are blushing," Tanzeela said and her voice turned annoyed. "But I don't like it, if you are here to meet him, just do that and leave, don't force your feelings on him. Got it? He is mine now."

Shalini was shocked when she heard that. She panicked and turned to her.

Tanzeela's eyes were angry, and Shalini started to sweat.

Tanzeela burst out of laughter, "Look at your face, I was just kidding, don't take it seriously."

"Joel is good at describing people," Richu laughed and Tanzeela stopped laughing.

Tanzeela shook her head and turned to Shalini, "See, I think you really love him very much, don't panic I won't steal him."

"It was too shocking, don't do this again. My heart was about to burst," Shalini laughed nervously.

"Who is this guy here?" Tanzeela asked and turned to Richu, dropping her smile to a cold stare.

"Hi, I am Richu. I am Shalini's buddy," Richu introduced.

"Hey, Richu. So, are you single? Wanna date me?" Tanzeela asked.

"No," Richu went uncomfortable and said with wide eyes. "I don't want to date anyone."

Both Shalini and Tanzeela laughed, "You don't want to…"

"He came here to guard you?" Tanzeela asked Shalini, turning to her.

Shalini took the glass of water from the table. "Yeah, something like that," she said, having a sip of water.

"He doesn't look trustworthy," Tanzeela said and looked at Richu.

Shalini coughed out the water from her mouth, laughing, "Sorry, sorry."

"Yeah, it's fine," Tanzeela said.

"I said the same thing earlier," Shalini continued laughing.

"I don't know in what way I look unreliable," Richu said and made a sad face.

"You must talk and get along with others. If not, you come off as unreliable."

Richu groaned, "Whatever."

Both Shalini and Tanzeela laughed. Time flew by as they started talking.

Looking into the clock, Shalini asked, "It's already late, Joel isn't home yet?" She was helping Tanzeela in the kitchen.

"He usually does that. He never shows up on time, he delays things, but one thing is he never makes mistakes, he is just slow."

"Don't say I am slow, come out and see the traffic," Joel walked into the house tiredly. He lightly punched Tanzeela's head and took out a plate to have dinner.

"You had dinner?" Joel asked Shalini, pouring him rice on the plate.

"Yeah," Shalini said, "It was good. Tanzeela is a very good cook."

"I cooked it," Joel said and walked to the dining room. Shalini turned to Tanzeela.

Tanzeela smiled crookedly, "I never said I cooked."

"Where is Richu?" Joel asked.

"He left. He waited for you till 08:00 p.m., but you didn't show up. So, he left," Tanzeela said.

Joel nodded.

"Shalini told me everything. Why don't you drag Raghav out of the auditorium," Tanzeela asked.

"He clearly said that he is not ready to meet her, what do you want me to do? You know him, right?" Joel said, looking at Tanzeela. "He will only come out if his mother is here, I don't think there is another way to drag him out."

"Is it easy?" Shalini said inquisitively.

"You have to do it. You want to see him, right? I will help you if anything is needed," Joel said and had his last bite. "I don't know if it will be easy for Raghav and Varun uncle but maybe you can."

Joel left after giving an idea to Shalini and having dinner. Shalini went to the terrace after showering and started processing his idea.

"What are you cooking inside you?" Tanzeela asked.

"Nothing, just, you know," Shalini said.

"Are you studious? I heard you did great in the board exam."

"Great huh?" Shalini asked, smiling and this question took her back to days after the annual day. "Let me recall and see if it was really great." Both chortled.

-CHAPTER 18-

With the annual day function behind them, the next hurdle for Ayesha and her classmates was the looming exams. Ayesha needed a bit of distraction to keep her spirits up, and Abdul stepped in to support her like never before. As the board exams drew closer, the pressure mounted, leaving no room for anything else in the students' minds. Every day became crucial as they dedicated themselves solely to their studies.

Ayesha's family couldn't choose either of the options given by the cardiologist and eventually, they also decided to go with the doctor's suggestion— a surgery before the 12th Boards exams but Ayesha had other thoughts, she refused to take the surgery and convinced both her parents and the cardiologist giving a pile of excuses with board exam one among them.

First-term exams got over in time, but it wasn't the end of their stress. The pending syllabus was intended to be completed before New Year. And the school management decided to start with the pre-board examinations in January. Ayesha got excused and became calm and focused on important things in her life. One at a time. Exams.

Who would have thought that this crisis— exams and captivity with academics— would aid someone from going insane?

Note: some go insane thinking about exams itself, those people are excluded. Ha ha.

Parents' way of motivation, "Good grades pave the way to prestigious colleges and lead you towards a promising future," is a tool used to hype everyone and to make them study.

Everyone was getting ready to bring out their best. Raghav struggled with theoretical subjects and it made him perplexed, but Shalini helped him out and in return, she was taught numbers.

Soon after the syllabus were done, pre-board exams marched forward. Shalini and Raghav found themselves pressed for time as they struggled to adequately prepare for all their lessons. Raghav hated pre-board exams and considered it as a waste of time. Shalini, on the other hand, had exact opposite thoughts.

The practice exam, organised by the management, gave some students an idea about how the board exam papers were like and how to manage their time efficiently, but Raghav cared less and he focused on the actual board than the exams in the middle.

During the final school devotional trip to St. Philomena's Cathedral in Mysore, the students received their hall tickets, marking the approaching exams. While the purpose was to uplift their spirits and encourage success in their exams, the students held additional wishes in their hearts. Praying for one another brought them a sense of tranquillity amidst the exam-related anxieties.

They sought a miracle and with their belief they felt the warmth.

He heals the broken-hearted and binds up their wounds. Psalms - 147:3

***

March 5th

Monday

First Exam— English

Maharishi Vidyalaya was the allotted exam centre, and at 07:30 a.m., students were summoned to cross-check their dress code and exam preparation.

The rules and dress code were already stated and everything was going according to the plan. The P.E teacher checked everyone and made sure the rules and regulations were followed.

To ensure timely arrival at the exam hall, the management arranged two buses for the students: one for the science students and another for the commerce students. Since it was a shared exam for both groups, this arrangement was made. The buses departed at 8:00 a.m.

Shalini, Raghav, Ayesha, and Abdul, together, went to the temple in front of the exam centre before walking to their respective classes.

Shalini alone was separated from the others in the seating arrangement.

At 09:45 a.m. the bell rang, and question papers were distributed in three different sets. And right after 15 minutes, the exam started.

It got over at 01:00 p.m., Raghav went to the other class to help Shalini and they moved out. They discussed the paper and had a debate. They checked their timetable on upcoming and gasped.

PHYSICS	7 MARCH 2018
BUSINESS STUDIES	9 MARCH 2018
CHEMISTRY	13 MARCH 2018
ACCOUNTANCY	15 MARCH 2018
MATHEMATICS	21 MARCH 2018
COMPUTER SCIENCE	23 MARCH 2018
ECONOMICS	26 MARCH 2018
BIOLOGY	27 MARCH 2018

The exams went smoothly, as per schedule. For some, exams preparation days were more than sufficient and for some it wasn't enough but somehow everyone managed to pull it off.

Board exams ended with Biology and all the students were summoned to attend a small farewell party after 03:00 p.m.

Juniors were also invited with their promoting to 12th grade on the very same day.

The farewell began with Raghav and Ayesha, who were asked to motivate the juniors.

Raghav and Ayesha, who had gone through a lot in those two years, came up with their one-liners.

Ayesha: "Stop the teacher and ask if you don't understand anything, make sure to use all the resources provided by the school perfectly, then you'll be set."

Raghav: "Don't panic, these exams are only to test your capacity and understanding. Try to be attentive in class and make your understanding better day by day."

Both of them shared advice from their respective fields of expertise, but they couldn't help feeling a bit uneasy about their own corny one-liners.

Writing each other's names on their school shirts is a popular tradition and a trademark of farewell functions and with no doubt the first one to get the shirt got filled with the inks and names of many was Ayesha. ***Many did love her for real.***

Abdul, Raghav, and Shalini's shirts were also slowly getting filled with lots of inky love. Raghav didn't expect any of that. Happiness sandwiched them in the small school play field. Many added their complaints secretly along with their names and especially Raghav's shirt was so full of complaints, that the names turned invisible.

Preethi was the first to write on Shalini's shirt. After writing her note down she said, "I moved on and I am leaving for Chennai tomorrow."

"Wow, that's great. I will miss you though," Shalini said with a smile and cute disappointment. She hugged her.

Preethi smiled, "What is next?"

Shalini smiled back, "Probably I would like to see you with your boyfriend."

"Raghav changed a lot," Preethi said looking at him. "Maybe you were both meant to be together from the beginning." She turned to Shalini who was speechless after hearing that out.

Preethi walked to Raghav and wrote her name on his shirt, with a kick on his ass.

Shalini was very happy as nobody gave her the pitied looks which she received on her first day at school. The last day was real and she had achieved what she craved.

Everyone's shirts were drenched with love, friendship, and memories more than mere ink.

The camera's shuttering sound roared in every corner.

Whatever happened from the beginning until the end, every problem, hate, arguments, stupid fights, and rivalry, everything was sorted out on the last day. Everyone had different paths to walk and go on and when they realised it, the sorrow of detachment— which was invisible behind the smiley face, slowly surfaced.

"The more and more happy memories you made with care,
Will give you heartache and worthy pain to bear."

The part from the song written by Raghav and sung by Shalini on the annual day echoed true.

A group photo was taken at the end with all the staff and students together.

The group photograph became a priceless asset for those who lived life at school.

"You are still the students at this school until results, so behave outside with care and don't embarrass us," Vaishali said, the mathematics teacher, before sending the students back home.

An eerie silence fell upon the once cheerful faces as the weight of the word 'results' reverberated in their minds.

The exam stress, which was expected to fade, transformed into apprehension of awaiting results.

-CHAPTER 19*

Raghav grew increasingly frustrated as he found himself confined to his room with nothing to do. The same person who once yearned to skip school despised the emptiness that filled his days without it.

Raghav was lying on his bed and received notification about his waiting friend requests while scrolling Instagram after a long time. He cared less and as he clicked on the panel shortcut, it directed him to JOEL's profile. It was Joel, a long-lost friend of Raghav.

He flinched when he accepted the friend request fortuitously. He closed his eyes and gasped after dropping his phone on the bed.

After school he hardly found time to spend with Shalini. And Abdul— Desperate to prepare for the NEET exam, he ignored his ringing phone and left Raghav's calls unanswered. Ayesha was a different story. She never gave up her pride in front of Raghav and their stubbornness was the likes of brother and sister.

Raghav sometimes tried calling his mother but, unfortunately, her phone was switched off during those days. He became more worried than discomfort he had before.

Lastly, he was left with no choice other than calling Joel, who had texted him his contact details a long time ago. He immediately called his number without any second thought and whispered, "This is stupid, I don't want to do this. He won't pick up anyway," as the call rang.

"Hey Raghav," Joel said, "Finally, you called."

Raghav exhaled nervously and his first question was, "Did you save my number?"

"Yeah, a very long time ago, Abdul gave it to me. So how are you?"

"Yeah, I am good. Never thought you would remember me and Abdul."

"How can I forget the idiot prodigy and the monk? We were 3 idiots. Weren't we? Maybe we still are," Joel grinned.

There was a long pause from Raghav's side as he was preparing to ask something, "Well, I don't know. Why did you flee without any note?"

"Yeah, so you are still furious with me over that. I know apologies won't work and I got no answers. Why don't you join me in college? Let's get along from the start," Joel became excited. "I dedicated my life to music. I am going to do a BPA in music, wanna join? I guess you are still into the piano?"

Raghav's eyes were wide open and he said, "I… I… I am not sure, I never thought of anything."

"Yeah, no problem, I will put an application for both of us, if interested let me know."

"Yeah sure…" Raghav said.

"Hmm, then how was your school life? Any girlfriend?"

This version of Joel was new, and Raghav realised everyone is bound to change with time just as he did, but he was clueless, he didn't know what to do when Shalini flashed into his mind. They talked for like 15 minutes and the call disconnected.

He then went to the gazebo to meet Shalini and they talked with each other for hours. They didn't even realise that their conversation, without a point, propelled like the river next to the gazebo.

Spending time with Shalini was racy compared to the time he spent in the closed room of nothingness.

***

Raghav went back home and found his father cooking dinner. He jumped into his room and accidentally stepped on the wooden scrap lying around in his room. Even after getting back to the piano, he didn't stop carving wood. He understood that his hands won't support doing both, but he was desperate for carving something memorable and decided not to stop until he does.

Whenever he tried something, Shalini always barged into his mind and his affection for her got deeper and deeper. He slowly started feeling uncomfortable looking at Shalini and thinking about her. He hated it and started whispering, "Have I fallen for her?" whenever she crossed him in his mind and in real.

Days fled and one fine day Raghav got to meet Elizabeth after a long time.

"Hi, Elize," Raghav said as he approached her with Shalini at the main gate of their house.

"Hi, Raghav, I was thinking about asking you something," Elizabeth said confusing Raghav and continued. "Why don't you join us for dinner sometime? I thought you would come home after my first invite, but you didn't show up?"

Raghav grinned nervously without an escape plan, but Shalini responded back saying, "He will come, mom. We still got 2 more things on our bucket list to finish, and dinner night at our house is among."

Raghav had no idea about it and his eyes went wide open. He looked at Shalini with disagreement, but Shalini's frown made him say, "Sure, Elize, sooner."

But then, an unexpected turn of events was disrupted. Raghav's grandfather, Raja Ram, fell ill and was hospitalized abruptly. Though his condition wasn't critical, Raghav and Varadarajan decided to stay with him for a few days.

Soon enough, Raja Ram made a speedy recovery, granting Raghav the opportunity to reunite with Shalini after a considerable period of time. ***Happiness passes quickly; it is nowhere near to sorrows which stay longer.***

Result date was announced over the media.

***

2018
May 26th
Result knocked doors

All the houses were bleak, there was no excitement in any of their faces, but all were eager except one guy who was not even aware of it— Abdul.

Abdul after his NEET exam spent more time with Ayesha and unfortunately, the result day was his rest day.

Raghav called and knocked some sense in him about the day, but he was ignorant. Already burdened by his disappointing NEET performance, the impending board exam results offered no solace to his troubled mind. So, he went back to sleep.

Shalini and Ayesha were on call, constantly refreshing the CBSE webpage.

"I messed up in mathematics, I am afraid that I might fail," Shalini continuously whispered.

"Don't be, during your 10th result also you were like this, but you did score good marks," Ayesha said.

"That was a miracle, as you said. Luck won't be on my side all the time, right?"

"Well, I am here," Ayesha smiled. "And I guess you would score more than me and Raghav this time."

"Hahaha."

Then they talked more about colleges and stuff. Ayesha had decided to apply for B. Pharma in PSG Coimbatore.

"What about Abdul?" Shalini asked.

"He said, he will do MBBS in PSG, the counselling should be in his favour. He tried so hard for that," Ayesha said, looking at the message Abdul sent *call me when the results are out.*

"Yeah, wish I had a boyfriend like him," Shalini said.

"Shu… Shu… Take your eyes off my boyfriend," Ayesha chuckled.

The page refreshed and results were out. Both Shalini and Ayesha put their mobile down and entered the codes to unlock their result.

488/500, Ayesha's score. She lost seven marks in mathematics, three in physics and two in English but scored a centum in Biology and Chemistry.

"Hello, Shalini… I got 488 in total, what about you?" Ayesha asked curiously.

Shalini's web page showed an error, and her heart skipped a beat, "It isn't showing, it is an error."

"Oh! Shit," Ayesha said.

Shalini while talking to Ayesha received another waiting call from Raghav, and she immediately merged both calls to the conference.

"Ayesha is on the call Raghav and she scored 488," Shalini said with panic. Ravichandran and Elizabeth both were around her. Ayesha asked for Shalini's hall ticket details so that she could check.

After sending it to her, Shalini relaxed a bit and remembered about Raghav and his result.

"Raghav, what about you? Sneaked in silently," she asked.

Raghav chewed the sweet his father fed, disclosing his result with embarrassment as he was nowhere near Ayesha. Her score made it obvious that he didn't make it among the top three in school.

He scored 462/500. He lost 18 marks in English, lost 13 in business studies and eight in economics. It was thanks to Shalini that he didn't fail in any of these subjects. Accountancy and mathematics were centum, and he somehow made it to the list of Mathematics centum students in In Shalini cleared her voice.dia.

Shalini freaked out on his scores and decided that her marks would be no better but Ayesha with a fire of excitement shouted, "488, you bitch."

"Why are you repeating yours again?"

"You dumb-bitch. You scored 488, we both scored the same total, but you scored a centum in four subjects, only one put you down, otherwise, you know."

Shalini hid her face and turned to her parents, "I scored a centum in four subjects."

Ravichandran's excitement manifested in exuberant leaps while Elizabeth found herself taken aback, her astonishment overshadowing her happiness. "How? No way," she whispered, punctuating her disbelief by playfully poking Shalini's arm. "I always knew you had the potential to excel academically," she exclaimed, pulling Shalini into a heartfelt hug, tears of joy welling up in her eyes.

"You scored 88 marks, in which subject?" Elizabeth asked.

Asking Ayesha was not necessary. Shalini herself knew and admitted with a great embarrassment, "Math."

Ravichandran controlled his laughter and fell on the sofa losing his balance. Elizabeth's face changed when she heard that. She wiped her tears and frowned at Shalini.

"Wait, what?" Elizabeth scoffed. "Don't you have any of my genes in you?"

Ravichandran busted out with laughter, Shalini went back to the conference call.

"What about Abdul?" Shalini asked.

"Yeah, he is on call," Raghav said. "Checking for his result."

"Hi, Shalini, congratulations," Abdul said.

"I think Shalini and Ayesha both are this year's toppers," Raghav said.

Abdul after checking his result, said "I don't think so."

"What?" All three said in unison, "How much did you get?" Ayesha asked.

Abdul was shocked as hell, he was speechless.

"I got, no… no… yes, wait," he checked his total through the calculator again and again for confirmation. "I got 492."

Everyone went out of breath; they were happy, surprised, and speechless just like he was.

"So, Abdul is the topper this year?" Raghav asked, waiting for some more shocking news.

"Abdul" Ayesha screamed out of happiness. "I love you."

"Yeah, this is shocking," Raghav said. "My ears are gonna bleed."

"This is the first time she actually said that," Abdul added with surprise.

Everyone laughed.

Abdul's English score suffered a two-point setback, while in Mathematics he lost five points, and in Chemistry, one. Though this marked the end of one of his major concerns, the impending NEET result loomed ahead, the biggest headache of all for Abdul.

They all went to school a week later as 450 and above

scorers were invited and only 9 students were there.

Preethi was one among them. The management appreciated the toppers and gave appraisal for their performance.

Abdul emerged as the school topper, securing an impressive score of 492. However, Preethi closely followed with 490, securing the second position. Shalini and Ayesha, with their scores of 488, secured the third position in the rankings.

Raghav was expected in the top three by the staff, though he didn't fulfil their expectation, he was happy. He changed.

A lot of change took place in those two years. The broken pieces were getting placed in their order correctly by itself... but some more were pending too. The chain which was broken by me was about to merge as expected. But I was not sure then.

***

2019

April 6th

11:50pm

"And after two to three days, NEET exam results were also out, and Abdul scored the marks he needed to get into the college he wanted to," Shalini said on the terrace with Tanzeela looking up in the sky at the shining bright stars. "We may not have been the most studious, but we found joy in each other's presence. Our bond fueled our studies, and that's what led us to excel."

"Ah," Tanzeela screamed, and looked at Shalini, "I hope I got similar company. I hardly scored four hundred and nine."

Shalini clapped, "Marks don't set up somebody's worth. You did great."

"Ahan, you think so," Tanzeela said and shook her head. "You are soft, and your words are sweet. I guess this is what made Raghav run away from you."

"What?" Shalini got confused.

Tanzeela cackled.

As time drifted on, the clock struck midnight, and they retired to their beds. Tanzeela swiftly fell into a deep slumber while Shalini's thoughts wandered to Raghav. "Does he think of me like I do?" Shalini whispered and covered her face with blanket out of embarrassment.

***

Joel was sleeping next to Raghav peacefully, but Raghav, on the other hand, was sitting on the bed, looking at the school group photo from his dairy— looking at Shalini— looking at her smile.

"I will meet you soon, but this… is not the right time. I am sorry," he mumbled.

CHAPTER 20

Tanzeela after showering, walked out half-naked with a towel wrapped around her. Joel was on the way to her house. So, she hurried and changed herself before he could knock on the door.

Hoping for some dramatic turn of events, I anticipated a mishap where Joel would coincidentally, miraculously arrive home and stumble upon Tanzeela in a compromising state. However, fate did not play along, and nothing of that sort unfolded. Don't curse me.

When Joel actually knocked on the door, Tanzeela was ready and she let him in.

Shalini was on the call with her father. A few minutes later after breakfast, all three got seated on the sofa.

"What did your father say?" Joel asked Shalini.

"He is fine with me staying here, he is just worried. Nothing else," she said.

Joel nodded.

"Did you think of anything? Like how to reach Raghav's mom?" he asked.

Tanzeela was busy with her college work, so she stayed out from their serious conversation.

"I will ask Raghav's father, he might help me," Shalini said.

"I tried talking to him a week ago," Joel said. "He gave me a number of someone who is close to Raghav's mom."

"Did you talk to that person?"

"No," he stopped and said, "I will send it to you, try calling her."

Shalini nodded.

"I am embarrassed to talk with aunt," Joel continued.

"Why?" Shalini got curious as she didn't know his story.

Joel sighed and walked out, shaking his head as he didn't want to talk about it.

"Do you want to see Raghav's mother?" Tanzeela asked, retrieving a large book from the bookshelf. Flipping through the pages, she continued, "And how about Raghav's and Joel's childhood photos? Would you like to take a look?"

This made Shalini more curious and she rushed to Tanzeela.

The photograph displayed Raghav, his mother, Abdul, and Joel. Despite their rugged appearances, they all had an undeniable cuteness. Raghav and Joel seemed so inseparable in the picture that it was hard to believe they had ever been apart.

Joel pulled out the picture from Tanzeela's hands, his face was red as he said, "This is embarrassing, guys."

"This picture tells a different story than Raghav's. You were this close to him, so why did you…?" Shalini intrigued him.

"Why do you think he is not dragging Raghav out from the Auditorium?" Tanzeela asked Shalini, looking at him.

"Because I don't want to betray him, he gave me another chance to be his friend. And all I want is to help him in a way which won't come off as betrayal. Probably!" he said. "I left him when he needed me the most. I wasn't a good friend to him," Joel swallowed in the sorrows.

"Don't say that. I believe you had your reasons," Shalini said and patted him on his back.

"I've wanted to ask you this so many times. Please, just open up and tell us. We're here for you, and now is the perfect moment to share." Tanzeela's eyes were filled with genuine concern.

***

Joel speaks

Okay! So, I was bad, I hated myself back then. I had complexes and had a feeling that I was not good enough like Raghav and others. I thought I would hurt their pride going forward. My thinking had nothing to do with them, I was the confused one.

I was a bit of an introvert, and Raghav was also the same as me, so somehow Raghav and I started off with small conversations that eventually grew into an inseparable friendship.

Abdul was obviously different from us. He had lots of friends, but they weren't enough for him. He intruded into our favourite game and he was good at that, he became our friend in an instant. And he too grew closer to us.

I don't know why? How? but I had an interest in music from the very beginning. I tried persuading my dad to enrol me in a music school, but he didn't, or he couldn't make that happen. A week later when I was passing through music school I wanted to join, that's when I met Raghav's mother. She came to me and asked, "I saw you with Raghav, are you, his friend?"

"Yes, aunty," I was confused. She looked a bit younger to be a mom back then.

"Are you going to join us?" she asked me pointing to the music school.

My face dropped, "I want to, but my dad… denied." I said. I was a child, and what did you expect?

"Oh!" Her face changed too. She took me in, got my parent's number, and talked to them for hours.

I didn't understand any of the conversations but later I realised that she was going to enrol me in music school along with Raghav, and she was actually a friend of my mother's— not a close one— but more likely a family friend.

I was happy. She was a kind and a very polite person, and I admired her. A week later, music classes began. Raghav chose piano and I was more into guitar, thinking it was manlier.

I didn't know that things were about to change from there on. Raghav was a fast learner. He completed his levels one by one, at a rapid pace, without taking any stress or effort to do it. He completed his first grade in no time.

His achievement made me think otherwise. I thought I had made a mistake. I got into music without realising how tough it was going to be, I was slow. I was slow in everything, unlike Raghav. I should have been happy for him, I should. But I couldn't. Instead, I developed jealousy. I got distracted from time to time looking at his progress, even though we chose different instruments. I couldn't bear that he was already very far away from me. *What am I lacking, which Raghav has?* I raised this question to myself and stayed with it.

One day after school Abdul took us to a nearby park and we played football with a crushed plastic bottle. It was fun and then we rested sitting on the swing.

"I am going to give my next grade exam in a week," Raghav said, with pride.

"That fast? I thought you had no interest in music," Abdul said.

Even though I doubted my passion for music, I never gave up and kept working hard but still I couldn't reach Raghav's level. Abdul's question was crap.

"I'm really not very interested in it, but I can't say I don't like it either. I love to see my mom happy and piano makes her happy."

I was embarrassed to learn music with the help of Raghav's mother and making no progress. I thought I was a failure.

"When are you going to start grade exams, Joel?" Raghav asked and I had no answer, but something made me say, "I am going to become one among, India's best guitarists."

They laughed. Was that cringe? I didn't know.

"That wasn't the question I asked, Joel," Raghav added.

"But that is my answer," I said and left.

They realised that I was angry, but they never imagined I would drift away from them slowly. Even I, myself, wasn't aware of it. I concentrated more on making my dream come true. I worked hard. I failed. I got up. I failed. And after three months I gave the first-grade exam when Raghav was ready with the second one.

What kind of person will hate to see his friend's achievement? But I couldn't stop hating him for leaving me far behind in music.

Then I heard that Raghav's mother was leaving somewhere far away for her dream job. I was happy for her though, and she came to me before she left.

"Hey Joel, how are you holding up?" she asked.

"Fine, aunty. Thank you very much for supporting me in

music. I will never forget your help," I said.

She smiled, "I am leaving for a job and I may come back after two or three years or more. I want you to stay with my son and help him hold up."

I nodded what else could I have done. I wanted to take care of that promise and for a year I supported him by staying beside him, but my jealousy didn't back off.

My father was transferred to Kerala with a promotion, and as my mother worked in a government job in Karnataka, she couldn't leave. It was the same situation as Raghav's family back then.

"I have a friend from the music industry in Kerala. I talked to him, he is very happy to teach you guitar," my father said and asked. "Want to come with me?"

I had to choose, whether to stay or to leave. It was not difficult. I wanted to leave with my father to achieve my dream without any distraction or jealousy towards a very close friend. At the same time, I was breaking a promise I had made to Raghav's mother. With many thoughts in my mind the promise was buried deep inside without any realisation.

If I was not jealous or distracted from anything, I would have chosen to stay with my mom even if it meant losing a chance to get trained by a professional. My older brother decided to stay with mom and I left with my dad.

I should say that I hurt Raghav the most and this is who I am. The decision I took made me who I am today. I don't feel jealous anymore and I will compete with Raghav face to face this time.

***

"I realized that if I had stayed, I might have dragged him down or harboured negative thoughts towards him. I didn't want that to happen, so I decided to leave," Joel confessed. "I wasn't a good friend; I was jealous of him. I resented him for surpassing me in music, but in the end, I did the same thing, or perhaps even worse. I broke the promise I made to Raghav's mother, and I left when he needed me the most. I feel so ashamed that I couldn't even confide in anyone about it. This is the first time I'm opening up to someone."

"And that's why you reclaimed the promise made and tried to protect it," Shalini said.

"Yeah, and I don't want to betray him again. That's why I want his mother to be back, to settle everything back to normal. To bring out every secret to light," Joel said.

"You got nothing to be embarrassed about, envying our friends and rivalry is the thing which helps us grow," Shalini said. "It's common."

Joel chuckled.

"What?" Shalini asked.

"I just remember something," Joel said smiling. "Granny Shalini and her life lessons!"

He laughed and Tanzeela busted out with laughter too.

Shalini could understand it and with embarrassment, she closed her face and whispered, "Curse you, Raghav…"

The more Joel and Tanzeela talked about him, the more Shalini was confused about why he ran away.

"Don't confuse me further. Let me bring his mom first," Shalini said.

With a pool of questions flooding in her mind, she wanted to uncover the secrets one by one.

*CHAPTER 21-

Against all odds, Shalini persevered throughout the day, determined to reach Raghav's mother. She faced many hurdles, and finally, after a relentless pursuit, she managed to connect with her.

Post dinner Shalini and Tanzeela walked to the terrace like they had done on the previous day to chit-chat with each other in the fresh air.

"Ouch, ouch," Tanzeela moaned as she sat on the ground. "So, go back in time, what happened after the results? Why do you think Raghav came here without mentioning it?" Tanzeela asked with utter curiosity.

Shalini shook her head, "I don't know. If he came here for studies, well appreciated. But I don't know why he didn't mention it. A lot happened after the results came out. We were so excited and nervous to slash out the last things from our bucket list."

Tanzeela already knew the meaning of a bucket list, specifically Shalini's bucket list. So, without any interruption, Shalini continued. "I had paraplegia. I hurt my lower spine during football practice and because of that I was traumatised. I hated going to the football field. I hated meeting my team with the wheelchair. I hated the fact that I hated it. I wanted to be free, so I challenged myself to get through it, by making pleasant new memories, and without Raghav, I couldn't imagine having done it alone. On the very same day my mom invited Raghav for dinner. Both, Raghav and I, decided to challenge the most distressful and disturbing moment of our life."

***

2018

June 10th

It was a chilly sunny afternoon, with drizzle hanging on the tree nearby. Raghav bid his time for Shalini to come standing in front of her house, hiding something behind his back. Easy to guess—it was a bouquet of peonies, a flower which brings good fortune.

Unfortunately, Raghav couldn't give it to her when she arrived as Ravichandran was the one who helped her to the gate. He couldn't hide it either so after making all the faces for a few minutes, Raghav finally handed out the Peonies to Shalini with a gasp.

Ravichandran on the other hand tried hard not to laugh at it, so he started making frowns with his rugged face. Shalini smelled the bouquet with happiness as they took off and she asked, "You brought these flowers for me?" They both crossed the school on the way to the NGO's football field.

"No, of course not," Raghav said. "Peonies were cute, so I just bought it, had nothing in mind," he smiled after telling a big fat lie.

"Then why did you give it to me?" Shalini was also smiling as she knew the answer.

"After buying them, I realised I had no use for them so…" Raghav dragged.

"So…?"

"I gave them to you. I heard it brings good luck."

"I also heard it has something to do with romance."

Raghav's ears turned red and he became quiet, silently blushing.

"I want to hug you so bad," Shalini said it out loud all of a sudden.

"What?" Raghav couldn't help but to get dumbstruck even though she did it very often. As they were about to reach, she looked at her legs and nervousness crawled up her spine.

***

As they entered the field, they found it bustling with activity. Various teams were scattered across the grounds, utilizing every available space for their practice sessions, even on a holiday. In one corner, children were engaged in their playful matches, while on the other side, girls were immersed in their own games. At the forefront, boys were fiercely competing, fully engrossed in the sport.

The kids in the corner, who were around 10–12 years old, were first to notice Shalini and they rushed to her shouting, "SHALINI," out loud.

Shalini laughed out with happiness and invited them into her arms.

One boy among the kids stopped midway and asked with a frown yet curiously, "Who is this guy? Your boyfriend?"

Raghav was frozen.

"Nope, who will love him?" Shalini said and smiled. "He is an idiot friend of mine," Raghav melted as she tugged at him.

Raghav had mixed feelings about Shalini and couldn't determine his relationship with her but Shalini, on the other hand, introduced Raghav as her friend without any hesitations and thus Raghav agreed with her.

"Annoying brat," he whispered about the kiddies and looked forward. From a distance, he noticed a group of girls who appeared to be around the same age as Shalini. They seemed to be engaged in a hushed conversation about her. Quietly and discreetly, they approached Raghav and Shalini, unlike the kids.

"Finally, you showed up again!" A girl with bob hair said and stood in front of Shalini.

Shalini high-fived her and held her hand tight, "Yeah, captain."

Others also assembled around them and Raghav was left behind. Kids slowly drifted back to their practice and Raghav became a bit uncomfortable standing there so he walked a few steps back and took a seat on the bleachers.

"We feel bad for you," Jersey number 12, Agalya, said. Shalini didn't want this to be said and it made everyone uncomfortable.

Shalini sniffled, "Don't be, it was just an accident. I got

used to it."

She said that, but Raghav felt something was different.

Rumi breathed hard and looked at Shalini with a sorrowful face, "Sorry, this happened because of me." The other players became silent.

"Who said that? It happened because I wasn't careful. You are an amazing player, don't let it bother you," Shalini said and comforted her. "It's very good to see you all and please stop this pity party. It is gross."

All laughed and Shalini started looking for Raghav to introduce him.

"What are you going to do now?" the captain asked.

"I thought there would be a match, aren't you playing?" Shalini asked.

"Today is the boys' turn to play, and we had decided to watch the game. There's an interesting bet going on with one of the boys' teams, where some are confident, they will emerge victorious. However, we're eagerly waiting for them to lose, and for us to win the bet," Agalya smirked.

"Wow, it is going to be interesting then," Shalini said and called Raghav towards her. "This is my best friend. Raghav."

"Only a friend? I thought you were dating?" Agalya said, smirking again.

Everyone laughed and Raghav was horrified with their laughter. Shalini was surrounded by physically strong girls and Raghav walked to her with shaky legs.

After introduction, everyone went to the bleachers and slowly the football field started clearing up.

The boys' match was about to begin but due to shortage of a player in one of the teams, Shalini pushed Raghav to play with them. He wasn't even slightly interested in playing so he gave a nonchalant shrug to Shalini.

"Just go and stand there, they will tell you what to do. It will be easy. Please, please..." Shalini said clearly and shoved him with her eyes.

He scooted to the ground with boots on. He was lucky to wear tracks from the beginning. He pulled them up for comfort and walked straight onto the field.

Raghav's opponent team was the one who made a bet with the girls on winning, so the girls cheered for Raghav and his team. Both the teams stood in their positions and clapped their hands in unison. The match began.

Raghav was placed as a right defender. He was so cocksure thinking that he wouldn't let the ball get past him, but the opponent team had already marked Raghav as the weakest spot in the team and decided to bring out his blunders. The ball was shot straight in his direction.

Raghav was quick to receive the ball and passed it to his ally, His receive was more like that of a regular player, which amazed everyone as it was not expected. But that was not the case, it was an absolute happenstance.

The ball once again went back to centre half. Raghav's team somehow got into the D box and shot the ball towards the goalpost. Failure, the goalkeeper was phenomenal. **0 - 0.**

The goalkeeper kicked the ball high and long enough to cross the centre half. The captain of the opposing team received the ball and sprinted forward. His first touch was perfect and his moves were flawless. Raghav got distracted by his fake shot while he assisted the ball to his teammate. He tapped the ball in and scored an easy goal. Bleachers of girls were submerged with disappointment. **0-1.**

"Are you panicking?" Raghav's teammate asked. He was thin and did not have a captain figure, but he was an experienced leader.

"No, I was just… just distracted," Raghav said. "I won't help the opponent because of my blunder again."

The captain smirked and the game resumed. Raghav received the ball and passed it to his teammates. The game started to get interesting. The opponents may have tricked Raghav the last time, but he too tricked the opponent with a nutmeg on a whim in response and approached the goal post. He took the ball along with him to the D box and shot the ball. The goalkeeper was again phenomenal. He saved the shot and sent back the ball into the centre half immediately. The other side was free to get in.

Raghav ran back to his post, but too late, the opponent

player shot the ball into the goal. Unexpectedly, the goalkeeper took care of that and sent the ball back to Raghav, making it easy for him to score again.

Raghav figured out how the goalie would move. He faked a shot and kicked the ball into the left corner swiftly while the goalie jumped to the right. GOAL!

1-1.

The score was one all at time out.

"You know how to play, don't you?" Shalini's captain asked Raghav from the bleachers.

"No," Raghav said and wiped off his sweat. "It is interesting."

Shalini was speechless. She just showed him a thumbs up, and with that, the second half of the game began.

Raghav enjoyed the game and was having fun. He laughed peacefully after a long time. The first 15 minutes of the second half were just here and there with no chance of a goal, no twists. It was bland.

Once again, the opponent captain showed up with a ball and a trick. Raghav tackled the ball from him, and they both started fighting to get the ball out from each other. But Raghav didn't give up.

"Don't lose the ball, Raghav," a spectator shouted.

Raghav had no option but to kick the ball outside the field. The opposing captain threw the ball to his teammate, the forward was interrupted and the ball was kicked out once again.

Everyone laughed. Raghav looked at Shalini from his position. She looked empty. She wasn't happy, wasn't sad, just empty.

Finally, the brat figured it out. Shalini turned to him and gave him an innocent smile. He smiled too. He was distracted again and let the ball past him.

The opponent scored the second goal, and their noisy joy made Raghav get back to his senses.

"We are going to lose our money," Rumi said.

"That won't happen I guess," Shalini said, looking at Raghav with full of hopes.

"How are you so sure?"

"Just a hunch."

The game resumed from the centre. Ten more minutes to the final whistle.

Raghav's teammates marched into the opponent's court with the ball. Raghav and others were also running up front to help each other. The time is what wasted with the ball being dribbled here and there.

The ball reached Raghav again. If he let the ball past him, the match would be over. He struggled, he smiled, he struggled and he smiled again, almost a minute before the game ended. Raghav found a tiny gap and passed the ball to the captain. The captain passed it to Raghav again, surprisingly, and without any tact, he just touched the ball, and it headed to a direct GOAL!

Two all, Time out. Game over.

"You should come and apply for practice, we can be a good team," Raghav's team captain said. The game was already over, so without any excuses Raghav declined the offer with just a smile. He didn't know many of his or the opponent's team members' names and he didn't bother to ask because he only had Shalini in his mind and ran back to her.

***

"It is already dusk. We must hurry, mom would be waiting," Shalini said as they were on the way to their house, crossing the tree shades and the warm bright yellow surrounding.

"How are you feeling? You were sad in the field," Raghav asked. "Were you worried that you couldn't play?"

"Where is this coming from? I was happy," she said with a nervous chuckle.

"I don't know if I am right, but good things never knock on the door. They straight away run into you surprisingly and vice-versa."

Shalini laughed, "Then I am looking forward to it."

He reeked of sweat with dirty clothes. After dropping off Shalini, Raghav went back to his house for a shower and change of clothes.

***

The dinner was ready by the time Raghav reached Shalini's place. Raghav with little hesitation walked into the house. He could see his past— when he was with his mother, living happily. He felt pain but it didn't cause him heartache, instead it made his heart melt. The pain he went through was healthy and he loved it.

That's when he realised all the things Shalini made him do and believe in had actually helped. He turned to Shalini and all he could think of was to hug her. Unfortunately, Ravichandran swept the thoughts out of his mind by shooking him off.

Ravichandran made him sit on the sofa and sat beside him.

"So, how was your day?" Elizabeth asked after taking a seat, facing Raghav.

"It was excellent, magnificent indeed," Raghav said, nodding.

"Aren't you tired of these questions mom?" Shalini asked, rolling in.

"Well, he was with you. That's why I am a bit worried," Elizabeth shrugged.

"This is too much," Shalini said. "He always loves my company, isn't it Raghav?" She turned to him.

"Yeah, of course," Raghav said nervously. The tone Shalini used was vulnerable.

Elizabeth shook her head with a smile.

"Shalini said you played football today!" Ravichandran asked.

"Yes, uncle. I never imagined it would be so interesting and fun. This is the first time I played *proper* football." Raghav said.

"Then let's go and play every weekend hereafter. I will join you," Ravichandran was hyped.

Raghav stuttered. He didn't know how to respond, whether to say, 'yes' or 'no.' Instead, he said, "I would love to, but… I'm not sure."

Ravichandran patted his back, "It's not a problem."

***

Everyone got seated for dinner. Elizabeth served naan and paneer butter masala to Raghav. Some more memories flashed to him when his mother used to serve him his favourite food, which was naan and paneer.

This time his eyes were filled with tears.

"What happened?" Elizabeth asked when she noticed his reaction.

"It was my favourite, and the last time I had this was with my mom," Raghav said. "She was a great cook too."

Elizabeth smiled and said, "Eat, and tell me how it is?"

Raghav took his first bite and carried on. Everyone started eating.

"So, Raghav, I have had something in mind for a long time." Ravichandran asked. "How did you get such low marks in 12th?"

"Hmm, I don't know. Probably I had lots to do, more than studies," Raghav said. It wasn't enough for them to understand.

"Oh!" was the only reaction they could give.

Raghav smirked and continued, "The marks I scored weren't that low, I am happy that I have managed to come this far. Shalini helped me a lot."

"What did I do? You were the one who helped me for real," Shalini said with naan in her mouth.

"Nope," Raghav said, "whatever."

"It is your happiness that is more important. Have a goal in your life, but being happy and making others happy should be the priority. The one who doesn't realise that, even if he is a billionaire or a celebrity, they are not gonna live a good life." Ravichandran said smiling, he looked at Shalini, "I taught this to Shalini from her childhood."

Raghav nodded just when his plate became empty. Elizabeth served him fried rice and refilled the plate. The dinning was filled with fun and laughter. Elizabeth served Raghav again and again which made his eyes watery.

"Raghav, eat... don't get too shaken up," Elizabeth laughed. Laughter continued.

Shalini was into the food, so she didn't care about things happening around her.

"In two to three days the colleges will announce the list of shortlisted candidates," Elizabeth sighed. "A new beginning to you all."

"Yes Elize, Abdul and Ayesha's admission was confirmed yesterday. He is lucky to get placed along with his girlfriend in the same college."

"Yeah, he is. I am praying every day for Ayesha's good health too," Elizabeth said. "She has again decided not to have the surgery for some more time?"

"She is afraid, nothing else. She will be fine," Ravichandran said. There were a few minutes of silence and dinner was wrapped up.

Before washing his hands, Ravichandran asked Raghav, "Why did you choose to pursue BBA?"

Raghav had no special answers to give, "I just chose it, never had anything else in mind."

"I enjoyed the song you played on the annual day. Why don't you try music as a career and BBA as a backup, you have a potential for that."

Raghav beamed and washed his hands.

Elizabeth added, "Uncle is right, don't give up on your piano."

Raghav couldn't answer and all he did was smile nervously. Later, Shalini took him to her room. Raghav's eyes were pinned on Shalini's bookshelves, which was almost the same as his mother's and he followed Shalini to the balcony.

Raghav couldn't help himself and he gasped with a laugh after the minutes of silence. His eyes were all over. He remembered everything that happened.

"I don't know why? But moving on is tough, I want to go back in time to those two years. I want to meet you again from the start. This time I will approach you. I will save you from that accident so that you wouldn't be in a wheelchair. I will persuade you until you accept me as your friend. Two years with you again and again and again, new fresh memories with no darkness, only light and warmth." Raghav said and turned to her, "You really made me see light, you made me cry, you made me smile. You really are something."

Shalini was so happy to hear that, "There are many more good things waiting for you in the future. You might love the upcoming years more than the ones which just got over and that's why life must move on..." she tittered. "What am I even saying? You made me ramble, you idiot."

"But I did understand," Raghav looked at his watch— an

old, antique, unisex watch— and something popped up in his mind all sudden. He looked at Shalini and asked, "Give me your left hand."

"My mom gave it to me, I am giving it to you. This watch was broken until you showed up," Raghav said and put it on Shalini's wrist.

"Why are you giving this to me?" she asked curiously with surprise.

"It is safer in your hands than mine. I will get it from you later," he beamed and looked away.

They went back to their room from the balcony. Raghav closed the balcony door but didn't lock it.

***

"Do you have a crush on somebody?" Shalini asked. They were playing 'truth or dare' as she didn't feel like saying bye anytime soon.

"I expected this question, I want to choose dare," Raghav said.

"Why? What's wrong with this question?" she frowned.

"Everyone in this universe plays truth or dare and starts with a question related to crushes, it's outdated. Try something else, I choose dare."

"Hmmhmm, call your father and tell him that you will be home soon," she smirked.

"What? No."

"Is that still bothering you? I thought you got away from your worst completely."

"I should have left earlier, I made a mistake."

Shalini with her cold stare waited for Raghav to call his father.

"Don't make that face, please. You look ugly," he said and dialled his father.

"Hello," the receiver said.

"Appa, I will be home soon, don't wait for me. Eat and go to bed," he said. His face was relieved as he said more than what he was asked to. He hung up the call after his father's response and Shalini grinned. The next turn was for Shalini and she chose truth.

"Did I change? Can I move on and be happy?" he asked.

"Lame question, mine was better," she said. "And you are asking about yourself."

"Just answer it," he said. "I want to know."

"Yes, you have changed from spoiled brat to annoying brat." Shalini snickered, "I am joking, you didn't change, you found yourself and accepted it and now we got to move on choosing what's best for us and live a life without regrets."

He laughed inwardly and she clapped her hands, "Next, truth or dare?" she asked.

He chose dare.

"Propose to me or kiss me on the forehead or lift me up and put me in the bed." She gave him more options to choose from in one turn.

"I am leaving," he got annoyed and stood up.

"I wouldn't have asked for it if you weren't my favourite person."

She insisted and wanted something to be done badly. "I want to see your face." She laughed.

He went to her bed and made it for her and he lifted her from the wheelchair and safely landed her on the bed. He knelt down saying, "My turn and last one, truth or dare?"

"Truth."

"How much do you miss playing football?" he asked and looked into her eyes. "You wanted the hardest question…"

She became silent and gave a smile pretending to be okay but she wasn't, she took some time before answering. "I cannot say how much. It's tough, but I miss it very badly. I hate to admit it but I couldn't overcome the fact that I cannot play football hereafter.

He held her hand, bent down, and kissed her forehead—let's say touched her forehead with his lips as it wasn't much of a kiss but it was something that made both of their hearts flutter and cheeks go red.

"Everything will be alright…" he said and smiled. Shalini blushed. She was out of words when he said that. It was more than comforting. She couldn't understand what that feeling was.

Ravichandran tried to peek into Shalini's room and was hit on his head by Elizabeth and Raghav witnessed it by mistake as he walked out at the same time.

"Okay then, I'm leaving, Elize," Raghav said and looked at Ravichandran with pity.

"I will think about what you said uncle, and your advice was freaking awesome."

Ravichandran giggled and looked at Elizabeth. "Good. Visit here often, and feel free to be home," he was proud.

Raghav then walked out with a smile on his face and looked at the house for one more time when he passed the main gate. He couldn't make a move from there. He was perplexed with flooded thoughts and questions— the thoughts which were crazy and nonsense and the questions for which he never tried to find an answer.

But at that moment, he had an urge to figure out something to carry on.

CHAPTER 22

On her third day in Ernakulam, all Shalini did was travel back to her past memories and babble to Tanzeela. Apart from that her days were filled up with multiple calls and stuff.

Raghav was fresh in new clothes with lots of energy. He had three more days to perform on the big stage and as always, he resumed his practice.

Raghav, who was afraid to play piano once, started encountering days where he only played the piano and did nothing else. The memories which he thought might haunt him while playing the piano proved otherwise. He started to remember Shalini along with his mother with every key he played.

On one hand, he wanted to meet Shalini very badly and talk to her but, on the other, he didn't want to cause a fuss by showcasing the unrealistic things which happened in their life. Instead, he wanted to bury the truth and stay away from her until a new miracle emerged. With all those thoughts in his head, he couldn't concentrate the same way he had for the last two days without bathing.

"I shouldn't have taken a bath," he whispered.

***

"Where is Shalini?" Joel asked after reaching Tanzeela's house half an hour late.

"Terrace," Tanzeela said and offered him a cup of coffee. With the coffee cup Joel climbed up to the terrace and found

Shalini, who was also having hot coffee in the chilly morning enjoying the noiseless surroundings.

"Nice day, isn't it?" Joel said and stood beside her.

She nodded with a smile and took a sip of coffee.

"Did you talk to his mother?" he asked curiously.

"Yeah, I called you to talk about it yesterday but we couldn't connect," Shalini said.

"Sorry, my phone was switched off all day," Joel said and pouted.

"She is coming today," Shalini dropped a bombshell on his head.

"What!" He was astounded. "Really? How did you reach her this fast?"

Shalini smiled, "I talked to her last night and informed her about Raghav and his competition. Do you know how excited she was? She immediately booked an air ticket for today," she chuckled. "And she forgot to ask my name."

He nodded, "She was probably waiting for this day to come and sorry that she didn't ask your name."

Both laughed.

"I am selfish. I don't know if I am helping him or myself. Today I had a thought about why I didn't do it before, before when I was with him," she said. "This one question made me look back and I realised I wasn't doing anything. I was just bossing him around probably. I never asked him for suggestions or gave him the opportunity to talk about his likes and dislikes. I thought I knew all of it but…"

Joel exhaled and said, "Well, as you said earlier to me, selfishness is not always a bad thing. Everything has its time to come and today is the day Raghav is going to meet his mom, nothing else matters."

She closed her eyes and took a deep breath, "Maybe, you are right. I should not overthink."

"At what time she will be here?"

"02:00 p.m.," Shalini said and kept her empty cup on the saucer.

***

The previous night's conversation with Raghav's mother made Shalini learn something she never would have imagined. Keeping that in mind, she took off to Cochin airport with nervousness and excitement.

Shalini reached the airport exactly on time and found Raghav's mother walking out from the exit.

"Hi Aunty," Shalini said and helped Raghav's mother by pushing the trolley towards the bike.

"Shalini?"

"Yes, finally I got to see you."

"Suhasini," Raghav's mother offered a handshake with a smile. Suhasini was young despite her age. She was trendy and beautiful, which made Shalini standstill without a blink of an eye. She shook her hand, saying, "I thought I didn't get the chance to tell you my name yesterday."

Suhasini smiled, "I was sure that it would be Shalini, which is why I didn't ask. Sorry I should have," she pouted. "Varadarajan, talked a lot about you."

"Uncle did?"

"Yeah, he told me everything you did for Raghav."

"I didn't do anything, aunty, he did everything on his own. I just stood by his side," Shalini said and looked at her. "Life is hard for everyone to understand everything. Sorrow is the only thing which distinguishes what happiness feels like," she smirked.

"You read my book?" Suhasini said with surprise.

"Your book always felt similar to the things happening in my life, now I understand how it is connected."

Both, with a smile on their face, rode back to the college.

***

While on the way to college, Shalini brought peonies for Raghav as he had once brought for her. When they reached college Shalini took her straight to Opulence Hotel.

"I am nervous," Suhasini said following Shalini into the hotel.

"All this nervousness will only last until you see him. It will fade before you even realise," Shalini comforted Suhasini.

"I am grateful that he made a friend like you," Suhasini

smiled with nervousness. "You look cute, lovely, warm, and cheerful."

Shalini said, "You are making me feel uncomfortable aunty…"

Suhasini patted Shalini's head just when Joel got there.

"Aunty," he said, "you are still young!" He was surprised.

"And you have grown as much," Suhasini said as they hugged each other. Joel's eyes turned watery and he said, "I am sorry, I couldn't keep my promise."

"You did your best," Suhasini said and cheered him up.

Joel wiped his eyes and backed off, "I will bring Raghav right away."

"Does he know I am here?" she asked.

Joel shook his head. He made Suhasini sit on the couch and left.

Suhasini clenched both of her hands with nervousness.

Shalini calmed her down by asking, "When will your next book come out?"

Suhasini beamed, "Same day as Raghav's competition."

"Oh!" Shalini's voice went low.

"Don't make that face. I will manage somehow."

"Can I ask you for something, as a gift?" Shalini asked, pleased. "I want the first copy of the book with your autograph."

They both burst out laughing.

Shalini inculcated Suhasini about her plan and locomoted herself to the corner of the hall. She didn't want to ruin anything so she planned to hide herself until Raghav and his mom sorts their relationship.

Joel got in the auditorium, panting when Raghav picked out the piece of paper hidden behind his phone case.

Dear son,

I am sending you a congratulation letter for passing 12th grade. I don't know if your results are still out but both of us know what it would be. And I am proud of you.

Sorry for hanging up on you during the 10th grade results. I wasn't meant to do that and I am not writing this to you, as an excuse but because I am really sorry.

I know you are having a hard time.

But no matter how much you hate me, resent me,

As a mother, I love you. Always.

Raghav turned back after hearing the panting behind. He immediately put back the letter into his case and turned back.

"Someone is here to meet you," Joel said and approached Raghav.

Raghav asked, "Who is it, this time?"

"Someone, who you wanted to meet," Joel said. Raghav looked at his mobile lock screen— his family photo.

***

Suhasini, with nervousness and excitement, waited for Raghav. She tried to clear her mind, getting rid of all things which kept bothering her at that moment, giving her pain.

Suhasini's aim from the beginning was to carry out her mother's dream and to make it come true. Her mother couldn't survive after giving birth to Suhasini and her dream went to the grave along with her.

With a broken heart, Suhasini's father decided to raise his daughter. He gave up things he wanted to do and became a teacher. While growing up, Suhasini learned about her mother's dream and it went straight deep inside her mind.

When she passed 10th standard, she published her first story in a commercial magazine. She made a promise to her mother that she would become a successful writer on her behalf and with that she started working hard, making a lot of sacrifices for both her father and mother.

Then she got into college to study Journalism and met Varadarajan. With the passage of time and great love towards arts, both of them got along very well and eventually started dating each other.

Good things never showed up to her without bad news. Her father became sick and his last wish was to see his daughter getting married and having a child. But Suhasini's plan was different. She wanted to succeed in writing before making commitments. When she was forced to make a decision, she agreed to get married after completing her master degree whereas Varadarajan dropped out from college to pursue theatre acting full-time.

After two years of marriage, Suhasini gave birth to Raghav

and shifted to Karnataka from Chennai along with her sick father. After cooing at his grandson for six months, her father passed away peacefully.

Before he passed away, Suhasini got to hear about her father's dream which he had accidentally let slip from him once when he was drunk with Varadarajan. He wanted to be a columnist for Indian Times, Mumbai, but he couldn't because of his responsibilities and commitments. He got his reasons for not disclosing it because for a long time he believed it would disturb Suhasini but the booze made him spill out and put her in unease.

The fact that she stole her parent's dream disappointed her. She didn't talk about it to Varadarajan and concentrated on her work and living without letting her worries out. She partly tried to get into the writer's community from Mumbai to learn all about writing and secretly looked up a job opening in Indian Times. She wanted to fulfil the wish of both of her parents without hurting anyone around her.

When she received the offer letter from the writer's community to work with Rahul Batt— the famous group writer for a contract of five years, she became happy and once again was forced to decide. She already had a peaceful life with Varadarajan and Raghav but something was missing. She couldn't foresee which decision she would regret and she became confused.

But Varadarajan sorted it out for her and convinced Suhasini to take up the offer. He didn't want his son to be a burden with their regrets and Suhasini agreed.

When she went there, she faced lots of problems, from language barriers to sexual assault, but she tried hard to sustain herself. She stayed with her college mate without paying rent and the time she was giving for her family while working there, gradually decreased.

She visited home after a year for a week-long break, which wasn't sufficient but she enjoyed it and by the time when she had to go back, she was also accepted as the columnist in the Indian times. She thought things would go well from there on but things turned upside down. She couldn't manage both her work and her family, and she was put under a huge burden which she couldn't talk with anyone.

At first, everything was fine. She was happily working and managing things. But Varadarajan's change in behaviour made her worried. Every conversation they had ended up in a fight, a silly one but it hurt her the most.

One day after Rahul Batt's second novel's release— which was doing well in the market— he organised a group meeting at night past 10:00 p.m.

Suhasini left her mobile on the table and went into the meeting along with the other members. Wrong timing, Varadarajan called Suhasini to apologise for his stupid fight, half drunk. He called twice but no one picked up. The third time, an editor, a man, who was passing that way found her mobile ringing.

"Hello sir, ma'am is in the meeting. Can you call later?" the editor attended the call.

"What the fuck? Who the hell are you?" Varadarajan started building up groundless thoughts in his mind. "Why do you have her phone?"

"Sir, don't misunderstand," the editor said.

"How can I not?"

The editor hung up and informed Suhasini about the call with embarrassment. She felt bad for the editor and apologised to him. She called back Varadarajan at 02:00 a.m., but Raghav attended the call.

Suhasini got to know about the theatre shutting down and his alcohol addiction. She became worried about Varadarajan and asked Raghav to look after him.

She decided to go back during the break to comfort Varadarajan but the next Morning Varadarajan called her again.

"Hello," he said.

"Varun, what happened to you? Are you falling back into the grip of alcohol addiction?" she asked.

"No," he lied but it was obvious. "How do you know?"

"I know everything. Don't drink from now on, your theatre will get back to normal."

He became annoyed with her comfort, "I tried everything, okay? But nothing worked out. Alcohol is what makes me feel alive nowadays."

"Don't lose hope, Varun. I will come back home during the break."

"Don't please," he said. "Don't become like me, at least I want to see you being a successful person. Don't come back without making your dream come true."

"But–"

"No, I don't want you to become a failure like me," he became gloomy.

"You're not a failure."

"Yes, I am," he yelled. "I am a failure. See. I didn't even realise I was addicted to drinking."

"What about Raghav then?"

"He is growing up, he will understand."

She believed that Raghav would understand, she believed that Varadarajan would change, so she focused more on making her dream come true as soon as possible. She wanted to earn for the hardship she had experienced all those years so she stayed and didn't go home on her week-long holiday.

She proved herself as a columnist. Her earnings became the source of income to run the family after Varadarajan's theatre's failure. She felt more responsible to take care of the situation, and with that pressure, she couldn't spend her time talking with Raghav.

She started working on her book and with every stress put together, she suffered hard. But as Varadarajan believed in her, she reminded herself to believe in her family.

Varadarajan and Suhasini's relationship got weaker and weaker and they started hiding things from each other. They chose the hardest way to live instead of living honestly. They didn't realise their insincerity was the source of their distress. They fought with each other for small things, which made no sense and mishap continued.

Suhasini's book was rejected 17 times and she recreated her book at every rejection. She crafted it carefully.

Within a year a new publication accepted Suhasini's manuscript and proceeded to publish it.

With happiness, she called Varadarajan to inform him but Raghav picked up the call.

She shouted, "I did it," with teary eyes and joy. There was a minute of silence from the other side, "Raghav?" she asked but the call got disconnected. She was broken into pieces as she wasn't expecting that. She fainted and dropped her mobile from the terrace. She, too, was about to fall but the people around her saved her right on time and admitted her in the hospital. She was diagnosed with a mental breakdown and she had to rest in the hospital for a whole day.

She took some time alone to relax and started with her second book from her duology, *No matter how far*.

She started regretting giving up on her family for her dreams. Even after her first book's success, she couldn't be happy. She started questioning herself, wondering if what she chose to do was wrong? And that question didn't let her go home.

After the 12th board exam, she wrote a short letter to her son as she didn't dare to call anymore. She was afraid, so she posted her letter and expected a response, expecting a call and talk— a call to get things back to normal. But her expectation wasn't fulfilled. Instead, she got to talk with Varadarajan, who was very happy about her first book's success.

From beginning to end, after seven years of struggle, hardship, and asunder, they reached their endgame after Shalini's call.

Later a talk with Varadarajan made Suhasini aware of Raghav's accident which happened after the 10th grade results. She got to know about Raghav's past from everything after being in a wheelchair.

After wiping all sorts of negative things from her mind, she turned to the other side and found Raghav and Joel approaching her. As she stood up from the couch, all her nervousness faded and she cried without acknowledging it.

When Raghav got into Shalini's field of vision, he was in a wheelchair. She dropped the peonies with a shock. She was muddled, and she recalled the conversation with Tanzeela and Joel. Everything which made no sense to her slowly started mapping. She picked up the peonies and moved to the corner, hiding from Raghav in a devastated state/with a disturbed mind.

***

Raghav was out of words. He couldn't say anything to his mother. He just gazed at her. He wanted to scold her and showcase every bit of anger he had, but the anger turned into sorrow and with an aching heart he started to cry.

"How are you?" Suhasini asked and knelt down.

"Why are you so damn late," he cried out loud. "I missed you very badly."

Suhasini wiped Raghav's tears and hugged him like her life depended on it with the ever-yearned unshown affection, "I thought you would never talk to me again. I was scared to show up because of that. I was too scared thinking you would never want me back."

"You know, I even thought of doing that. I wanted to hate you so badly until I realised, I love you so much that my hate couldn't replace it," Raghav said sobbing and continued, "A girl came into my life and made me realise that."

"Shalini, is it?"

"You know her?"

"Varun told me everything, I know everything that happened."

"Appa was the one who suffered the most. He always needed you by his side, even though he never wanted you to come back without succeeding." He sniffled. "Because of his temper and drinking habit he chose to stay away from me just to raise me to be good. He believed I was strong enough to understand, but I didn't realise any of the sacrifices you both made so that I could live a regret less life unlike you".

Suhasini held his warm hands, "You talk big now."

"Will you go back again?" he asked. "Please at least stay for Appa."

"I won't go, Raghav," she said with a smile and watery eyes. She wiped her tears and smirked, "What about Shalini? Is she your girlfriend?"

"No," Raghav blushed and shook his head out of embarrassment. Joel walked to Shalini leaving Raghav to his mother.

***

"So, now do you understand why he chose to stay hidden?" Joel asked Shalini and stood by her side.

Suhasini and Raghav laughed together and were happy. He picked up the paper from his phone case and gave it to his mother. She kissed his forehead which made Shalini remember the forehead kiss she had got from him. Both Joel and Shalini couldn't hear their conversation but they were happy to see them together.

"I don't know how to react. I should be happy now, but I am all confused."

Joel smiled, "Ask him yourself. You wanted to slap him hard, right? Do it. He is all yours."

Shalini nodded and looked at the flower she had in her hands. Joel went back to Raghav and helped Suhasini to her room.

"Thank you, Joel," Raghav said.

"I am not the one you should be thanking," Joel said and boarded the lift with Suhasini.

Shalini stood behind a confused Raghav and held his wheelchair handle. She cried with a heavy wheeze saying, "Bastard."

He closed his eyes and his melancholy flashed as he whispered, "Shalini."

CHAPTER 23

"Ouch!" Raghav shouted after getting a tight slap. "It hurts." He was in his room with Shalini, who stayed silent staring at the floor.

"I heard your paralysis is gone. I am so glad," Raghav said and expected her to lift her head, but she didn't. He got worried and asked, "Why are you silent?"

"You keep quiet first. I am so angry. I want to calm down a little," she said and clenched her fist with the flowers in her hand.

"Are those peonies for me?" Raghav asked.

"I am going to kill you, why did you leave without a goodbye?" she said while choking his throat and shaking him front and back.

Raghav with both of his hands tried to escape her grasp and made her relax a bit. When she did, he coughed.

"Did you bring those flowers to give, after killing me," he said and laughed.

"Say, why did you leave me all alone?" Shalini asked and calmed down. She gave him the flowers without looking at him.

"I thought it would be for the best. Staying away from you without dragging you down, without making you worry, and to keep you away from the strange thoughts you have in your mind right now."

"It's you, right? Don't tell me you have something to do with my cure and your situation."

"Okay, I will not tell you", he smiled, shaking his head.

Shalini hit him on the head as always and wailed, "Tell me."

Raghav laughed, "Do you really think you were paralyzed

because you fell on your back?"

"That's what the doctor said,"

"What if I say that those two years of your life in the wheelchair were actually for me and I should be the one to be paralyzed instead of you?"

"I don't get you," Shalini said.

"Even I don't. A stupid man claimed that it had to do something with him."

And I never thought he would describe me as a stupid man, yes it was me. My stupid mistake made them pay a huge price and I gambled somebody's freedom to correct it. Stupid man is probably not a wrong thing to say.

***

Raghav continued speaking

After that dinner night, after playing a game of truth or dare. I realised two things. I wanted to be happy and you didn't like the way you were living i.e., struggling in the wheelchair.

I was informed by the same stupid man with shady green hair that I could take on one's disability. I thought it was stupid and immediately swept that out from my mind.

But that night, I wanted that ability to be real. I didn't care about anything. I wanted you to walk again, to play football again and to see you happy— the real happyhappy. I believed that would be my source of happiness too.

I know I was neither God, nor Harry Potter or anyone who could do magic, but I wanted that stupid man's words to be true.

I sat on the road between my house and yours and I called Joel.

"Hey! How are you, Raghav?" he asked.

"I want to join your college, just promise me one thing— will you take care of me? Help me out with something?"

He was so happy to do that favour for me. And after that call, I went back to my house and hugged my father with panic. He was waiting for me and his eyes were tired and wet as if he had cried.

"Did you eat?" I asked.

"No," he said.

I served him food on his plate and asked him to dig in.

"I want to learn fine arts in music with Joel in Kerala. My application was selected and I want to leave tonight?" I asked when he started eating and I had cleared out all my mind.

He slowed down his eating and said, "Why so sudden? And why do you look confused?"

"I don't know. I just want to leave. I am confused because… nothing makes sense."

He didn't understand a thing but he thought otherwise, "You want to go away from me? Do you still hate me?"

I shook my head fast, "No, no Appa. I have another reason which may sound crazy so I will tell you later, but I don't hate you. The truth is I love you more than anything."

His tears dropped on his plate. "Dad, don't cry," I said.

He shook his head and said, "I am not crying. I am happy." He smiled and started eating in a hurry.

"I still remember the fear you had in your eyes when I tried to hurt you. Are you still afraid of me?"

"Yeah, I am still afraid of that day and afraid of you but you are my father. I had never seen you like that before, and even after that, you changed for me and I don't want to let you down."

"I failed in everything. I dropped out from my college to pursue my dreams and failed to protect them in the end. I promised to make your mother's dream come true but I gave her a hard time. I promised to protect you but, not only did I fail to keep that promise but I dragged the family down too."

I shook my head, "Mom couldn't come because she was forced to stay because of her work and our family situation. You could have asked her to come, but you wanted to keep the promise you made to her. You stayed away from me because you hated yourself for going crazy that day. You believed that I might end up being like you if you tried to get along. You were stupid but you desperately wanted to protect me as promised. Your theatre failed because… I don't know the cause but I am sure it's not because of you. You have always been a disciplined person, who follows certain principles in life. I always admired you for that. I was the one who failed to understand things back then and started blaming mom and you."

He smiled, "Shalini huh? She really brought my son back."

I blushed and said with embarrassment, "Appa…"

I went to my room and started packing. When I walked out of my room with the suitcase, my father was not in the dining room and his room's light was on. I had never visited his room before but that day, I walked in while he was changing his clothes. I looked around and found pictures of me hanging on the wall—me holding a shield with an annoyed smile, the picture from fresher's party in 2016 and another picture of me playing piano along with you, the picture from the annual day.

At that moment, I couldn't help but to ask him, "Why? Why didn't you raise me like other parents, why did you leave me to struggle alone?" I screamed.

I looked at his eyes and saw the pain he had held in all those days. He couldn't say anything.

"You know right. Shall we leave then?" he asked with a smile and desperation after I calmed down.

"Wait… I have one more job that needs to be done before that," I said, scratching my forehead for an idea.

***

"Do you remember the day I got into an accident?" Raghav asked.

Shalini nodded.

Raghav continued

I planned to jump off the cliff to commit suicide instead to jumping in front of the vehicle. With all my guts I stood at the edge of the cliff to jump for over thirty minutes but I couldn't do it. I wasn't strong enough to die; I was afraid of both living and dying.

Later with despair, I was walking back to the gazebo, trembling with fear, when a bike passed by me into the camber curved road behind. The biker ran into a little puppy who tried to safeguard its life but ended up losing its legs. It wailed. The biker didn't stop.

I saw the tears in the puppy's eyes and went to it. Another car was on the way but I didn't realise that.

Everything happened so fast that I tried to give up my life to save that puppy. I didn't expect the car driver to be kind, he took me to the hospital.

I cursed him for saving my life and after all the treatment I went through, I was finally left alone in the room with the dripping sound. It was peaceful for a few minutes but later that stupid man ruined it. That was the first time I saw him.

I thought he was from the police, who came to investigate the suicide, but he wasn't. He talked like he was the puppy's owner and he said he would like to repay my kindness by giving me a blessing.

A blessing to take over somebody's disability. It didn't sound like a blessing but as a curse at first and he sounded stupid as always. His stupidity made me furious and I threw him out of my room and completely wiped his words out of my mind and finally one day I wished to remember it and I wanted his curse to be true.

Before leaving for Kerala, I came to your house jumping off the fence, climbing up to your room. I knew it would be useful to leave the balcony door unlocked. I was alone with no idea what to do, but somehow that stupid man stood behind me and whispered, "Just wish her good luck while holding her hand." I held your hand and wished, I just did everything that he told me to.

And then I came to Kerala, and after a week I got severe pain in my back and neck. My legs went numb and I fell down.

I was hospitalised for a few days and I came out in a wheelchair. It wasn't my hallucination, but it was real and he was real.

I heard your paralysis wore off. I was happy. I was so happy that I thought I did something for you. I was happy that I fulfilled your wish. I was happy that my wish was fulfilled.

But all that I believed was a lie. I didn't do a thing for you. I met the stupid person again on the same day before you showed up here.

I thought it was some kind of magic, some kind of grace falling upon me and you, but it wasn't.

***

Shalini blinked her eyes twice with confusion.

Raghav continued with a smile, "I have to say this, you saved my life twice. You saved me even before we got to meet each other. You always say this, friends are meant to share each other's burden, but–" he chuckled. "Our bond was so strong that you shared my disability with you in order to save me, even without realising it."

Raghav got into a car accident while Shalini was hurt during a practice match. Both of them fell on their back at the exact same time. This made things easy for me to interchange the effects of each other.

The two years of school life Shalini and Raghav spent together were real with Shalini's leg being the only anomaly and the present moments with Raghav as the crippled was the product of the fate that I induced.

I was there when Raghav tried to jump off the cliff. I did know that he wasn't going to jump, and that was the day Raghav and Shalini had to encounter their fate, but I ran into a puppy. I made the puppy run in Raghav's direction by mistake, and because of that trivial mistake I made, Raghav could have actually died. A change in one's fate would affect the whole chain connected to it, so to correct it. I gambled Shalini's legs to save Raghav's life from the change in fate I created. Shalini had to live with Raghav's disability as I had switched. And I awaited the day for Raghav to accept back his disability to himself to put back fate in order.

And this happened.

Raghav continued, "The stupid man, in the end, wasn't stupid at all."

"Yeah, but you are. I don't know why but I want to believe it. I don't want to hear any more explanation or logic behind this. I know life itself doesn't make sense." Shalini said and knelt down. "Is this forever?"

She pointed to the wheelchair.

"Of course not, I am not stupid enough to steal back my disability if it is forever," Raghav said and smiled. "You dummy, my injury was incomplete from the first. I went through the treatment for six months with my father and things are good now. I might walk again, with proper improvement," his smile widened.

"I should have guessed. Everything was suspicious back

then. Everyone's memory of me became cloudy. You went missing. I should have guessed," she said.

Raghav smiled, "What happened to you was a miracle, and to me a misfortune, there is no difference," he placed both of his hands over her chubby wet cheeks. "I remember everything we did together and I guess you do too. Those memories are only meant for us to remember and we must treasure them."

"Since when did you get this mature?" Shalini smirked. "Am I seeing an old grandpa in front of me?"

Both giggled. Raghav wiped her wet cheeks and asked, "Okay now tell me, how did you find out that I was here?"

"Before that, I want to give you something," Shalini said and remembered her rehabilitation to walk again and her struggles. She was looking out for him.

"What is it?" he asked, bending forward.

She slapped him one more time, "This is for Abdul, Ayesha, and Preethi. Do you know how hard I worked to find you? Obviously, my hard work didn't pay off. Preethi was here last month with her boyfriend to meet her future sister-in-law and she happened to find you were here accidentally."

"She has a boyfriend?"

"Is that important?"

He smiled and said, "Do you know what happened to me after leaving you?"

"I don't know about you, but—"

"I realised that I am in love," both said in unison. "With you."

Both laughed out loud. Their eyes met, their heart fluttered, they forgot their surroundings and slowly leaned forward to kiss.

An abrupt vibration in Shalini's pocket, brought her back to her senses and she held back saying, "I am still angry with you."

She picked up her mobile and checked the message she got.

DAD: *What are you doing?*

"Nice dad, nicely done," she whispered with anger.

Raghav gasped loudly with closed eyes. "I don't know why but I suddenly feel so energetic."

Shalini murmured something.

"Do you love me?" he asked.

"No, I am not going to answer until you propose to me fairly," she said.

"Why don't you?"

"I won't then, don't ask me this question," she frowned and moved back.

"Okay. Okay, I will," Raghav tugged her towards him. "Hmm," Shalini kept staring. "Don't look at me like that, I feel nervous."

Shalini took her eyes off him.

"You know, there are only a few things in life that truly motivate us, that inspire us to take steps forward. For some, it may be a flower, for others, it may be a passion. But for me, it's you and the ever-evolving person you are. The more I get to know you, the more I realise there's so much more to discover, and it feels like a lifetime won't be enough to fully understand you. Every passing second, every new moment, I find myself wanting to love you more, almost as if it's beyond my control." His cheeks turned a shade of pink as he mustered the courage to say, "I want us to be there for each other through thick and thin, to experience happiness and sadness together, and to create a beautiful future side by side. So, I have to ask, would you do me the honor of being my girlfriend?"

Shalini blushed with a smile and nodded saying, "You really are a son of a writer."

"I didn't know how long I waited for this day to come. Both you and mom are here, the best day in my life," he said with overflowing happiness.

"Just let me clarify this to you, once again if you leave me again without a word, I will make you sit in these wheels forever."

Raghav laughed, "Sorry, *meri Jaan*," he hugged her and patted her hair. "I missed you a lot, I won't do that again."

Both of their eyes were watery but they had a real smile on their faces.

CHAPTER 24

2019

April 11th

Sixth day in Ernakulam

The day Raghav performed on the big stage.

The day of Ayesha's Surgery, which made Abdul kneel at the mosque for hours.

The day of Suhasini's book release event, which the author herself couldn't participate in.

After breakfast with Raghav and his mother, Shalini climbed upstairs to the terrace to get some fresh air exercising her leg muscles which required warm-up. Climbing from the third floor to the terrace in the seven-story building had her drenched in sweat and she was panting fiercely as she reached the top.

She took a huge breath and exhaled which made her calm down a little. Her calm self-reminded her mother and the days she missed talking to her. Expecting the least of an acknowledgment she called her finally.

"Hey, mom," she said with a nervous smile.

Elizabeth scoffed, "I thought you just decided not to talk with me since you were too busy with your in-laws and Raghav."

"Mom!"

"Raghav called me just minutes ago, he apologised for creating this situation."

"And what did you say?"

"I scolded him a little and then I talked with his mother. She was so sweet. She exalted you so much and she said she adores you."

Shalini blushed.

"Did something happen between you and Raghav there?" Elizabeth raised a question.

"No, nothing happened."

"Well, Raghav told me he proposed to you and you nodded 'yes'."

Shalini bowled over and opened her mouth wide, "He said that?"

"I knew from the very beginning that you had feelings for him," Elizabeth exhaled. "I am not against it."

"Really?" Shalini asked.

"Don't be too amazed, I have something big to give you, get your ass back home soon," Elizabeth ordered.

Shalini smiled nervously and hung up. Due to the low battery her phone died.

"Something big, huh?" Shalini whispered. "Was that a threat?"

She panicked. She needed more air to calm down this time. She looked at the clear warm sky again and took a long deep breath.

***

Suhasini, after showering, received a call from her publisher. She answered it immediately and had a little chat.

She convinced the publisher to conduct the event without her and that was when she noticed the letter Raghav had given her three days ago. She was so busy spending her time with Raghav that she completely forgot about the letter.

She hung up the call while picking up the letter. She sat on the bed, unfolding it.

It was the same letter she sent to him to congratulate him on passing 12th grade. The first half of the paper was her message to him and the other half was written by Raghav as a response a year ago but he couldn't send it to her.

She read it.

Mom,
How are you doing?
I hope you are doing well.
I was the one who hated you all these days. I was the one who chose not to talk with you and blamed you for not talking with me.
I too made your life hard, but I understood my anger was just because I love you so much and I cannot hate you anymore.
I miss you mom. I hope you come back soon and give me the same warm hug you always gave.

With a hasty knock on the door, Suhasini realised the need to wipe the tears and she answered the door.

"Hey Shalini, come in… come in," she let her in and closed the door.

"Were you crying?" Shalini asked.

Suhasini shook her head, "I was just talking to the publisher."

"So, your book is going to be released soon," Shalini said and sat on the bed.

Suhasini took out a package from her bag and tossed it to Shalini, "The book is out now."

Shalini grinned and opened the package promptly.

"Wow," Shalini gasped.

Suhasini took the book from Shalini's hands and sat beside her. She signed at the first page of the book and said, "This is not a fan service or something and I have never done this before, but this is for you because you asked for it," she said with a smile. "Ouch, this is so embarrassing,"

Both laughed, Suhasini gave back the book, and Shalini hugged her and exhilarated, "Thank you."

Shalini flipped the pages and smelled it.

"I think I should meet Raghav now, I got something to give him," she said.

"Let me guess a smack or two," Suhasini said.

***

Raghav was on a call with someone as he was working on his piano notes in the auditorium, which was empty. Shalini silently approached Raghav to startle him, but he sensed someone was behind him and turned around. She was about to scream to startle him, but he turned back, which made the stupid startling game into a failure and he burst out with laughter.

Raghav removed his specs and made her sit beside him. "Ayesha is on call," he said and put the call on speaker.

"Hey, Ayesha," Shalini said.

"Shalini?" Ayesha raised her voice. "I tried calling your phone but it was switched off, what happened?"

"Low battery, I guess," Shalini said. "So, when is your

surgery?"

"At 06:30 p.m."

"Are you scared?"

"I was earlier, but after talking to Abdul and Raghav, I completely forgot about it," Ayesha grinned.

"Get back home soon. You must attend my football finals as promised," Shalini mellowed.

"And I even promised Abdul that I will kiss him when I get back," Ayesha said with excitement.

"Ah, then I have nothing more to say. Your arrival is confirmed," Shalini awed.

Both laughed.

"Have you and Raghav kissed?" Ayesha asked.

Shalini recoiled, "Let's talk later after your surgery. All the best. Bye."

Ayesha smiled, "Later then?"

After ending the call, Raghav asked, "When will we?"

"Over my dead body," Shalini stood up embarrassed.

"But you were ready the other day," he said.

"I was never ready. Think of your program today and do good and then we can have this silly conversation," she said and turned her blushing face to the other side.

"Are you embarrassed?" he asked curiously, but without answering or showing her face she walked out silently.

Raghav smiled, shaking his head and got back to his work.

Time passed, everyone started practising for the evening. Suhasini's book was officially released. All the procedures before the operation were going on, one by one, making Ayesha a bit uncomfortable.

Raghav prayed for Ayesha before getting ready for the program. Shalini went to the temple nearby and prayed for Ayesha and Raghav. Abdul spent his whole day in the mosque and waited for the operation to get over successfully, praying to God.

YUNUS (10:57) Men! Now there has come to you an exhortation from your Lord, a healing for the ailments of the hearts, and a guidance and mercy for those who believe.

***

The clock struck 06:00 p.m., and the program started.

The guests assembled and got seated in the college theatre. Students slowly filled the seats on time.

Shalini, Raghav, and Suhasini, who were on the way to the theatre, found Tanzeela wearing a white lace dress waiting for someone. She looked gorgeous and took Shalini's breath away.

"Wow, you look fabulous," Suhasini said as they approached her.

Tanzeela grinned.

"Who are you waiting for?" Raghav asked.

"My brother is coming today with his girlfriend. I sent Joel to pick them up but I completely forgot about his lack of punctuality. Will he make it in time?" Tanzeela asked anxiously.

Raghav smiled, "You have to worry about your brother. Think about Joel's driving now."

Tanzeela frowned sadly.

"He will make it, don't let it bother you. You are going to perform too," Raghav said.

And after all the guests' speeches, the program finally began.

Many were lined up before Joel. He was lucky that many students' names began with the alphabets before J, and Joel was the 16th contestant.

When all the Previous 15 contestants were done, Joel was called. Shalini, from the audience seat, bit her nails and worried about him.

He didn't make it on time and instead some other boy showed up, and the name was rearranged to another Joel who was 17th in order. Joel still had luck on his side and one more opportunity to perform.

The 17th contestant from the 16th slot took 12 whole minutes with his flute, playing different classics. Again, Joel was called and this time he showed up. He looked stressed, and his hands were trembling.

"Do it, Joel," someone from the crowd shouted.

Joel played his first note and waited for the sound to flow all over the theatre and the tempo began.

With nimble fingers dancing across the strings, his guitar

wove a tapestry of Western classics. The melodies flowed effortlessly, his left-hand gliding in perfect sync with the tempo. The audience watched in awe as he played, entranced by his skill and artistry. For nearly five minutes, his music held them captive, leaving mouths agape.

The line-up moved forward one by one. Everyone showed their talent. Some of the performances were exaggerated.

Raghav was the 25th contestant. When he was called, he rolled along with his wheelchair on the stage to the piano, bowed down to others, and his pitch receiver was set so that he could control the pitch through his mouth.

Everyone made an awkward face towards him. He didn't care and opened the piano. Some of them were excited from the very beginning. Suhasini with both of her hands joined together, prayed repeatedly for him to do a good job.

Raghav played Ravel— *Gaspard de la Nuit: Ondine.* Unleashing his musical prowess, he transformed the surroundings into a haunting spectacle, captivating the audience like a scene from a horror film. The guests rose to their feet, cheering him on with wild enthusiasm. But then, he shifted gears, playing a composition of his own creation for the remaining five minutes— a melodic embodiment of a love that defied convention.

Suhasini, moved by the song's profound message of love that endures from birth to death, found tears streaming down her face. At that moment, she deeply comprehended and embraced its meaning. Not only Suhasini but also other music lovers in the audience were touched to the core, their emotions flowing freely in tears.

As Shalini immersed herself in the performance, she felt an alternate reality, a world untouched by the accident that forever altered their lives. At that moment, she envisioned a life where Raghav never faced adversity, where their connection was built on pure warmth and light. As the performance drew to a close, Shalini found herself overcome with tears, deeply moved by the emotions stirred within her. Others in the audience, too, were caught up in the intensity of the moment, their tears flowing without even realising it.

When Raghav was done, he picked up the mic and named the song he played, *Phiilia Gaia*— highest form of love, and mother.

Some guests stood up in the end and clapped their hands, giving him a standing ovation. Nobody expected his performance to be the best.

Joel's song excited others whereas Raghav's made others cry. They performed equally well. The contestants weren't easy to judge. Everyone made their mood swing.

Thirtieth contestant was Tanzeela, and as she was called, Shalini got ready to see her sing for the first time. Shalini was thrilled when she heard Tanzeela was a singer from Raghav. But she was also sad for not sharing about each other's life and plans as they were busy talking about the past and Raghav. They sometimes talked about Joel and that made Shalini understand the feelings Tanzeela had towards him and she tried to confirm it, but Tanzeela stubbornly refused to accept.

Tanzeela stood up on the stage and gave a pleasant smile before starting as she began to sing the opera song in Tamil, her powerful voice filled the air, sending shivers down the spines of the audience. The clarity and precision with which she hit the high notes were awe-inspiring. It was a truly remarkable performance that left everyone in awe. The song she sang was not just any ordinary composition; it was a lifeline, with lyrics penned by Raghav himself as a continuation of a song he had initially started during the annual day song selection. The synergy between their creative talents was evident, creating a truly unforgettable musical experience.

Tanzeela bowed down. She, too, got a standing ovation and she left proudly. After her, eight more contestants took part and everyone literally rocked. This competition wasn't the competition to award grand prizes but to impress the guests so that they could recommend the best students to participate in the foreign concerts. And some of the guests could even offer the contestants a position as a full-time member of their music community.

Raghav, Joel, and Tanzeela's route were cleared and they were requested by more than three communities to join.

Everything was great. They were happy. Suhasini hugged Raghav and congratulated him. After dinner, Raghav sent his mother back to her room so that she could rest a bit before the next day's early morning flight.

Shalini, Raghav, and Joel after dinner were gathered and looked for Tanzeela.

After turning here and there Shalini found her. She approached her with others and said, "Tanzeela, you were breathtaking, it felt like I made it to heaven."

"Awe that's too much," Tanzeela said and looked behind Shalini.

"What are you doing here alone?" Joel asked.

"Actually, I wasn't alone. My brother went to answer a call, and his girlfriend went to bring me a drink," Tanzeela said and looked behind. "Ah! There she is."

Shalini and Raghav turned to the new girl and it was Preethi.

"Preethi!" Shalini said with shock.

"Oh!" Preethi was surprised. "So, you came all the way here," she asked Shalini and turned to Raghav. "Hey."

"Hey, Preethi," Raghav said. "Nice to meet you."

"Both of your performances were rocking and wow," Tanzeela said with a smile and gave a thumbs up to both Raghav and Joel.

"So, you know each other?" Tanzeela asked.

"Yeah, she was the one who gave me info about Raghav hiding here," Shalini said and looked at Preethi.

"We are all connected in a weird way OMG," Tanzeela said and smirked.

"So, you found your soulmate in the end," Raghav asked.

Preethi blushed, "It's just been six months since we started dating. He is fun and athletic."

"He is not fun at all," Tanzeela added.

All laughed together.

"Ah! There he is," Preethi said and pointed at him.

When Shalini saw him, she was, once again, surprised, "Aaqil?"

"Shalini?" Aaqil gasped.

Raghav and Preethi ha-ha-ed with annoyance.

"So, you know each other from before? The connection is getting way weirder, care to explain?" Tanzeela said.

"He was my senior in the football club when I was in Chennai," Shalini said.

"Tonight, is getting funny," Aaqil said.

Then, they had a long funny conversation together with overflowing laughter. Hours later Shalini received a call from Abdul. She answered it and walked out of the crowd and noise.

"Ayesha's surgery is done. Thankfully she didn't have any cardiac arrest," Abdul said but he wasn't happy.

"But why do you sound sad?" she asked nervously.

"She was put into an induced coma because of her syndrome. Doctors just asked us to wait until she regains her consciousness," he said, sobbing. "I don't know how many days this girl is going to stay unconscious."

"It is just a medical procedure, don't be afraid of it, everything will be okay soon. Did you talk to her father?"

"I talked and comforted him a little,' he said.

"Yeah, you get some rest. You are at home, right?" she asked.

"Yeah, I just reached," he said.

"Get some sleep," she said and hung up the call. Her face dropped and all the happiness she had minutes ago was wiped off.

Tanzeela with her brother and Preethi left early with a bye. Shalini later informed Raghav about Ayesha's condition when they were on the way to the hotel along with Joel.

Raghav got angry and stopped. He clenched his fist and said, "Shouldn't we be happy for at least a moment?"

Shalini had no answers to feed. Instead, she said, "We have to believe in Ayesha and wait."

CHAPTER 25

The next day both Suhasini and Shalini left. The rooms they stayed in became quite- lifeless and Raghav realised the emptiness in his heart and yet those sad feelings were somehow comforting to him. Shalini dropped Suhasini at the airport and drove her bike straight to Coimbatore.

She gave a heartfelt thanks to her brother for lending his bike to her for a whole week and boarded a train straight to Bangalore.

The next morning when she reached the Bangalore station, Ravichandran was waiting for her. He drove his Jeep back home with her and they had lots of funny conversations on the way.

When Shalini reached home, she had to go through Elizabeth and her silence. She tried everything to grab her mother's attention, but nothing worked, and she eventually got annoyed.

After breakfast, Shalini went to Elizabeth to have a square conversation.

"Mom, please talk to me. Scold me, beat me up but don't stay up silent," Shalini said and sat beside her in the swing. "It doesn't feel right,"

"Does it hurt? Just think how much I was worried when you left without informing me," Elizabeth said. "I know, my Shalini got her reasons but not always things go as planned, as parents it is not easy to stay without worrying about their kids,"

"Sorry Mom, I made you worry. You can even give me the big thing you were holding all these days."

"What do you think it is?" Elizabeth asked and stood up

furiously.

Shalini had no idea and she shrugged.

Elizabeth walked into the house and came out with a file and pen. "Read it and sign,"

Shalini checked the file, and she reached the top of the world. It was the application form to join AIFF- All India football federation -fall 2019 selection.

"Mom! Mom!" Shalini shouted with excitement- signed the application papers and hugged Elizabeth tightly. "I never thought this would be the big thing you were holding all these days, I love you, Mom."

"Okay, stop drooling," Elizabeth grinned. She patted Shalini's back asking, "Did you hear anything about Ayesha?"

Shalini turned downcast and took seconds to say, "No luck. It's been 2 days and still... She will be alright, right?"

"You know... she is a good brave girl. She must," Elizabeth continued patting.

***

8 days left until Shalini's football finals and she started receiving excuses from some of her invitees. The first one to walk off was Tanzeela as she was hired to sing at Goa's music festival in a band. The next important invitees were Preethi and Aaqil and they were stuck with their semester exams.

Shalini gave a miserable smile with their excuses and she couldn't do anything. Her expectations dropped, and her only wish was to have Raghav on her side to support.

God would be great to grant that wish, but he never concedes wishes for granted.

On the 21st of April, the football match stood up in no time, but Raghav was missing.

"Ahem! This is the finals; we have made it this far successfully and have only one more game left to show our actual worth. Don't try to lose girls..." Danya shouted to her teammates in the dressing room. She was the captain of Shalini's team, and she was the first one to notice Shalini being sluggish in the group who were excited about the day.

"You are in a slump Shalini, I noticed you in the past 3

matches and you are no good. Is there any problem?" Danya yelled a little around everyone.

Shalini flinched and shook her head. "Nothing… just…"

"It seems you got excuses,"

Shalini lifted her head stiffly, "Today I will prove you… I am not in a slump,"

"You gotta show me how much you got in your head with your goals," Danya said, "And this is for everyone."

Shalini relaxed herself, relieving the thought about Ayesha- who still showed no improvement, about Abdul who was devastated and Raghav who didn't show up.

While in the process of relaxation, Shalini's mobile popped up with the message and she grabbed the mobile in a hurry.

'I am on the way,' Raghav's message and Shalini somehow got pumped up with energy.

Alley Institutes of Science and Technology- Shalini's college
VS
MV College of Business- the opponent

Ravichandran and Elizabeth were on the bleachers and cheered up Shalini when she marched out to the field with other players. Abdul was also there in his flooded thoughts surrounded by noises and cheers.

The match began and Raghav didn't make it on time. Red Jersey were Shalini's opponent and they started with the pass, the ball was dribbled into Shalini's direction, and without any effort or showing special moves, Shalini pulled the ball out from the FWD and passed it to her team. She received the ball back and tackled the DFs with high-speed Samba and flicks, shooting the ball into the goalpost. But no luck, the opponent's goalkeeper was awesome and without wasting any time she kicked the ball to her teammate in the centre.

Shalini ran back to the centre but it was too late and the Reds managed to reach the penalty area and with an air elastico to outmaneuver the Blue team's DF they shot the ball on the upper post to confuse the goalkeeper. The ball rebounded back and with just a tap from the Reds, they made a GOAL.

(Opponent) 1-0 (Blue team)

Bad timing but Raghav showed up with Joel to the match exactly after the first goal. While the ball was taken to the centre, Shalini found Raghav and Joel rolling towards their seat and she waved her hands to them. Raghav encouraged Shalini with his gesture and thumbs up, and Shalini got fired up even more than before— her extreme level of concentration and excitement surfaced when the game resumed from the centre.

***

In Raghav's house— Varadarajan was cooking in the kitchen when he heard the front door getting open. He gazed out and found Suhasini walking into the house which made him drop the ladle and his jaw.

"Hey! Varun," she said and gave a warm smile.

He tried to talk, but he couldn't. Instead, he picked up the ladle and hid in the kitchen.

"Welcome back, you finally made it home," he said.

She dropped her luggage and ran into the kitchen. She hugged him from behind and cried slowly saying, "I am sorry, I made your and Raghav's life miserable. I am so sorry… sorry."

She sobbed and Varadarajan turned to her. He wiped her tears saying, "You already sobbed over it on a call. You are the one who paid off the hardship we faced. You didn't make our life miserable, but it was our choice."

"You already comforted me over the call," Suhasini beamed.

"But never kissed," both chuckled and he asked, "Did you miss me?"

She looked into his eyes, "I missed you, I missed your lovely eyes, your rough cheeks," she said and ran her hands over his cheeks. "I missed you a lot Varun."

"I realised something when you were not here; I am nothing… nothing without you so please take me with you hereafter."

"I too had the same thought; I am going to shift here again."

"Yeah, and I heard my hero is back as a drama teacher in fine arts school."

"It's been 2 months since I started teaching acting again. I am also promoting my theatre school by giving free theatre workshops in different schools. Everything is getting back on track."

"You happy?" she said, messing with his hair. It was all romantic until the onion left in the flame got burned.

"Oh shit! Oh shit!" Varadarajan said and turned off the gas. Together they laughed. "And my hero burned that onion, and it's still kinda messy."

"Wanna eat out?" he asked.

She nodded her head, "Let's go to Shalini's football match; we still got time,"

With a big nod, Varadarajan cleared his kitchen mess and got ready. He uncovered his old vintage bike RX100— which he bought during the birth of Raghav.

"You were using it?" Suhasini asked.

"No… I just occasionally washed it and kept it clean. It's in good condition."

Happy memories flashed up and they contemplated for minutes having a nostalgic reminder of every tiny-tiny thing— which made them happy— and which was missing when they were away.

He kick-started the bike and with a wide smile, they took off.

***

When Varadarajan and Suhasini reached the football field it was half-time. The scores were 1-0 and the Shalini team couldn't score a goal in the first half.

In the middle of the serious discussion with the team Shalini happened to find Suhasini and Varadarajan and she gave them a smile. Looking at them, Shalini formulated a plan, and she proposed it to her team.

Danya agreed with Shalini and to implement they had to pair up players— a pair who completely trust each other— and because of that the position plan had to adjust and the team were ready to compromise it.

The second half started, Shalini and Danya paired up and they backed up each other. With a one-two they moved past the

DMFs into the red team's post and another pair from the blue team marked the Red's DF in their way. In the blink of an eye the ball hit the net of the goal post resulting in one all.

(Opponent) 1-1 (Blue team)

The field was filled with cheers on blues and Shalini wanted to score 2 more goals to have a safe win.

The game began from the Centre once again, the opponent rushed the ball into the blue's territory and right in front of D box, one of the Reds shot the ball to the goal post but Shalini's team goalkeeper was wide awake, and she saved the goal in an extremely cool way. Cheers continued.

Ball was pushed to the field and both the teams kept pushing the ball out the field frequently for four times until Danya fed up and baited the opponent FWD to push while positioning herself in a way, she earned a corner for her team.

5 blue jerseys stood before the opponent's goal post while being constantly marked. Danya kicked the ball from the corner to her team mates but due to unforeseen circumstances the goal was not made instead pushed away from the goal post and the golden opportunity got wasted. The unforeseen circumstance was clearly a fluke for the Reds on defence.

The Red team fluked back the ball and rushed to the other side having Blues to follow them. With a high pass from the Centre, the Red's jersey no.11 near the Blue team's goal post trapped the ball with an extreme positioning in the air which felt surreal. With nothing but a goal in mind, a volley shot towards goal was made however the fatigue kicked in. In a battle demanding every ounce of concentration of all players, the physical toll played a heavy role, with Shalini's team goalkeeper being the only exception to remain unwavering and analysing the whole play. ***If I had been a human, I would have married her. Ha ha.***

She saved the ball and had 10 minutes left for the game to end. The game became so intense that the first 7 minutes fled and nothing happened.

In the last remaining tick-tocks, Shalini was asked to play solo whereas all the FWDs in blue promised to back her up. There was no time to think and accept but to agree and fight. Shalini's mind was afraid to get injured and she didn't want to risk but her body wanted otherwise— it sought an adrenaline rush with nothing but a pure desire to remain in the field in success, she entered into the ZONE unconsciously and she rushed the ball into Red's with an overflowing excitement. Unexpectedly she pulled an ultra-fast step overs to overcome the DFs and a roulette to top it leaving the crowd in awe, with a penultimate one-two and mid high pass from Danya to overcome the final DF within a split second a direct shot from Shalini to score a goal and boom.

RED: 1-2 : BLUE

TIMEOUT

Shalini knelt and remembered the conversation she had with her father, the day before she went to Kerala to bring back Raghav.

***

2019

April 4th

Shalini was bewildered by the thought of meeting Raghav and as she walked up to the terrace, she found Ravichandran with a newspaper and a cup of tea.

"Dad, I found where Raghav is," Shalini said and sat beside him in the chair.

"Aargh, it took a year to find that bastard," Ravichandran said, looking at the newspaper.

"Yeah, but I cannot understand why I went to the extreme, to find a person who left on his own without a note," Shalini gasped.

Ravichandran kept the newspaper on the table and took a sip of the tea before saying, "Well, you know how people grow up?"

Shalini shook her head.

"People grow up learning things from others and you will never feel complete until you find someone who makes you feel real-alive. I wasn't until I found your mother, even though she was tough, she was badass, but still, we fell in love because she completes me, and together we are one." He had another sip of tea and giggled, "I hate to say this but you might have felt complete with him— and without him, you couldn't feel that anymore that's why you looked out for him."

"No Dad, I don't know," she said, shaking her head. "But will it change like people's feeling,"

"No… feeling completeness and having feelings are two different things— feelings change from time to time. If you moved on you weren't complete and if you want to kick his ass to have him with you… you know. You wouldn't have gone extreme if you didn't feel complete."

"I want to slap him hard- not to kick his ass," Shalini said.

"Not the point," he chuckled. He continued, "Another question, why do you think some people leave just like that without a note?" he asked and put the empty cup over the table.

"Because," Shalini said and stopped; she couldn't figure out why. "He hates me?"

"One of the possibilities," he said and looked at her daughter. "Otherwise, he loved you so much that he might have thought that leaving you alone would be much better…"

"But what good it does? After he left, I just turned crazy looking out for him,"

"Yeah, and he might also be suffering; we don't know that until you find out," he said. "I know you are confused about whether to leave, but it is up to you to decide. I won't stop you or push you,"

"I think I want to go, I want to find out if he hates me or not,"

"He cannot hate you, that is for sure, you are my lovely daughter indeed," Ravichandran said with a grin.

***

"Yes Dad, he didn't hate me, he loved me even more, and I feel complete with him, he makes me feel happy and strong." Shalini whispered, kneeling on the football field. "And I can finally understand the term love is not something which describes our relationship; we are a much more than that,"

Red's jersey no.11 gave her hand to Shalini and lifted her up, "You are strong; it felt good playing with you."

Shalini hugged, "Me too."

All the players from both teams shook hands with each other and expressed their fair play.

Everyone feels complete with the person who supports their interest- who gives strength, who gives them motivation- to win. If not- a shoulder to cry on, a hug to feel the warmth. Completeness makes them move further.

As a writer, Suhasini felt strong when she writes, but she felt complete only with Varadarajan to move on.

As a theatre actor, Varadarajan felt motivated when he shared his skills and art with the next generation, but his motivation faded when he lost in his dreams. He could have gone in the wrong way but thinking about Suhasini and waiting for her to win kept him strong. He felt complete only with Suhasini to move one.

As doctor, teacher, sportsperson, and musician everyone needs one thing or another to keep them strong and motivated, but completeness can only be achieved with the shoulder and support they get from the person they love. And sometimes only love can fill the gap when a situation turns incomplete.

Being complete is what makes people go on and live.

I shouldn't have shown myself to the puppy, I shouldn't have let the puppy to change one's fate, I shouldn't have swapped one's disability for another... not only humans but nature also makes mistakes sometimes, god also makes mistakes sometimes, but correcting the mistake is important- as a human if a mistake is corrected, he grows. Similarly, as in nature, if a mistake is corrected, it is called a miracle.

And miracles made Raghav and Shalini complete even after an unprecedented fluctuation in fate introduced by me.

And it will be a miracle if their relationship falls apart. Ha ha, Just kidding.

***

After the tournament cup was presented to the wings of freedom, the football field was opened for the public to rumble. Joel rolled Raghav to the field along with Ravichandran, Elizabeth, Suhasini and Varadarajan, but Abdul stayed.

Shalini from afar shouted, "I did it," So that Raghav could acknowledge but another girl from her team stood beside her and shouted the same to her boyfriend and in addition, she ran towards him, with a jump she hugged him tightly. Shalini's and Raghav's parents dropped their jaws, and they turned back to Shalini who was approaching Raghav with a smile.

She knelt down and hugged Raghav lightly, "This feels good,"

Joel felt a bit uncomfortable and said, "Your parents are here too."

The situation was awkward and all gave lifeless laughs to cover. Looking at all of their faces Shalini got reminded of Abdul and she asked, "Where is Abdul?"

Abdul was on the bleacher with his sad, depressed, confused and scared face- he was looking at Shalini, Raghav and others.

"Abdul come on," Shalini shouted as she found him. He gave a smile with his sad eyes, and when he got up, he received a call from 'She' on his mobile. It was a video call and he answered it quickly.

"Hey, scaredy-cat," Ayesha said, "I heard you cried a lot the other day,"

Abdul didn't speak a word and tears fell out with a smile on his face.

"Why are you crying again, Idiot?" she said, chuckling.

"Yeah, I don't know," Abdul said and wiped his eyes, "I was so worried about you…"

"Where are you now?" Ayesha asked.

"In Shalini's college," he said.

"You went to her match? How many days have passed?" she pouted.

Abdul nodded. "You didn't even check the dates."

"No, I never thought of checking. It was good to sleep, though,"

"Guys, Ayesha is up," Abdul shouted from his place and ran over to them.

Raghav and Shalini got super excited, and when they heard him, tears walked out even before they realised.

The cloudy atmosphere slowly shifted to a beautiful evening. Ayesha spoke with everyone and had fun over the call. While checking out faces one by one, Ayesha found Joel.

"Who is that Handsome?" Ayesha rose curiously.

Abdul blocked Joel and said, "I am still here, Ayesha."

Everyone laughed, Raghav held the mobile and introduced Joel to her.

"When are you going to get discharged?" Shalini asked.

"Tomorrow," Ayesha said. "And sorry I missed your game."

"Yeah, no problem, at least keep up your promise with Abdul."

"You dummy," she screamed out of embarrassment.

Happiness was surrounded everywhere on the football field as I walked out.

I am air and I rejoined the fate in its circle. Once again, I ran into a different puppy, but this time I stopped it and gasped. I didn't want to work hard anymore. Making mistakes is easier than clearing up the mess later.

***

Ayesha came back to Karnataka after a few days- she secretly fulfilled her promise to Abdul. Two months passed and another bucket list was made. They made promises to meet each other every semester holiday and at each time they struck off the stuff from the list. They balanced their life, dream, responsibilities, friendship and love. However, tough days still followed.

The abandoned dark gazebo, which was only used by Raghav earlier, became livelier and many people started using it. Autumn leaves gave more base around gazebo which reflected the pass of time.

In December, during a semester break, they assembled at the gazebo. Raghav held Shalini's hand and looked at the watch he gave, which was working just fine.

Abdul slept over Ayesha's lap and relieved his collegiate stress. They talked about the boring yet funny days they had individually, and they created stories. They had lots to talk about, and occasional meetings strengthened their bonds.

With that, days fled,

Months passed,

Years born...

Small fights and disappointment never left any of them alone, but believing in one another, sharing the burden and having honest relationships helped them tackle all the unexpected situations.

With the birth of 2020, Raghav slowly regained his legs back. The additional yet useful character in the story died— the wheelchair.

A lot of offers piled over Raghav's desk to participate in

orchestras and concerts yet Raghav wanted to do more, he wanted to study business and conquer more with his skills.

When everything was right on track again, a misfortune arose and this time not to the individual but to the entire world.

Colleges got shut down, and everybody had to lock up their houses. Being in house arrest for a long time made all four sick and they occasionally sneaked out to the gazebo. With the flow of time all four decided to have a group photo along with the special gazebo, which held a lot of memories.

Varadarajan took on the role of photographer as the preparations for the photo shoot began. Raghav and Abdul donned stylish grey and green suits, while Shalini and Ayesha adorned themselves in vibrant rose red and elegant shady white attire, respectively. They posed with confidence and grace, channelling their inner models as the camera captured their essence. Over 20 photographs were taken, each capturing a unique moment and showcasing the individuality of the group.

"One more, one more," Raghav and Ayesha insisted.

For the final picture, Ayesha and Shalini took their seats, while Abdul leaned affectionately against Ayesha's shoulder, planting a gentle kiss cheek to cheeks. Raghav, with open arms, embraced them all, creating a heart-warming scene frozen in time as the camera captured the moment.

Epilogue

The entire world got shut down, Because of one stupid. *Not me.*

Varadarajan once again fell into crisis.

"I am the world's unluckiest person," he said.

"No, the whole world is now unlucky, Varun. Things will return to normal soon," Suhasini said. But she didn't understand; the soon was very far. "My book got sold over a million copies by this year,"

That made Varadarajan happy. Their house finally has a door plate made of wood, amateurish but lively.

SUHASINI & VARADARAJAN
DOOR NO. 221

***

Ayesha and Abdul, in front of textbooks, were having a video call chat.

"Let's get married soon," Ayesha said.

"Why so urgent?" Abdul asked.

"I am afraid some other girl might end up making your heart flutter,"

"From where you are getting these weird thoughts?" he asked with a smile, blushing.

"Because mine did, my heart fluttered on a boy in my class."

"You!" he scoffed as his smile dropped, and he shouted furiously. "Let's get married soon…"

Ayesha chortled. "That's what I said earlier,"

She laughed her head off, leaving Abdul confused.

***

"Joel, I love you! I can't hide it anymore," Tanzeela said over a call.

"Where are you now?" Joel asked.

"In my house; I am going to my parent's tonight," she said.

"Just wait" Joel rode his bike to Tanzeela's house in a hurry.

When he reached there, he asked in person, "I am not late, am I?"

She shook her head.

"Can I kiss you? I went crazy without talking to you all these days," he said, and they began smooching along with her nod.

***

Preethi introduced Aaqil to her parents, standing beside him in her house.

"You love him?" Preethi's father asked, sitting on the sofa.

"Yes, Dad," she said.

"Don't you think teenage love won't last long?" her father asked with a bossy sound and crossed legs.

"Yes, uncle. At first, I thought the same, but later I understood that we couldn't live apart." Aaqil said.

"Yes, Dad. We broke up with each other over 37 times, but no matter what, we couldn't live apart. So, we are sure our love is different," Preethi insisted.

"Do his parents know?" Preethi's mom asked calmly.

They both shook their heads together.

"Then why the hell you came here." Her mom yelled and changed the atmosphere.

Preethi and Aaqil looked at each other and smiled.

With a lot of agreement and disagreement, they somehow managed to get their blessings as they desired.

***

"Eat well on time and be safe," Elizabeth said, sending off Ravichandran for work like sending him off for war.

"Love you," he said with a smile hidden behind the mask, taking off with his jeep.

When Elizabeth stepped back into house, Shalini was lying on the sofa chatting with someone, grinning.

"Who are you chatting with?" Elizabeth asked.

"Richu... he is saying he has fallen in love with our classmate Jelsia." Shalini said.

"What? Richu? No, not possible," Elizabeth said. "He said he wanted to be a monk,"

"Yeah, he really did shave his head, but his hair grew up along with love on our class rep; let's see how much he is going to get manned up?"

Elizabeth pouted, shaking her head and went back to the kitchen.

Shalini's phone rang. "Hey, Grandpa," she said after picking up the call.

"Aren't you coming to the gazebo today?" Raghav asked.

"Hmm, I will... just wait for me," she said and got up to change.

"I love you," he said nervously.

Shalini smiled and hung up the call.

Raghav, who was waiting in the gazebo, accidentally found a strange man walking on the road; ***yeah, it was me.***

Raghav climbed up to the road and stood there maintaining a 10-meter gap between me, he shouted "Who are you, man? Why are you all green?"

He asked me, and I turned to him, "You can still see me?"

"Mr. Air…" He sighed, "I thought only your hair was green."

"Yeah, only my hair was supposed to be green, but because of some stupid, even I am suffering from my fate mixing up with the virus."

Raghav laughed hard, "Oh! You look pitiful but don't come near me." and he wore his mask.

"Ok, let me go then,"

"Should I ask you one more question?"

"What?"

"You are green because of the virus, right?"

"Yeah," I said.

He chuckled, "What if? What if? I mean, what colour will you change if someone farts?"

That question made me so embarrassed, and I just ran away weeping.

Some humans are pathetic.

"I hate you, Raghav, I hate you..." I shouted, I wanted the world to hear it, but not even a fly could do. I am really pitiful. SAVE ME...